CLIVILIUS
INTERCONNECTED STORIES. INFINITE POSSIBILITIES

© 2024 Nathan Cowdrey. All rights reserved.
First Edition, 16 May 2024
ISBN 978-1-4457-4123-9
Imprint: Lulu.com

Step into Clivilius, where creation meets infinity, and the essence of reality is yours to redefine. Here, existence weaves into a narrative where every decision has consequences, every action has an impact, and every moment counts. In this realm, shaped by the visionary AI CLIVE, inhabitants are not mere spectators but pivotal characters in an evolving drama where the lines between worlds blur.

Guardians traverse the realms of Clivilius and Earth, their journeys igniting events that challenge the balance between these interconnected universes. The quest for resources and the enigma of unexplained disappearances on Earth mirror the deeper conflicts and intricacies that define Clivilius—a world where reality responds to the collective will and individual choices of its Clivilians, revealing a complex interplay of creation, control, and consequence.

In the grand tapestry of Clivilius, the struggle for harmony and the dance of dichotomies play out across a cosmic stage. Here, every soul's journey contributes to the narrative, where the lines between utopia and dystopia, creator and observer, become increasingly fluid. Clivilius is not just a realm to be explored but a reality to be shaped.

Open your eyes. Expand your mind. Experience your new reality. Welcome to Clivilius, where the journey of discovery is not just about seeing a new world but about seeing your world anew.

Also in the Clivilius Series:

Luke Smith (4338.204.1 - 4338.209.2)

Luke Smith's world transforms with the discovery of a cryptic device, thrusting him into the guardianship of destiny itself. His charismatic charm and unpredictable decisions now carry weight beyond imagination, balancing on the razor's edge between salvation and destruction. Embracing his role as a Guardian, Luke faces the paradox of power: the very force that defends also threatens to annihilate. As shadows gather and the fabric of reality strains, Luke must navigate the consequences of his actions, unaware that a looming challenge will test the very core of his resolve.

Paul Smith (4338.204.1 - 4338.209.3)

In a harsh, new world, Paul Smith grapples with the remnants of a hostile marriage and the future of his two young children. Cast into the heart of an arid wasteland, his survival pushes him to the brink, challenging his every belief. Amidst the desolation, Paul faces a pivotal choice that will dictate where his true allegiance lies. In this tale of resilience and resolve, Paul's journey is a harrowing exploration of loyalty, family, and the boundless optimism required to forge hope in the bleakest of landscapes.

Glenda De Bruyn (4338.206.1 - 4338.209.4)

Dr. Glenda De Bruyn's life takes a perilous turn when her link to a government conspiracy forces her to flee. Thrust into Clivilius, she confronts medical crises and hints of her father's mysterious past. As danger and discovery entwine, Glenda's relentless quest to uncover her family's secrets propels her into the unknown, where every clue unravels the fabric of reality as she knows it.

Jamie Greyson (4338.204.1 - 4338.209.3)

Haunted by shadows of his past, Jamie Greyson navigates life with a guarded heart, his complex bond with Luke Smith teetering on the brink of collapse. When Jamie is thrust into a strange new world, every moment is a test, pushing him to confront not only the dangers that lurk in the unknown but also the demons of his own making. Jamie's quest for survival becomes a journey of redemption, where the chance for a new beginning is earned through courage, trust, and the willingness to face the truth of his own heart.

Kain Jeffries (4338.207.1 - 4338.211.2)

Kain Jeffries' life takes an unimaginable turn when he's thrust into Clivilius, far from the Tasmanian life he knows and the fiancée carrying their unborn child. Torn between worlds, he grapples with decisions concerning his growing family. Haunted by Clivilius's whispering voice and faced with dire ultimatums, Kain's resolve is tested when shadowy predators threaten his new home. As he navigates this new landscape, the line between survival and surrender blurs, pushing Kain to confront what it truly means to fight for a future when every choice echoes through eternity.

4338.207.1 - 4338.212.2

KAREN OWEN

CLIVILIUS
INTERCONNECTED STORIES. INFINITE POSSIBILITIES

"When the familiar world shifts, it's not just the scenery that changes, but also the eyes with which we view it."

- Karen Owen

4338.207

(26 July 2018)

THE BUS

4338.207.1

"Oh my god, I can't believe it's still here!" I announced, my voice tinged with a mix of surprise and nostalgia, as I leaned in close to Jane in the bus line. The familiar streets of Hobart, with their quaint mix of old and new, were a backdrop to our daily rituals, but today, they held a different allure. The cobblestone paths intertwined with sleek modern pavements, a showcase of the city's journey through time. Old brick buildings, with their stories etched in weathered façades, stood proudly beside glass-fronted boutiques, reflecting the city's fusion of history and modernity.

Jane, always the epitome of friendship in my life, bounced on her feet, surprised by my sudden enthusiasm. Her head swung around, her face lighting up with recognition and warmth. "Oh Karen," she laughed, her voice a comforting melody in the mundane symphony of our commute. "You almost scared me to death." Her eyes sparkled with amusement, a surprising contrast to the usual reserved glances we exchanged amidst the hum of bus routines.

I laughed along, feeling a brief respite from the day's stress. "I needed a good chuckle after the day I've had," I confided in Jane. She was a part of my daily life, a friend who shared in the drudgery and dreams that filled our bus rides to and from work. The warmth of her presence was like a beacon, guiding me through the fog of my mundane concerns, reminding me of the small joys tucked in the corners of everyday life.

"You too, hey?" Jane replied, her voice a mixture of sympathy and shared understanding. It was a simple acknowledgment, yet it carried the weight of shared experiences and unspoken solidarity.

As the bus line moved, I gestured for Jane to lead the way. She climbed the bus steps with her usual determination, a trait I've always admired, tapping her bus card with a practiced flick before finding us seats in the almost full vehicle. "Here. I've saved you one," she said, patting the seat beside her with a smile that seemed to cut through the dreariness of the day.

I settled beside her, my long legs cramped in the confined space of the bus seat, an all too familiar discomfort in our daily commute. "Sorry," Jane remarked, her voice laced with genuine concern as she noticed my attempt to find a comfortable position, "Didn't look like we had many options."

"We never do this late in the day," I responded, my gaze drifting out the window at the darkening sky, the fading light a reminder of the day's end. "It's basically dark already." My voice carried a hint of resignation, a reflection of the weariness that comes with the setting sun, especially in the heart of winter.

"I know," Jane agreed, her eyes reflecting the bus's dim interior, creating a soft glow that seemed to encapsulate her innate warmth. "Middle of winter. Days will start getting lighter again, soon," she added, her voice a mirror to the dreariness outside, yet somehow managing to carry a tone of reassurance, as if to say we've weathered worse, and we'll weather this too.

I shivered slightly, the mention of winter intensifying the cold I felt seeping through the bus windows, an invisible but palpable presence that seemed to claw at the warmth within. I tugged my jacket closer, a futile attempt to ward off the chill, the fabric a thin barrier against the creeping cold. The bus, with its steamed-up windows and the soft murmur of tired passengers, felt like a microcosm of the world outside - a world bracing against the cold embrace of winter, holding onto the warmth of human connection.

Jane shifted her bags on her lap, a subtle reminder of the everyday struggles we often overlooked in our conversations. The mundane reality of our lives returned, grounding us back to the present moment within the cramped confines of the bus. "So why are you so late today?" she inquired, her voice laced with the familiar timbre of curiosity that had been a constant in our years of friendship. It was a simple question, yet it opened the floodgates to the frustrations I had been holding back all day.

I sighed deeply. "Oh," I started, my voice heavy with exhaustion, "We've got no staff and incompetent management to thank for that." The words came out more bitterly than I intended, a reflection of the pent-up frustration that had been simmering beneath the surface.

"So nothing unusual," Jane quipped, her sarcasm slicing through the tension. It was a familiar comfort, her ability to inject humour into even the most frustrating of situations, a reminder not to take everything so seriously.

"No. I guess that's not unusual, is it," I mused, the corners of my mouth turning up in a reluctant smile at Jane's remark. My mind briefly wandered to the day's challenges, the endless meetings, and the mounting paperwork. "I've been working on a submission to local council to expand a parcel of land for the further protection of a species of Lucanidae," I said, the frustration in my voice giving way to a sense of purpose. It was a project close to my heart, an opportunity to make a real difference in the conservation of a species I had spent years studying.

"Oh, right," Jane replied, her tone shifting to one of genuine interest, albeit tinged with her usual lack of understanding of my passion for entomology.

I chuckled, a little resignedly, feeling the weight of the day's frustrations melt away in the face of Jane's lightheartedness. "It's a Stag Beetle," I clarified, my voice carrying a healthy dose of pride.

"Of course," Jane said, her voice warming with a smile that I could almost see without looking. "I know how much you love bugs." Her words were casual, an attempt to connect over a subject she knew was close to my heart, yet the terminology she used was a gentle nudge to my professional sensitivities.

I corrected her, a little more sternly than intended, the scientist in me bristling at the oversimplification. "No, they're not bugs. They're..." My voice trailed off, a momentary flash of frustration passing through me, not at Jane but at the endless battle of correcting common misunderstandings about my work.

"Beetles," Jane finished for me, her laughter echoing softly in the cramped space of the bus.

"See, you do know," I said, a smile finally breaking through my exhaustion, a flicker of amusement lighting up my tired eyes.

Jane's face showed a mix of amusement and understanding, the soft glow of the bus's interior lights casting a gentle hue on her features. "Oh, I know. I just forget sometimes. I'm not as up to date with these things as you are," she admitted, her humility a grounding force.

Despite the respect we held for each other's passions, I glanced at her, feeling a brief disconnect in our worlds, a momentary realisation of the spaces between our shared experiences. "It's not something new," I remarked, my voice tinged with a hint of defensiveness, "They've always been beetles. They're in the Tasmanian Threatened Species Protection Act."

Jane's expression turned serious, the levity of the moment fading as she recognised the importance of what I was sharing. "Oh, I don't doubt they are," she assured me, her tone sincere.

Before I could respond, Jane shifted the conversation, effortlessly steering it away from the minutiae of my work to the practical matters of the evening. "So, with you being so late tonight, how are you getting back home? Is Chris waiting for you at the usual spot?" she asked, her concern evident in the furrow of her brow and the slight tilt of her head, as if trying to gauge my situation before I even articulated it.

Worry creased my forehead, my mind racing through the logistics of the evening. "I'm not sure yet. Earlier I told him to go home as usual and I'd let him know what time to come and get me. But I haven't been able to reach him as yet. I may have a lengthy walk ahead of me," I explained, the words heavy with the dread of facing the cold, dark trek alone.

"Don't be silly, dear friend," Jane said, her voice a warm blanket of concern in the chilly air of the bus. She touched my arm gently, a reassuring pressure that spoke volumes of her willingness to go above and beyond for a friend. "Message Chris and tell him not to worry about it. I'll take you home tonight." Her offer was generous, selfless, the kind of gesture that underscored the depth of our friendship.

I hesitated, torn between relief at the thought of avoiding the cold walk and concern for Jane's own commitments. "You can't do that," I protested, my voice laced with worry. "Wouldn't Valerie have dinner ready and waiting for you by now?" I asked, more out of concern for her than for myself. The thought of Jane disrupting her evening plans for my sake was a discomforting one, even in the face of my own predicament.

Jane's insistence cut through my protests like a beacon of unwavering determination. "Of course I'll take you. We can't very well have you walking all the way from Berriedale to Collinsvale in the cold and dark now, can we," she said, her voice imbued with a resolve that I had come to admire and rely upon in her.

Just then, my phone erupted with its loud ring, slicing through the gentle hum of conversation like a sudden clap of thunder, jolting me from the comfortable cocoon of our discussion. "This is probably Chris now," I said, my voice a mixture of hope and apprehension as I fumbled with the device. My fingers, slender and more accustomed to the delicate handling of insects than the frantic scramble of modern technology, struggled with the urgency of the moment. The phone felt awkward, slippery, almost resistant in my hands as I pressed it to my ear, longing for Chris's familiar voice to dispel the looming shadow of the evening's uncertainties.

"Hey Karen," Luke's voice came through the phone, cheery and unmistakable. There was an instant comfort in its familiarity, a gentle reminder of the many mornings we'd shared on the bus, each of us ensconced in our own worlds yet linked by the camaraderie of our routine commute. His voice, usually a beacon of cheerfulness, now carried an added weight, bearing the promise of news or a message that could potentially alter the course of the evening.

"Can you hear me okay?" he asked, his voice slightly muffled by the phone's speaker.

My eyebrows furrowed in concentration, as I attempted to connect more deeply with the voice on the other end. "Yeah. You're a little soft, but I can hear you well enough," I replied, adjusting my grip on the phone as if by doing so I could somehow clear the static distance between us. The bus's hum, a constant, monotonous drone, and the intermittent chatter of passengers formed a backdrop of noise that I struggled to tune out, each sound a reminder of the public nature of this personal moment.

"Oh good," Luke said, his voice tinged with a hint of relief, as if he too had been holding his breath, awaiting confirmation that our connection, tenuous as it might be amidst the cacophony of public transport, was secure.

A pause hung in the air, thick with the ambient sounds of the bus's steady rumble and the faint rustling of Jane's bags beside me. My patience, already frayed from the day's relentless stress, waned further, a thin thread on the verge of snapping. "I'm on the bus with Jane," I interjected, my voice a blend of irritation and eagerness, hoping to fill the silence that stretched uncomfortably between Luke's words and my anticipation.

"Oh. Hi Jane," Luke called out, his voice lifting slightly in a clear attempt to bridge the physical distance with a semblance of warmth and camaraderie.

I turned to Jane, conveying the greeting with a gesture, "Luke says hi," I relayed, my tone carrying a hint of the affection we both felt for him. Watching her face light up with recognition, I saw the blend of warmth and motherly concern that Jane reserved for Luke, a reflection of the fondness we both harboured for him, akin to the young son neither of us had. It was a moment of shared understanding, a brief connection sparked by Luke's greeting, bridging our separate worlds.

"She says you're a slacker. We haven't seen you on the bus all week," I teased, echoing Jane's earlier jest with a playful tone. The words, light and teasing, were an attempt to recapture the ease of our usual banter, a gentle ribbing that belied the deeper currents of care and concern beneath.

"Ahh. I know," Luke's voice came through, tinged with a sheepish acknowledgment of our mock accusation. "I've had the week off." His admission, simple and honest, carried a note of justification, a reminder of the ebb and flow of our daily routines and the occasional, well-deserved break from them.

"Fair enough then," I replied, a smile tugging at my lips, a spontaneous reaction to the easy excuse. *Can't really argue with that*, I thought to myself, a silent acknowledgment of the countless times we had all shared our frustrations and dreams during our morning rides.

The conversation lulled again into an awkward silence, the kind that often creeps in when words struggle to bridge the gap of distance. It was a silence filled with the weight of unsaid things, a gap in conversation where the heart's unvoiced concerns and the mind's unresolved thoughts lingered, a palpable void that even the most casual of exchanges could not fully dispel.

"You busy tomorrow morning?" Luke finally broke the silence, his question catching me slightly off guard amidst the low buzz of conversation and the rhythmic hum of the bus moving along its route. The sudden shift from our awkward lull to this direct inquiry jolted my thoughts back into focus, like a diver surfacing for air.

"Well," I began, my mind momentarily shifting gears to the plans Chris and I had laid out for our day off. "Chris and I have to make an early start in the morning to fix the small hole in the retaining wall. It keeps running mud underneath the backdoor when it rains." The words painted a picture of our humble, hands-on life, a testament to the small battles fought in the upkeep of a home. But then, a lighter thought floated to the surface, carrying with it the promise of shared moments and simple pleasures. "But if you come over at nine, Chris might cook you up a fresh duck egg omelette," I offered, the thought of Chris, apron-clad and wielding a spatula with the same precision he applied to every task, bringing a sense of warmth and homey comfort.

"That'd be lovely," Luke replied, his voice weaving through the phone with a hint of enthusiasm, a soft glow of anticipation lighting up the words.

"Okay. See you at nine then," I confirmed, a mix of curiosity and apprehension blooming at the prospect of Luke's visit. It was a plan set in motion, a small event in the grand tapestry of life, yet it held the weight of friendship and the shared familiarity that comes with knowing someone over the course of many rides and conversations.

"Okay. Bye," said Luke, and the call ended, the finality of the disconnect echoing slightly in the space around me. I stared at the phone, a sense of bemusement washing over me. The interaction had been brief, a few exchanges carried over the airwaves, yet it left a trail of questions in my mind. *What prompted Luke's call? Was there more beneath the surface of his casual inquiry?* The phone, now silent in my hand, was a bridge back to reality, a reminder of the connections we weave, sometimes in the most unexpected of moments.

"Not Chris then," Jane observed, pulling me back from the reverie of thoughts that Luke's call had spiralled me into. Her voice, always a grounding presence, now carried a note of curiosity, probing gently at the edges of my distraction.

"No," I echoed, my response trailing off slightly as my thoughts continued to linger on the call. The bus's steady hum and the occasional rattle from the journey provided a familiar backdrop to the moment of introspection.

"Everything okay?" Jane asked, her tone now laced with concern, the words cutting through the ambient noise of our surroundings.

I shrugged, feeling a ripple of unease that seemed to resonate with the vibrations of the bus. "I don't know. That was all very odd." My voice carried a tinge of uncertainty, reflecting the turmoil of thoughts and feelings that Luke's call had stirred within me.

"It was a bit, wasn't it. Does he visit your place often?" Jane's curiosity was now fully evident, her gaze fixed on me with an intensity that sought answers. Her question wasn't invasive but rather an extension of her concern.

"Only that one time with you," I replied, the memory of Luke's previous visit surfacing in my mind like a photograph slowly developing in a darkroom. It had been an ordinary day, much like any other we had shared, yet now, in light of his call, it seemed to hold a different significance, a piece of a jigsaw that I hadn't realised was incomplete.

Jane's expression shifted to one of surprise, her brows knitting together in thought. "Very odd indeed," she mused, echoing my own sentiments.

"Hmm," I mused aloud, my mind racing with possibilities. The situation was unusual, perplexing even, for Luke to reach out like this, and even more so for him to express a desire to visit. Despite the oddity of the situation and the whirlpool of questions it sparked, a part of me, a steady, unwavering part, trusted Luke. Over the years, the three of us had formed a bond, one that was built on the countless mornings spent waiting at the same bus stop in Berriedale, woven through with conversations filled with laughter, shared frustrations, and the camaraderie of our daily commute. This bond, I realised, was the anchor that attempted to keep my swirling thoughts from drifting too far into doubt.

Jane nudged me gently, her touch pulling me from the whirlpool of thoughts that Luke's call had initiated. "We're nearly there. Quick. Send Chris that message," she urged, her voice a perfect blend of concern and practicality. It was a reminder of the immediacy of our surroundings, the need to transition from the abstract musings about Luke's intentions back to the concrete actions required by the here and now.

"Yeah. Alright," I replied, my voice a mix of distraction and agreement. My fingers moved over the touchpad of my phone with a familiarity that belied the turmoil of thoughts whirring within me. As I composed the message to Chris, informing him of the change in plans for the evening, a nagging thought lingered at the back of my mind, casting a long shadow over the simple act of sending a text. *What do you really want, Luke Smith?* The question echoed in my head, a persistent murmur that refused to be silenced, adding a layer of mystery and unease to the otherwise mundane end to my day.

4338.208

(27 July 2018)

THE MISHAP

4338.208.1

Wiping my hands along my thighs, I left a muddy trail across my already dirt-stained jeans, each streak a badge of honour from the morning's labour. The work had been unexpectedly arduous, a battle of wills against the earth itself. "That took a bit longer than I expected," I admitted, my voice tinged with a blend of fatigue and satisfaction. The retaining wall, with its crumbling stones and stubborn refusal to yield, had tested our resolve, but together, Chris and I had managed to overcome its challenges.

Chris huffed loudly, his exasperation laced with a playful note that belied his feigned annoyance. "We would have been finished half an hour ago if you hadn't been so distracted by those bugs," he teased, his eyes twinkling with humour, reflecting the shared joy of our domestic adventures. His comment, though teasing, was a nod to the idiosyncrasies that defined our relationship, the acceptance of each other's passions and quirks.

"They're not bugs!" I retorted with a mix of jest and passion, unable to resist defending my tiny, misunderstood subjects. The surge of fervour for my entomological interests was a familiar feeling, a part of who I was. I paused, ready to launch into a detailed clarification, but the warmth in Chris's gaze reminded me of his teasing nature. He understood my work, perhaps better than anyone else, and his playful jibes were often a prelude to genuine, engaging discussions about the natural world that surrounded us.

Chris's chuckle, deep and resonant, cut through my momentary defensiveness, a sound that grounded me back to the present. He glanced at his watch, a gesture that spoke volumes about the practical aspects of our lives that still awaited attention.

"So when is this friend of yours supposed to be coming around?" he asked, his tone weaving curiosity into the fabric of our post-labour conversation. It was a gentle shift from the playful banter that had marked our morning, an inquiry that brought Luke's impending visit back into focus amidst the satisfaction of our completed task.

"I told him to come at nine," I replied, my gaze drifting to my own watch, a practical accessory that seemed almost out of place against my mud-splattered self. Time, it appeared, had slipped away with more haste than I had realised, its passage marked not by the ticking of hands but by the progress we had made on the wall.

"Well, it's quarter past now," Chris continued, his voice carrying a hint of concern.

"You may as well get yourself cleaned up and start cooking breakfast," I suggested, already turning my attention back to the day's remaining tasks. The practicalities of hosting, even in an informal setting like ours, necessitated a degree of preparation, albeit with a casual approach that matched our lifestyle.

"You're not going to wait for him?" Chris asked, his surprise evident in his tone. His punctuality and perhaps a touch more formality in hosting stood in contrast to my more laissez-faire attitude. It was a difference that often complemented our partnership, blending his meticulous nature with my more spontaneous spirit.

"A tasty duck egg omelette waits for nobody," I declared stubbornly, a half-smile playing on my lips. The thought was both whimsical and grounded in the simple pleasure of enjoying the fruits of our own land. There was a deep satisfaction in the notion that, despite any delays, the day would unfold with the comforting rhythms of home life.

"Okay then," Chris said, his expression softening into an understanding nod. His acceptance was a reflection of the shared values that underpinned our life together, a mutual appreciation for the balance between duty and delight. He headed towards the outdoor washroom, his steps unhurried and relaxed, embodying the laid-back lifestyle that had drawn us to Collinsvale. His movement, in harmony with the natural ebb and flow of our day, was a visual reminder of the contentment we found in this simple, yet richly fulfilling life.

I stood back for a moment, admiring our handiwork on the retaining wall. We had replaced the rotten wood that had been the source of much annoyance, especially during the rainy season. The new wooden slats lay neatly in place, a testament to our hard work and determination to maintain the integrity of our home's landscape. I bent over, taking in a deep breath of the fresh timber scent, a natural perfume that always brought me a sense of accomplishment and peace. There's something profoundly satisfying about the smell of fresh wood; it's like the earth's own scent of victory, a reminder of nature's enduring presence and the tangible results of our efforts.

Just then, I noticed a small harlequin beetle crawling up my sleeve. "Hey there, little harlequin," I murmured, a gentle smile spreading across my face as I observed its progress. There was a certain serenity in these moments, a connection to the smaller inhabitants of our garden that often went unnoticed. Carefully, I held out my palm, encouraging the beetle to change course. Its brilliant red and orange markings stood out vividly against the small black body, a tiny splash of colour in the earthy tones of our garden. The contrast was striking, a vivid reminder of nature's diversity and beauty in even the smallest of its creatures.

"What beautiful colours you have," I whispered, almost in awe of the tiny creature's vibrant appearance. It was moments like these that fuelled my passion for entomology, the simple yet profound beauty found in the insect world. I lowered my palm to the edge of the garden bed, letting the beetle make its way into the mix of leafy plants. For several minutes, I stood mesmerised, watching as it explored its new environment with an unbothered grace, a tiny explorer in a vast world of green.

A light growl from my stomach broke the spell. "Right," I said to myself, reluctantly tearing my gaze away from the captivating sight of the harlequin. The physical reminder of hunger brought me back to the immediate needs of the day. "Time to clean myself up and eat." The promise of a hearty breakfast, especially after a morning of hard labour, was a welcome thought. The physical satisfaction of completing the wall, combined with the brief interlude of natural observation, had heightened my anticipation for the meal.

As I walked towards the house, the anticipation of a delicious meal mingled with a lingering curiosity about Luke's unexpected visit. *What could have prompted his sudden desire to connect?* The thought was intriguing, a puzzle piece in the day's unfolding narrative that added an element of mystery to the otherwise routine satisfaction of a job well done.

❖

Three sharp knocks echoed through the quiet of the morning. The day's newspaper, a sprawl of articles and reports that had been engaging my attention, suddenly felt less pressing. Setting it aside, I rose to answer the door, my movements tinged with a mix of curiosity and slight irritation at the interruption.

"You're late," I said, opening the door to reveal Luke standing there, his expression a mix of apologetic and slightly flustered. The sight of him, unexpectedly on my doorstep after no communication of his tardiness, sparked a flicker of annoyance tempered by the undercurrent of our longstanding friendship.

"I know. I'm so sorry," Luke replied, his voice carrying genuine remorse. The sincerity in his tone, the slight downturn of his lips, all spoke of his regret.

Stepping aside, I opened the door wider, a silent gesture of forgiveness and an invitation to enter. The minor irritation at his tardiness dissolved in the face of his evident contrition. "Don't mind the clutter," I warned him casually as he stepped over the threshold. The house, always brimming with my work, was a chaotic mix of organised disarray. A landscape of papers, books, and various research materials that had somehow found a harmonious existence amidst the chaos. "Most of it is research papers and journals," I added, almost proudly, a nod to the passion that consumed much of my time and energy.

Luke smiled, a gentle, understanding curve of his lips, as he walked down the hallway. His eyes briefly glanced over the short stacks of papers, each pile a silent witness to the endless hours of study and research that defined not just my professional life but my personal identity as well.

Meanwhile, a discomforting churn in my stomach reminded me of the morning's hearty breakfast. A twinge of unease that whispered of a slight disagreement with my usually resilient digestion. There was something unsettling about that last duck egg, a reminder that even the most mundane choices could have unforeseen consequences. The discomfort was a subtle undercurrent to the morning's unfolding events.

"Something smells good," Luke commented as he stepped further into the house, the lingering aroma of the morning's cooking enveloping him like a warm, inviting blanket.

"We ate without you," I said bluntly, my tone matter-of-fact yet devoid of any real censure. The statement was simply a reflection of the day's reality, an acknowledgment of the passage of time and the continuation of life's routines, even in the face of delays. "Chris is in the garden. You can cook something for yourself if you like," I suggested, the words carrying an unspoken caution against the duck eggs that had unsettled my stomach. It was a subtle warning, one born out of concern yet masked by the casual offer of self-service.

"Nah. It's all good. But thanks for the offer," Luke replied, his easygoing nature shining through his response. His ability to brush off inconvenience with a smile, to remain unfazed by the minor disruptions of daily life, was a quality I had admired in him.

"Please sit," I offered, guiding him towards the kitchen chair nearest the small window. This particular spot was a personal favourite of mine, not just for its proximity to the natural light that flooded the kitchen but for the view it offered. The window framed the magnificent view of the enormous oak tree in our garden, a sight that never failed to bring me a sense of peace and contentment. That oak, with its sprawling branches and sturdy trunk, was more than just a tree; it was a symbol of endurance and growth, qualities that resonated deeply with me.

"I'll make us some tea," I announced, turning on the kettle and reaching for two mugs that had almost dried on the kitchen sink. The routine act of preparing tea was a comforting one, a small ceremony that marked a pause in the day's events, an opportunity to offer hospitality and share a moment of tranquility. My gaze drifted to the cupboard, filled with an assortment of tea bags - from the robust flavours of black tea to the soothing whispers of herbal blends. *Which tea shall we have?* I pondered, glancing over at Luke.

He sat there, staring at the table, his fingers interlocking and then quickly switching direction. Luke's odd mannerisms, though familiar, sometimes puzzled me. It was intriguing, this mix of habitual gestures and the thoughtful silence that often enveloped him. Despite our lengthy conversations on the bus, conversations that spanned from the trivial to the profound, revealing his intelligence and depth, he remained an enigma wrapped in the casual ease of everyday interactions.

Peppermint tea seemed like a good choice, its refreshing clarity mirroring the fresh start of our unexpected morning together. Dropping a teabag into each mug, I waited for the kettle to boil, stealing another glance at Luke. His fidgeting had become increasingly noticeable, a silent dance of restlessness that contrasted sharply with the serene view outside the window. A soft chuckle escaped my lips as I recalled Jane's initial encounter with Luke. Her excitement in making a new friend, something so pure and spontaneous, had been infectious, leading to our own unique friendship with him. Jane's text message from that day still resonated with me: *I did it! I made contact!* Without her, I doubted I would have ever engaged with Luke, given my own tendency to keep to myself, a habit that had only deepened as the years added layers to my introspection.

Turning sixty in a few years, I found Luke's boundless enthusiasm for life quite refreshing when it wasn't exhausting, a vibrant streak of colour against the more muted tapestry of my own experiences. His energy, seemingly untethered by the reservations that time had woven around my own outlook, often sparked a flicker of amusement in me, a reminder of the diverse tapestry of human expression. *But that constant fidgeting...*

"Would you stop fidgeting!" I exclaimed, my patience finally giving way, the words slipping out in a mix of jest and exasperation. It was a rare outburst from me, a deviation from the norm that underscored the comfort and familiarity our friendship had reached.

Luke's reaction was immediate. He pressed his palms flat on the table, a clear sign of his attempt to restrain himself. "Sorry," he said, his voice tinged with a mix of surprise and compliance. The swift change, the sudden stillness, was almost more jarring than his previous movements. It was a moment that highlighted the delicate balance between our personalities, a dance of differences and similarities that had somehow meshed into a friendship both unlikely and undeniable.

The kettle whistled, its sharp cry cutting through the tension like a knife, offering a brief distraction from the growing unease. I poured the hot water into our mugs, watching as the steam rose, curling and twisting, merging with the soft morning light that filtered through the kitchen window. The simplicity of this act, the brewing of tea, seemed almost ceremonial, a grounding ritual amidst the swirling undercurrents of unspoken questions and hidden truths.

The moment of casual enthusiasm abruptly ended, giving way to a sense of purpose that gripped me with unexpected intensity. "Why are you here?" I asked Luke directly, my tone firm, unyielding. The question had been hovering at the edge of my consciousness, a shadow that had lengthened with each passing minute of his visit. There was an unusual tension in the air, palpable and thick, a departure from the typical easy-going nature of our previous encounters. "You've only come here once before and that was only because Jane brought you along." The words tumbled out, stark and loaded with the weight of unspoken implications, marking a clear line between the casual nature of past interactions and the seriousness of this moment.

Luke's response was a throat-clearing that sounded both rough and awkward, an audible manifestation of the unease that had begun to settle over the room. It was a sound that seemed to echo off the walls, amplifying the silence that followed, a silence filled with anticipation and the unspoken questions that hung between us.

"Is there something you want?" I pressed on, placing a steaming cup of peppermint tea in front of him. The gesture was automatic, yet imbued with a sense of ceremony, a bridge between the comfort of routine and the unfamiliar territory we were venturing into. I then pushed aside a few piles of books to take a seat across from him, my movements deliberate, echoing the seriousness of my question. The clearing of the space, both physical and metaphorical, set the stage for a conversation that felt as significant as it was unexpected.

My gaze met his, steady and searching, seeking the truth behind his visit. The warmth of the tea contrasted sharply with the chill of uncertainty that had crept into the room, a tangible reminder of the complexities and intricacies of human relationships. In that moment, the kitchen became a crucible for the unfolding of truths, a place where the simple act of sharing tea laid the groundwork for revelations that could alter the course of our friendship.

Luke leaned over his cup, the steam from the peppermint tea swirling up towards him. "Mmm peppermint," he commented, his voice carrying a note of appreciation for the choice. However, his evasion of my direct question did nothing to ease the growing knot of curiosity and concern within me. It was unlike him to dodge a conversation so blatantly, especially one that held such evident weight.

I watched him over the rim of my cup as I sipped the hot tea, the warmth of the liquid a sharp contrast to the cool unease settling in my stomach. His avoidance was becoming more apparent with each passing second, and it left me with a sense of frustration. *He still hasn't answered my question*, a thought that repeated itself, a mantra of growing irritation.

Unexpectedly, Luke stood and moved toward the living room, his actions abrupt, almost erratic. "Where are you going? Is everything okay? The bathroom is down the hall and to the right, if that's what you're looking for," I called after him, my voice a mix of confusion and irritation. I remained seated, a deliberate choice, unwilling to indulge in what seemed like an unnecessary drama. My position was a statement in itself, a refusal to chase after explanations or to play into what was beginning to feel like a deliberate obfuscation.

The sound of magazines being shuffled reached my ears, the noise out of place in the quiet of the morning. It deepened my frown, each shuffle a note in the growing symphony of my confusion. *What in the world is he up to?* I wondered, the mystery of Luke's behaviour growing by the second. The simple act of making tea had morphed into a scene filled with tension and unanswered questions, a far cry from the peaceful morning I had envisioned. The disparity between the serene start to the day and the current atmosphere was stark, a reminder of how quickly dynamics can shift, leaving one to navigate the unexpected currents of human behaviour.

"Karen," Luke called from the living room, his voice croaky, pulling me out of my brewing storm of irritation. The tone, so unlike his usual self, piqued my curiosity despite my best efforts to remain annoyed.

Reluctantly, I stood up, the chair scraping against the dining room floor in a harsh echo of my internal state.

"Everything okay?" I asked as I made my way into the living room, my tone dry with exasperation, expecting perhaps some trivial matter that had caught his attention.

"Just watch," Luke instructed, his demeanour having shifted from the awkward evasion to something serious and intense. The change was disconcerting, adding layers to the enigma he had become this morning.

"What am I looking for?" I asked, my frustration evident, feeling like I was being drawn into a scenario I had no script for. Luke's cryptic behaviour was beginning to grate on me, his presence, usually a source of intriguing conversation and light-hearted debate, now a cause for a growing headache.

Then, Luke pulled a small object from his pocket and aimed it at the closed living room door. The door, a mundane fixture in our home, was about to become the centre of an inexplicable phenomenon. My skepticism hung in the air, a thin veil about to be shattered.

A small ball of light shot from the object in Luke's hand, bursting into a kaleidoscope of vibrant colours that sprawled across the door's surface. I gasped, my initial shock giving way to awe as the colours danced before my eyes, painting the ordinary wood with an ethereal glow that seemed to pulse with life. "That's incredible," I murmured, the words slipping out in a hushed reverence, my irritation replaced by a sudden, inexplicable calm. The frustration that had been building was swept away, replaced by a childlike wonder at the spectacle before me.

"I know," Luke replied, his voice holding a hint of pride. There was a depth to his tone, a resonance that suggested this was more than a mere trick or illusion. The pride in his voice was not just for the display of light but for the shared moment of astonishment, a connection rekindled through the unexpected and the unexplained.

I stepped closer to the door, mesmerised by the collision of colours that sent sparks flying through the air, a spectacle that defied the mundane reality of our living room. "Can I touch it?" I asked, my voice laced with awe, my hand instinctively reaching out towards the beautiful, swirling display. The colours danced, almost inviting, yet there was an undercurrent of caution that Luke's presence reinforced.

"Not yet," Luke cautioned, his tone firm yet laced with an urgency that halted my advance. "Don't touch it yet." His warning was clear, but it sparked a wave of confusion and a touch of stubborn defiance within me. "Why the hell not?" I demanded, my curiosity morphing into frustration. *This is my house, after all.* A space where I felt in control, where every item and corner was familiar and safe. The idea that I should refrain from touching something within my own walls was both irritating and perplexing.

"Because..." Luke began, his explanation poised on the edge of revelation, but he was abruptly cut off.

"Karen!" Chris's voice rang out, a familiar anchor in the escalating surrealism of the moment. He entered through the back door, his presence a reminder of the normality that had been so starkly disrupted.

"In here, Chris," I called back, my attention torn between the extraordinary scene unfolding before me and the arrival of my husband. His entry felt like a lifeline, a return to reality, or so I hoped.

As the living room door opened and Chris began to speak, his words were swallowed by the sudden onslaught of bright blue and rainbow flashes that filled my vision. The world seemed to tilt, reality bending in ways that my mind struggled to comprehend. My body felt like it was being pulled apart, a sensation both terrifying and surreal, a physical impossibility that was nonetheless happening. "Chris!" I screamed, reaching out for him in desperation, seeking the solidity of his presence, a grounding force against the unfathomable.

"Karen!" Chris yelled back, his voice a beacon in the chaos. His hand found mine, a brief connection in the midst of disarray. But the feeling of his hand in mine was fleeting, torn away as the colours shifted to reveal a clear blue sky, a vision so vastly different from the interior of our home.

Then, a voice spoke, not audibly, but directly into my mind, a presence that was both foreign and intimate. *Welcome to Clivilius, Karen Owen*, it said, its words resonating within me with a clarity that was undeniable. The message marked the beginning of something entirely unknown and utterly bewildering.

CLIVILIUS

4338.208.2

"Karen!" Chris's voice was a mixture of panic and relief, slicing through the disorienting calm that had enveloped me moments before. As he grasped my arm, pulling me back from the precipice of the unknown, a rush of emotions flooded through me. I spun around instinctively, letting him draw me into a protective embrace, a harbour in the tumultuous sea of confusion and awe that surrounded us.

"I thought I'd lost you somehow," he confessed, his voice strained with a torrent of emotions, the fear of having witnessed my disappearance etching deep lines of concern across his face. "When I saw you disappear like that." The words hung between us, a stark reminder of the surreal journey we had unwittingly embarked upon.

Gently, I pulled away from his grip, needing to affirm the reality of our surroundings with my own eyes. The landscape that greeted us was unlike anything I had ever seen or imagined. Oranges, browns, and reds painted a barren, sandy terrain that stretched endlessly into the horizon, a tapestry of colours that spoke of an unfamiliar beauty and desolation.

"What the hell just happened?" Chris's voice, thick with confusion and fear, echoed my own inner turmoil. "And what the hell is Clivilius?" His questions, laden with the weight of our sudden displacement, mirrored the swirling vortex of thoughts and fears in my mind.

"I think this place is," I replied, my voice barely above a whisper, the realisation of our situation settling like a heavy cloak around my shoulders. The reality of our presence in this strange world called Clivilius was slowly dawning on me, a truth as undeniable as it was incomprehensible.

Chris gasped, his eyes widening as he took in the surreal environment for the first time. The familiarity of our world, the comfort of our home, had been replaced by this vast, uncharted wilderness that lay before us, a realm that defied explanation and challenged the very fabric of our understanding.

I reached out, my hand hesitantly making contact with the large, translucent screen that seemed to be the source of our bewildering transportation. To my surprise, it was solid and cold under my fingertips, a contrast to the warm, vibrant kaleidoscope of colours that had previously engulfed us. "Luke!" I called out, my voice tinged with a desperate hope, clinging to the belief that he could somehow guide us in this moment of uncertainty. "Luke, where are you?" The words felt heavy in the silent expanse, each syllable a drop in the vast emptiness that surrounded us.

But there was no answer, only the haunting silence that seemed to stretch endlessly, a void where even the echo of our voices seemed to disappear. It was a silence that weighed heavily, amplifying the surreal sense of isolation and confusion.

"Help me," I urged Chris, nudging him with my elbow. We needed to find Luke, to grasp some understanding of the situation, to anchor ourselves in the swirling maelstrom of this strange world.

Confused but compliant, Chris joined in the search for our missing friend. "Luke!" he shouted, his voice echoing against the clear, unyielding wall that stood as a barrier between us and the answers we sought. His call, filled with concern and confusion, merged with my own efforts to pierce the silence.

"Luke!" I screamed again, my frustration and fear manifesting in the pounding of my fists against the barrier, the solid, cold surface a jarring reminder of our predicament. A growing sense of desperation took hold, a fear that we were truly lost in this unknown land.

Suddenly, the unemotional voice that had greeted me upon our arrival cut through the tense air, its authoritative demand for calm a sharp contrast to the tumult of emotions raging within me. *Karen Owen. Calm yourself!* it demanded. *Remember the things that Luke has told you.* The instruction, reminiscent of the cryptic conversations I had shared with Luke, sparked a flicker of recognition, a glimmer of understanding. *You know how to ask*, it instructed, a directive that hinted at a way forward, a method to navigate the bewildering landscape.

The voice, devoid of emotion yet carrying a weight of authority, served as a beacon in the fog of confusion, a reminder that we were not entirely without guidance. The mention of Luke's dreams, the cryptic hints he had dropped in our conversations, suddenly took on a new significance. It was a puzzle piece, a clue to unlocking the mysteries of this place and possibly finding a way back home, or at least understanding why we were brought to Clivilius. The realisation that there might be a method to this madness, a way to ask, to communicate, or to navigate this foreign world, ignited a spark of hope, a determination to grasp the threads of knowledge Luke had left me and weave them into a lifeline.

Chris, fuelled by desperation, slammed his fists against the wall, his voice breaking with emotion. "Help us, please!" The rawness in his plea, the fear and hope mingling in his voice, echoed painfully in the barren landscape that surrounded us. But deep down, a quiet resignation had begun to settle within me, a striking contrast to Chris's fervent outbursts.

I knew it was futile. Sinking into the fine dust that carpeted the terrain beneath us, I pressed my back against the cold screen, the solid, unyielding surface offering no comfort, only a chilling reminder of our predicament.

"He'll come back for us. Won't he?" Chris's voice, filled with uncertainty and a hint of desperation, broke the heavy silence that had fallen between us.

I sighed, a deep, weary sound that seemed to carry the weight of our situation. "I don't think it matters anymore." My voice, though quiet, was laden with a resignation that felt as vast as the landscape stretching before us.

Chris sat beside me, confusion etching his features. "What do you mean, it doesn't matter anymore?" he asked, his voice laced with a disbelief that mirrored the turmoil swirling within him. His inability to grasp the full magnitude of our situation was palpable, an uneasy reminder of the chasm that uncertainty and fear was carving between us.

"We're not going back," I stated, the realisation heavy in my heart, a declaration that felt as final as it was sudden. The words, once spoken, seemed to hang in the air between us, a sombre acknowledgment of the journey that had brought us to this moment and the uncertain path that lay ahead.

"We're not? But what about work? And the house? And the animals?" Chris's questions tumbled out, each one a poignant reminder of the life we had left behind. His voice, tinged with panic, was a mirror to the internal chaos that the thought of never returning home wrought within us. Each question was a thread in the fabric of our former lives, pulling at the edges of the new reality we found ourselves ensnared in.

Suddenly, a distant sound broke the stillness—a muffled woman's voice, echoing across the barren landscape. It was a beacon of hope in the overwhelming silence, a sign that we were not alone.

"Someone's coming," Chris whispered, his voice laced with panic as he pushed me lower to the ground, a protective instinct kicking in.

I brushed his arm away, annoyed by his fear. "Don't be such a fool," I scolded him, my irritation at his immediate leap to fear overruling the shared apprehension of our situation. Pulling myself to my feet with a newfound resolve, I stood defiantly against the unknown. "Hey! Over here!" I called out, waving my arms towards the source of the voice. This was no time for fear; we needed answers, and perhaps this stranger, whoever she was, could provide them.

Chris's hand gripped my jeans, his fear palpable, a tangible weight that sought to pull me back down to his level of caution. "What are you doing? She could be dangerous!" he cautioned, his voice trembling with the terror of the unknown, his imagination conjuring myriad threats that the stranger might pose.

I looked down at him, a mix of frustration and determination in my gaze. "Get up," I commanded, my voice firm, refusing to let fear dictate our actions. In this unknown world, hesitation and fear would not serve us; they were luxuries we could ill afford. The need for answers, for understanding, outweighed the instinct to hide.

The tall, slender woman gradually slowed her jog as she approached us, her gait smooth and controlled, despite the evident exertion. "Hello," she called out, her voice tinged with a hint of curiosity. Her approach, cautious yet open, suggested a willingness to communicate, to bridge the gap between strangers in a strange land.

Chris, still visibly shaken, hesitantly rose to his feet, his eyes locked onto the approaching stranger, his body tense with the anticipation of the unknown. The moment hung between us, charged with the potential for both danger and discovery, a delicate balance that could tip with a word, a gesture, a misunderstanding.

Yet, there was something in the woman's demeanour, a calm assurance that suggested she was not a threat, that she too was navigating the uncertainties of this world.

"I'm Glenda," she introduced herself, catching her breath from the exertion of her approach. Extending her hand towards me, her gesture was friendly, yet measured, a balance of openness and caution that mirrored my own feelings in this encounter. The sun, casting long shadows across the sandy terrain, seemed to pause, highlighting this moment of human connection amidst the unfamiliar landscape.

"Now is that a good wi—" Chris began, his tone laced with suspicion, the words trailing off as if he were about to question Glenda's intentions or perhaps the wisdom of trusting her so readily.

"Oh stop it!" I scolded him, delivering a quick, admonishing whack across the back of his head. It was neither the time nor the place for his usual skepticism, not when we were faced with the potential for understanding and alliance in this bewildering world. My frustration with his instinctive wariness bubbled to the surface, a sharp contrast to the curiosity and cautious optimism that Glenda's presence inspired in me.

"I'm Karen," I said, shaking Glenda's hand firmly, the contact a tangible affirmation of our mutual desire to connect, to bridge the gap between the known and the unknown. "And this is my husband, Chris," I added, gesturing towards Chris, who stood somewhat awkwardly beside me. His stature, noticeably shorter than mine, did nothing to diminish the strength of his presence, though at that moment, he seemed to shrink further under the weight of the situation.

Glenda then turned to Chris, offering her hand with the same warm openness she had extended to me. "Nice to meet you, Chris," she said, her accent distinctly Swiss, a melodic lilt that spoke of her origins, adding yet another layer of intrigue to her character. Her acknowledgment of Chris, despite his initial suspicion, was a gesture of goodwill, an olive branch extended in the hope of mutual understanding and cooperation.

"Where is Luke?" Glenda inquired, her eyes searching mine for an answer, her sense of urgency a clear reflection of the weight she placed on his absence.

I shrugged, the motion conveying the confusion and anxiety swirling within me. Words seemed insufficient to encapsulate the whirlwind of emotions I was experiencing.

"I don't think he's coming," Chris chimed in, his voice carrying a mix of resignation and frustration.

"He didn't arrive with you?" Glenda pressed, her surprise evident in the arch of her eyebrow.

"No," I responded, the word heavy on my tongue. "I don't think this is how he meant for things to happen." The words felt inadequate, a feeble attempt to rationalise the chaos that had enveloped us. My mind was still reeling, trying to piece together the bizarre sequence of events that had catapulted us into this unfamiliar world.

"It was an accident?" Glenda asked, her voice seeking clarification, a lifeline in the form of understanding, however partial it might be.

I took a deep, steadying breath, trying to marshal my thoughts into coherence. "I don't really understand it, but Luke made the most beautiful colours appear on the back of the living room door. I wanted to touch it, but he told me not to." My recounting felt surreal, as if I were describing a scene from a dream rather than an event that had irrevocably changed the course of our lives.

"He did?" Chris interjected, his tone a mix of surprise and a hint of accusation, as if the revelation shed new light on the events, casting them in a different, more personal light.

"Yes. And then you came bursting through the door and then, well, here we are," I explained, my voice flat, the words spilling out in a torrent of resigned acceptance. The absurdity of our situation, the sheer unpredictability of it, seemed to defy logic.

Chris's eyes widened in disbelief, a visual echo of his inner turmoil. "You're blaming me for this?" he asked, his confusion palpable. The question, laden with incredulity, underscored the complexity of our situation, the intertwining of actions and consequences that had led to our current predicament.

"Well if you had just come through the kitchen like you usually do, this wouldn't..." I began, my voice trailing off, my frustration at the unforeseen impact of our seemingly innocuous actions evident in my tone. The realisation that our ordinary, everyday decisions could have such extraordinary repercussions was a harsh lesson in the unpredictability of fate and the fragile nature of reality as we knew it.

"Guys. Guys!" Glenda interjected firmly, her voice like a beacon of reason piercing through the fog of our escalating argument. Her intervention was a necessary jolt, pulling us back from the brink of a blame game that served no purpose. "I don't think this is really anybody's fault," she said, her words attempting to diffuse the tension that had wound itself tightly around us.

"Of course it is!" Chris exclaimed, unable to contain his agitation. His frustration, simmering just beneath the surface, now boiled over. "It's Luke's fault!" The accusation hung heavily in the air, a tangible manifestation of his need to assign blame, to find some reason in the unreasonable.

Glenda and I fell into a momentary silence, absorbing the weight of Chris's accusation.

"Accident or not," Chris continued, his voice laden with a mix of anger and desperation, "It was ultimately Luke's carelessness that got us in this situation."

"Hmm," I muttered, my mind churning over Chris's point. The reality was that Luke indeed had a lot to answer for, his actions, however unintentional, having catapulted us into this strange world. Yet, laying blame felt like grasping at straws in a storm, a futile attempt to regain control over something far beyond our understanding.

"When can we go back home?" Chris asked Glenda, hope flickering in his eyes like a fragile flame in the darkness.

"We're not," I said sharply, the words slicing through the hopeful tension. My interruption preempted Glenda's response, laying bare the harsh truth that had slowly been dawning on me.

Glenda looked at me, her expression a complex tapestry of surprise and confusion, as if my declaration had shifted the ground beneath her feet.

"This is our home now," I declared, imbuing my voice with a sense of finality that I barely felt. It was a declaration not of acceptance but of resignation, a stark acknowledgment of the reality that confronted us.

"It is?" Chris and Glenda echoed, their voices overlapping in a chorus of disbelief. Their reactions, so perfectly mirrored, were a poignant reminder of the shared disorientation and uncertainty that this strange new world had thrust upon us. The very notion of calling this place 'home' seemed absurd, yet in the absence of a clear path back to our world, the concept of home had become as fluid and elusive as the sands beneath our feet.

My brow furrowed in contemplation, a storm of thoughts swirling within me as I tried to piece together the fragments of past conversations, searching for a thread that might connect to our current, bewildering predicament. Then, a memory surfaced, a flicker of insight amidst the confusion. "Do you remember the times we sat in bed at night, and I used to joke to you about those crazy dreams Luke would tell Jane and I about on the bus?" I asked Chris, my voice tinged with a mix of nostalgia and urgency. I was seeking a connection, a clue that might explain the inexplicable, linking Luke's fanciful tales to the surreal reality we now found ourselves in.

"Yeah," Chris replied, his expression shifting from confusion to one of dawning realisation, as if my question had turned a key within him, unlocking a door to understanding that he hadn't realised was there.

I bent down, the action deliberate, and scooped up a handful of the dust that blanketed the ground beneath us. Its texture was unfamiliar, yet it held within it the key to understanding our situation, a tangible piece of the puzzle that Luke had unknowingly provided us. "Hold your hands out," I instructed Chris, my tone firm yet filled with a burgeoning sense of awe. "I think it may actually all be real," I said, as I let the dust cascade gently into his open palms, each grain a witness to the truth of our situation.

"Shit," he gasped softly, the expletive a whisper of acknowledgment, a quiet surrender to the vast, incomprehensible truth that enveloped us. The reality of our situation, once the subject of disbelief and speculation, began to sink in, settling into the marrow of our bones with the undeniable weight of truth. The dust in his hands, a physical manifestation of our presence in this world, was a silent, eloquent confirmation of the unimaginable journey we had embarked upon, spurred by the dreams of a friend who had always seemed just a bit out of step with the world as we knew it.

Unexpected Excitement flickered in my eyes, the thrill of the unknown propelling me forward as I bombarded Glenda with questions. "How many people are there? Are we close to the capital? And what of the facility?" I asked, my words tumbling out in a rapid stream, a reflection of the whirlwind of thoughts and memories spinning through my mind. Each question was a desperate grasp at understanding the scope and structure of this unfamiliar world, a world that had, until now, existed only in the realm of Luke's dreams and our unimaginable reality.

Glenda's expression morphed into one of confusion. "Capital? Facility?" she echoed, her voice laced with perplexity. "What facility?" Her questions, simple yet profound, punctured the bubble of excitement that had enveloped me, a sharp reminder of the vast differences in our understanding and experiences.

"You know, the breeding facility," I clarified, my voice carrying an assumption of shared knowledge, believing that Luke's vivid dreams, which I had once dismissed as mere fantasies, would have some basis in the reality of this world.

Glenda stared at me blankly, her lack of recognition a cold splash of reality on my fervent hopes. The disconnect in our conversation was evident, a chasm of understanding that neither of us knew how to bridge.

"I don't think Glenda knows what you're talking about," Chris pointed out, his voice tinged with disappointment. His observation, though gentle, felt like a confirmation of our isolation.

Glenda's expression turned sombre. "There's only a few of us. We're just a tiny settlement," she admitted, her admission dampening the initial thrill of discovery. Her words painted a picture of a world far removed from the bustling civilisation I had envisioned, a stark, lonely outpost on the fringe of the unknown.

"Take us," I said, the mixture of excitement and doubt in my voice betraying the tumult of emotions within me. Despite the uncertainty and the growing realisation that my preconceptions might not align with the reality of Clivilius, the desire to understand, to see and experience this world firsthand, remained undiminished.

"Sure," Glenda nodded in agreement, her willingness to guide us a sliver of light in the murky waters of our situation.

BLANK CANVAS

4338.208.3

We trudged silently behind Glenda, our feet sinking into the thick dust that blanketed the rugged landscape of Clivilius. With each step, a cloud of fine particles rose, coating our clothes and skin in a layer of the planet's essence. The terrain was harsh and unyielding, marked by small hills that seemed to challenge our resolve with every incline we traversed. Our exhaustion grew with the landscape, reflecting the distance between our expectations and the reality we now faced.

Eventually, signs of habitation materialised before us, breaking the monotony of the barren landscape. My heart sank as I took in the sight of the so-called settlement. It was a disappointing contrast to the images that had been conjured in my mind when Luke had shared his dreams. "Not much of a settlement, is it," Chris remarked, his voice tinged with disappointment, a sentiment that resonated deeply with my own feelings.

I surveyed the scene before us: several large tents and a small campfire constituted the entirety of the settlement. It was primitive, a far cry from the utopian world Luke had painted in our conversations. The disparity between expectation and reality was jarring. "Is this it?" I asked, my voice laden with dismay, unable to mask the disillusionment that clawed at my chest.

"This is it," Glenda confirmed, her voice carrying a sense of pride that seemed incongruous with the modesty of our surroundings. "Welcome to Bixbus." Her pride, despite the simplicity of the settlement, hinted at stories and struggles we had yet to understand, a depth to this place that went beyond its physical appearance.

"Bixbus?" Chris echoed, his confusion palpable. The name added another layer of mystery to our already bewildering situation. "I thought we were in Clivilius?"

Glenda chuckled lightly. "Oh, we are in Clivilius, but we've called our own little settlement Bixbus." Her explanation, while simple, spoke volumes about the human capacity to adapt and to carve out a sense of belonging, even in the most unusual of environments.

Chris responded sheepishly to the revelation of Bixbus, his demeanour a mix of confusion and subdued excitement, a reflection of the internal struggle we both faced in reconciling our dreams with our reality. And I, I fell into a deep, contemplative silence, my thoughts swirling as memories of the bus rides with Luke and Jane flooded back. Those conversations, once filled with laughter and speculative dreams, now felt like distant echoes of a past that was irretrievably lost.

We had often mused about a world ready for a fresh start, a blank canvas where the mistakes of our past could be washed clean, a place where we could live in harmony with nature. Chris, with his inherent love for the land and sustainable living, had always been more enthusiastic than I about these discussions. His passion, his vision for a future that was both simple and profound, was one of the things I admired most about him. It was a vision that had always seemed just within reach, a tangible future if only we dared to grasp it.

But standing here, in the underwhelming reality of Bixbus, I realised how unprepared I was for this new life. The barrenness of the landscape was suffocating, a sharp contrast to our discussions that were filled with lush greenery and thriving communities. Here, the emptiness stretched as far as the eye could see, a visual representation of the isolation that now enveloped us. The vibrant world we had envisioned, where nature and humanity existed in a delicate balance, seemed a naïve fantasy in the face of this desolate reality.

Where are all the people? The trees? The animals? And where is the capital? These questions hammered in my mind, a relentless tide of confusion and disappointment. I sucked in a huge gulp of air, trying to calm the rising panic, to find some grounding in this unfamiliar world. *This is the capital! Bixbus is the capital!* The realisation hit me like a physical blow, a cool tingle running up my spine as the full weight of our situation settled around me.

A young man emerged from one of the tents, his presence momentarily diverting our attention from the desolation that surrounded us. The small Shih Tzu that followed at his heels offered a flicker of normality, a reminder of the world we had left behind. "Duke?" I asked, crouching down to greet the little dog, the sight of him a small beacon of comfort. It was strange how the presence of something as simple as a dog could momentarily lighten the weight of our circumstances.

"You know him?" Glenda inquired, her curiosity evident as she watched my interaction with Duke. Her question, simple yet filled with implications, hinted at the unexpected connections that seemed to weave through our small gathering.

"Not really," I replied, my eyes meeting hers. "I've seen pictures. Is Henri here too?" My question was driven by a mix of hope and the desire for familiarity, for any thread that could link this strange new world to the one we had known.

Glenda pointed towards the tent, her laughter lightening the moment as the shorter, fatter Shih Tzu made a half-hearted attempt to follow Duke. The sight of the dogs, so carefree in their actions, offered a brief respite from the overwhelming reality of our situation.

"Hi," the young man greeted us. "I'm Jamie." His introduction was straightforward, yet his presence here, in Bixbus, added another layer to the unfolding mystery of our arrival.

"Ahh," I said, a realisation dawning on me. "Luke's partner." The pieces of the puzzle began to click into place, though the picture they formed was still incomplete.

"Yep," he replied, his expression sombre. The weight of his single word carried an undercurrent of emotion, a reflection of the complexities and challenges that lay beneath the surface of our casual meeting.

"This is Karen and her husband, Chris," Glenda announced, formally bridging the gap between us.

"Bus friend Karen?" Jamie asked, his eyes narrowing in recognition.

I chuckled, a small release in the tension that had built up since our arrival. "Yes, that'd be me." The acknowledgment of my identity, once so closely tied to my daily routine and interactions on Earth, now felt like a title from another life, a reminder of the distance we had travelled, both physically and metaphorically.

"I'd normally say nice to meet you, but this is hardly a fun place to meet in," Jamie said with a palpable lack of enthusiasm. His words, though perhaps intended as candid, seemed to echo the barrenness of the landscape, amplifying the sense of isolation that had begun to settle in my heart since our arrival in Bixbus.

Feeling my pulse quicken, I realised the truth in Luke's description of Jamie. His negative energy was almost tangible, casting a shadow over our already grim situation. It was a presence that we could ill afford, especially now, as Chris and I grappled with the reality of our new life. Chris, already burdened with his own fears and doubts, didn't need this additional weight, this confirmation of our worst fears.

I glanced quickly between Glenda and Jamie, making a decision. The need for space, for a moment to think and regroup, was pressing. "Do you mind if Chris and I take a moment for a quick chat, just us?" I asked, my voice steady despite the turmoil churning within me. It was a request for distance, for a brief respite from the collective anxiety that Jamie's introduction had exacerbated.

"Sure," Glenda responded, her tone laced with understanding. "A river runs behind the tents. Might make a more pleasant spot for you."

"Thanks, Glenda," I said, a genuine note of gratitude in my voice. Her guidance felt like a lifeline, a path to a momentary escape from the overwhelming reality that awaited us in Bixbus. I took Chris by the arm, gently leading him away from the group and towards the river, seeking a moment of solitude. The prospect of the river, of water running free and clear, offered a symbolic promise of renewal, a chance to wash away the immediate dread and perhaps find clarity in the midst of our confusion.

"Karen, what are you doing?" Chris asked once we were a safe distance away, his voice laced with confusion and a hint of concern. The tranquility of the river did little to ease the tension that had built between us.

I turned to face him, feeling the seriousness of our situation wash over me like a cold wave. The lines on my face deepened. "Listen to me. I remember Luke telling me about a very specific dream. It was about the role that you and I would play in the new world," I began, my words tinged with a mix of urgency and hope. It was a leap of faith, invoking Luke's dreams as a beacon in our current darkness, clinging to the possibility that there was more to his stories than mere fantasy.

"Come on, Karen," Chris interjected, his skepticism a sharp contrast to the earnestness in my voice. "That was all just fantasy. All those times you and I talked about it, none of it was real." His disbelief, though understandable, felt like another obstacle to overcome, a reminder of the chasm between hope and reality.

"Chris," I cut in, my voice firm with determination, not allowing his doubt to derail the moment. "Quiet yourself," I urged him, needing him to truly listen, to open his mind beyond the confines of our past discussions and entertain the possibility that there was a deeper truth to uncover.

Chris complied, albeit reluctantly, closing his eyes and taking several deep breaths. It was a visible effort to find some semblance of inner peace. His shoulders relaxed slightly, a sign that he was at least willing to entertain my request.

"What does your mind show you?" I prompted gently, watching him intently. It was a question born of desperation and hope, a plea for him to connect with something beyond our understanding, to find a clue or a sign that would guide us forward.

As Chris mumbled quietly, his words blending with the soothing sounds of the river, I gazed across the wide expanse of water, allowing myself a moment of silent reflection. *Clivilius, if you are there, help him see,* I silently implored, my heart clinging to the slim hope for some guidance, some sign.

Chris's eyes fluttered open, a newfound confidence in his gaze that took me by surprise. "I think you're right, Karen," he affirmed, his demeanour shifting from skepticism to something that bordered on belief. It was a transformation, however small, that filled me with a sense of relief and renewed purpose.

Just then, the sound of a vehicle near the tents drew my attention, cutting through our quiet conversation. "Shall we?"

I asked, feeling a surge of curiosity. Despite the uncertainty and complexity of our situation, the arrival of others at the small camp was a chance to see who else was here.

Chris shrugged, his silent gesture of agreement an acknowledgment of our shared interest. Together, we walked back to the camp, the bond between us momentarily fortified by our mutual curiosity.

As we approached, two young men were stepping out of a dust-covered ute, their presence an anomaly in the desolate landscape of Bixbus. I couldn't help but wonder, *Where did they come from?* My observations during our arrival hadn't revealed any tracks or signs of other settlements, adding another layer of mystery to the already perplexing situation of Clivilius.

"That was bloody awesome!" one exclaimed, his voice filled with exhilaration as he high-fived the other. Their carefree demeanour and laughter were starkly out of place in the grim reality of Bixbus, yet it brought a momentary lightness to the air.

"Apart from clogging up the engine!" the other laughed, his mirth echoing in the barren landscape. Their joy, though infectious, felt like a distant memory to me, a reminder of a time when such simple pleasures weren't overshadowed by the weight of survival in an unfamiliar world.

"Guys!" Glenda interjected, her voice cutting through their jovial banter. "We have two new guests," she announced, her tone shifting to a more formal register, introducing us as if our arrival was an event of some significance within the small confines of their community.

"I wouldn't call them guests," Jamie's voice sliced in, his tone laced with cynicism. "They're not going anywhere." His words, though harsh, rang with an uncomfortable truth, casting a shadow over the brief moment of levity. The group fell into an awkward silence, the air suddenly heavy with the implications of his statement.

"I'm Paul," the taller man broke the silence, extending his hand towards us, a gesture of welcome that momentarily bridged the gap between our worlds.

"Chris Owen," said Chris, his grip firm as he shook Paul's hand. "And this is my wife, Karen," he introduced me, a hint of pride in his voice.

"Nice to meet you, Karen," Paul said, turning his attention to me. His handshake was firm, yet friendly, a warmth in his grasp that belied the harshness of our surroundings. It was a simple human connection, yet it held within it the promise of understanding, of potential friendship.

Meanwhile, the younger lad introduced himself to Chris and then to me. "Kain," he said, his handshake equally firm. "Jamie's nephew." The introduction brought a flicker of recognition across my face, connecting the dots of our arrival to the web of relationships that constituted this small community.

"Ahh," I responded, acknowledging the connection. Paul gestured towards Jamie, who was still standing near the front of the centre tent with Henri at his feet, a silent sentinel amidst our growing acquaintance. "I see you've met Jamie then," he said, a note of camaraderie in his voice.

"We've only just met," I replied. "But Luke told us a lot about him over the years." My words, meant to convey familiarity, seemed to echo strangely in the open air, a reminder of the distance between what we knew of Jamie through Luke's stories and the man standing before us.

"Us?" Chris interjected, a note of confusion in his voice. "I've never heard his name before." His statement, while true, highlighted the selective nature of the narratives we shared, the pieces of our lives we chose to reveal to one another.

"Not you, darling. Jane," I clarified, turning to face him.

"Who's Jane?" Kain asked, his curiosity piqued.

Paul's exclamation cut through the growing list of questions. "Oh, you must be one of Luke's bus friends!" The recognition, while accurate, felt reductive, framing my connection to Luke within the confines of a daily commute. I was more than just a 'bus friend', but perhaps to these people, that was all I was.

"Yes," I replied simply, my response a concession to the role I played in their understanding of Luke's world. My mind wandered, pondering the nature of my relationship with Luke. We had been close, sharing moments of laughter and serious discussions in the confines of a city bus, yet standing here, in the shadow of Clivilius, I wondered if our connection had been as profound as I had believed.

"But where is Luke?" Kain asked, his gaze shifting between Chris and me, his question cutting through the tentative bonds we had just begun to form with our introductions. His inquiry, innocent yet laden with implications, seemed to cast a shadow over our small gathering, reminding us all of the person whose absence was as palpable as the dust under our feet.

"He's not here," I answered, the words heavy on my tongue, feeling a pang of disappointment and confusion that seemed to resonate with the barren landscape around us. The absence of Luke, the catalyst for our journey to this world, loomed large, a silent question mark hanging over us.

Paul looked questioningly at Glenda, seeking an explanation, his expression one of concern and confusion.

"Appears this was another accident," Glenda explained, her tone resigned, as if this were not the first time unforeseen events had shaped the course of their lives here in Bixbus. Her words, though sparse, hinted at a history of unpredictability and challenges that we were only just beginning to grasp.

Kain muttered something under his breath, his comment almost inaudible, a low murmur that seemed to carry the weight of shared understanding among those who had lived in Bixbus longer than we had.

"Not to be rude," Paul said, his curiosity piqued, breaking the momentary lull that had fallen over our group. "But what do you actually do?" His question, though direct, was a bridge back to normality, an attempt to understand us beyond the circumstances of our unexpected arrival.

"I'm an entomologist," I responded, feeling a sense of pride in my profession swell within me, a reminder of the life I had led before finding myself in this unforeseen situation. It was a piece of my identity that remained unchanged, a constant in a world that had been turned upside down.

"A what?" Paul asked, his confusion clear.

Kain jumped in with a simplified explanation. "She studies bugs." His attempt at clarification, though well-intentioned, missed the nuance of my work, reducing it to a colloquial understanding.

"Oh," said Paul, the deep lines of confusion still riddling his face.

I corrected Kain, my tone patient but firm. "Insects. Not bugs." It was a small distinction, but an important one, a clarification that spoke not only to the specifics of my profession but also to the importance of understanding and precision, qualities that seemed all the more vital in this new and unfamiliar world.

Paul's confusion seemed only to grow as I delved into the specifics of my profession, but I persisted, driven by a need to make him understand the significance of my work, even here, in Clivilius. "Well, insects need an environment to thrive. I work with the University of Tasmania to understand how they contribute to ecosystems and work with local communities and environmental groups to petition for greater protections," I explained, my voice laced with the passion I felt for my field. It was important to me that they grasp the essence of my work, the belief that even in this strange world, the principles of ecological balance and conservation should still apply.

"That's great!" Paul responded, his enthusiasm genuine even if his understanding seemed superficial. His reaction, though encouraging, left me wondering about the relevance of my life's work in a place that seemed so removed from the environmental causes I had championed back on Earth.

He then turned his attention to Chris, perhaps seeking something more relatable in his profession. "I do yard work," Chris stated simply, his voice carrying a hint of pride. It was a straightforward declaration, yet it encapsulated so much of who Chris was: a man of the earth, someone who found satisfaction in the tangible results of his labour.

"Yard work?" Kain echoed, his curiosity clearly piqued by Chris's concise description. The concept, so mundane back on Earth, seemed to intrigue Kain, perhaps for its simplicity or the direct interaction with the land it implied.

Instead of elaborating with words, Chris chose to demonstrate. He crouched down and scooped up a handful of the pervasive dust, the action symbolic of our current reality. It was a poignant gesture, highlighting the stark contrast between the yard work he was accustomed to and the barren, dust-covered landscape of Bixbus. Here, the very soil we stood on looked to pose a challenge unlike any we had faced before.

"It's everywhere!" Paul exclaimed, stating the obvious.

Chris let the dust cascade through his fingers, his gesture thoughtful and deliberate. "Yeah. I've noticed that," he said, his gaze lifting to meet mine. In his eyes, a mixture of determination and acceptance reflected back at me. "But if this is our home now, we'll find a way." His words, simple yet profound, warmed my heart. Despite the uncertainty, the daunting challenges that lay ahead, and the desolation that surrounded us, I felt a surge of hope knowing Chris was by my side, ready to face whatever came our way.

"Call me crazy. But I trust Luke," I declared to the group, my voice steady, infused with conviction. It was a statement of faith, not just in Luke but in the vision that had brought us here, despite the inner turmoil and doubt that ebbed and flowed within me.

Jamie's scoff cut sharply through the air, a discordant note in the tentative harmony we were trying to build. "You're definitely crazy then," he remarked, his voice dripping with skepticism.

I stood firm, refusing to be drawn into a petty argument with Jamie. Throughout my career as an entomologist, I had faced disbelief and skepticism, had learned to defend my beliefs and the importance of my work against those who lacked vision or understanding. Jamie's dismissive attitude, though disheartening, only fuelled my determination, my resolve to prove the value of hope and vision.

Filled with resolve, I addressed the group, my voice clear and unwavering. "A beautiful masterpiece starts with a single brushstroke. This is our blank canvas. Let's create a masterpiece. Together." My words, a call to action, hung in the air, an invitation to each of us to join in shaping this new world, to move beyond survival and begin the work of building something meaningful.

Despite the challenges, the lack of resources, and the overwhelming sense of the unknown, I believed in the potential of what we could achieve together. My declaration was more than just words; it was a commitment to the future, to the belief that, together, we could transform the barren landscape of Bixbus into a thriving community, a new home that reflected the best of what we could imagine and create together.

DIRTY MIRACLE

4338.208.4

"I better check-in with Joel," Jamie said, breaking the silence that had enveloped us. "Nice to meet you both," he added, his voice trailing off, dissolving into the air as he disappeared into the tent. The fabric swallowed him whole, leaving behind a ripple of curiosity in his wake.

"Joel?" I questioned, unable to mask the intrigue in my voice. The name felt like a piece of a puzzle, a clue to the intricate tapestry of lives intertwined in this makeshift community. It was strange, this sensation of being both an outsider and yet intimately connected through shared circumstance. Everyone here, it seemed, carried their own hidden stories, their personal struggles tucked away like letters in a drawer, in this unfamiliar world that we were all trying to navigate.

"Jamie's son," Glenda clarified, her voice a soft undertone in the bright sun. There was a depth to her words, an unspoken understanding that behind each name was a saga, a battle fought in the quiet spaces of our hearts.

"He's not been well," Paul added, his voice quick, laced with concern. He threw a glance towards Glenda, a silent exchange that spoke of shared worries and unvoiced fears. His attempt at optimism was evident, an effort to cast a ray of hope in the shadow of uncertainty. "I'm sure he'll be fine after a few days' rest." Yet, the worry in his eyes, the slight tremble in his voice, betrayed his true feelings, revealing the fragile veneer of hope.

"Yes," Glenda concurred, her agreement tinged with a resignation that seemed to echo in the air between us. Her sideways glance at Paul was a dance of empathy and concern. "Perhaps you and Kain would be best moving back in there for a short time," she suggested, her gaze drifting towards Jamie's tent.

Paul's expression faltered for a moment, a crack in his carefully maintained cheerfulness. But he quickly recovered, mustering a smile that seemed to draw strength from somewhere deep within. "We have another tent," he declared, pointing towards the ute with a semblance of cheerfulness that belied the undercurrents of tension.

"Brilliant!" Glenda exclaimed, her voice carrying a relief so palpable it felt like a balm to the unease that had settled over us.

I nudged Chris gently, hinting that it was our turn to lend a hand. As we made our way towards the ute, Kain was already in the midst of unloading, his movements methodical, almost meditative. "Looks like they got a little dusty," he observed, a lightness in his tone as he expelled a breath, sending a small cloud of red dust swirling into the air. The particles danced in the sunbeam, casting a brief, fiery glow before dissipating into the vast, open expanse.

I watched, momentarily captivated yet troubled by the sight. The dust particles, suspended in the air like tiny, drifting embers, seemed to carry with them a silent warning. *Breathing hazard*, the thought echoed in my mind, a reminder of the invisible dangers that lurked in this beautiful yet harsh landscape.

"Here, let me take that," Chris's voice broke through my reverie, his offer to Kain breaking the pattern of my thoughts.

"Thanks," Kain responded, his nod carrying a weight of gratitude.

"May as well put it next to ours, I guess," Paul's suggestion came from a practical standpoint, yet there was an underlying invitation in his words, a subtle nod towards inclusion and unity. He pointed towards a third tent, its solitary position on the left marking the spot for this new tent, a new addition to this makeshift community.

Chris nodded in agreement and headed towards the indicated tent. I watched him go, appreciating his willingness to help despite the uncertainty surrounding us.

"Tent pegs," Paul's voice drew me back. He handed me a small, rectangular box, its contents essential yet so easily overlooked.

"Thanks," I replied. Clutching the box, I turned towards Chris, my sneakers pressing into the soft, yielding earth, leaving faint impressions behind. "Chris," I called out, hastening my steps to catch up with him.

As Chris let the box drop to the ground with a heavy clunk, the sound echoed around us. I reached his side just as he was examining our provisional shelter, placing the smaller box of tent pegs atop his. The solid thud of the boxes connecting felt symbolic, like the sealing of our fate in this new, uncharted life.

"What do you think?" I ventured, my voice tinged with a mix of hope and apprehension. I was eager to hear his thoughts, to find some solace in shared perspectives about our new living quarters.

"Looks like this is another ten-man tent, just like the other three," he observed, his finger tracing the picture on the label. His brow furrowed as he took in the vast expanse that surrounded us. "It could be worse, I guess." His attempt at optimism did little to dispel the unease that had begun to grow within me.

My frustration and confusion surged, breaking through the façade of calm I had been struggling to maintain. "I just don't understand," I confessed, the words spilling out amidst a sigh. A bead of sweat traced a line down my forehead, a reminder of the relentless heat and the dust that seemed to permeate everything. The uncertainty of our situation was a constant, oppressive companion, its weight ever present. "I Just…I…" My voice trailed off, lost in the vastness of our surroundings.

Chris squatted down and scooped up two handfuls of the omnipresent dust, letting it sift through his fingers in a silent, poignant gesture. "I don't understand how any of this is actually real," he admitted, his voice low, almost lost against the backdrop of our desolation. "But it feels real." His words mirrored my own thoughts, a reflection of the disbelief and bewilderment that gnawed at the edges of my consciousness.

"I just thought there'd be more," I murmured, almost to myself. My gaze wandered over the sparse, unforgiving landscape, seeking something, anything, that might offer a hint of solace, a promise of more than just dust and survival.

"Well, looks like there can't be much less," Chris replied, his tone laced with a wry resignation as he stood. His comment, meant to inject a dose of dry humour, instead served as a blunt reminder of our predicament.

Standing there, beside Chris, I couldn't help but feel a profound sense of dislocation, as if we had been uprooted from our lives and planted in a foreign soil, expected to thrive. The vast, open sky, the relentless sun, and the endless expanse of dust – they were all constant reminders of our vulnerability, of the sheer magnitude of the challenge that lay ahead.

Determined to carve out a semblance of normality amid the uncertainty, I gently took Chris's arm, my voice laced with a resolve that I hoped was infectious. "Come on," I coaxed, feeling the rough fabric of his sleeve beneath my fingers. "We may as well keep ourselves busy until we figure this all out."

The air was thick with dust and a tangible sense of unease, yet I found a strange comfort in the act of doing, of moving forward even when the path was unclear.

Chris released a sigh, a soft exhalation that seemed to carry with it the weight of our shared apprehension. Yet, he acquiesced, allowing me to lead him towards the ute where our next box awaited.

As we approached, the sound of Kain's voice floated towards us, suggesting a reshuffling of roles that momentarily caught me off guard. "Chris and I can help," I found myself saying, my voice louder than I intended, propelled by a desire to be useful. "We're used to camping when we go on our short research trips. Shouldn't take too long." It was a small piece of our past, a reminder of a time when our biggest concern was data collection, not survival.

Glenda's smile, warm and genuine, was a beacon in the dimming light. "That'd be great," she responded, her gratitude evident.

Paul, unsure of his role now, asked, "So what am I doing now?"

The silence that followed was telling, a mirror to the disconnect that lingered beneath the surface of our interactions. It was then that I pondered on Glenda's place among us. The realisation that, apart from her and me, everyone was linked by familial ties struck a chord. It dawned on me that Glenda, much like us, must have been chosen for her unique skills, yet her story remained unasked, untold. *What does Glenda do?* The question echoed in my mind, a mystery amidst the myriad of unknowns.

Glenda's voice broke through my reverie, her directive to Paul clear and purposeful. "You're helping us put up the tent."

"Great. Let's get to it," Paul's response was almost too eager, a sudden shift from his previous uncertainty. Watching him, I couldn't help but speculate about the man behind the enthusiasm. His background, perhaps rooted in the digital world, seemed at odds with our current necessities. It was a reminder of the diverse paths that had led us here, to this moment of communal effort under the vast, unforgiving sky. Each of us, with our disparate backgrounds and skills, now faced the common task of building a new life from the dust of the old. In this endeavour, every hand, every skill, was invaluable, even if its application had yet to be discovered.

❖

As we delved into the task of setting up the tent, I found myself immersed in the intricacies of poles and fabric, a task that demanded my full attention. This focus was a gift, allowing me to momentarily sideline the barrage of questions and fears that had become constant companions in my mind. The physicality of the work, the feel of the canvas and the metallic coolness of the poles, anchored me in the present, a reprieve from the uncertainty that clouded our future.

Watching Paul and Glenda bicker over the instructions, I couldn't help but smile. Their exchange, filled with mock frustration and exaggerated gestures, was a slice of normality in our otherwise abnormal situation. It was strange, considering the unusualness of our circumstances, how such a simple interaction could weave a thread of lightness through the heavy fabric of our reality. It reminded me that humanity finds ways to adapt, to seek moments of connection and joy, even in the most dire of situations.

My initial impressions of Glenda had been hastily formed, a surface-level assessment that failed to capture the depth of her character. As I observed her navigate the task with a calm efficiency, her actions spoke volumes of her experience and practicality. She moved with a confidence that was both impressive and inspiring, her hands deftly securing the tent's structure, her instructions clear and purposeful. It was evident that she was no stranger to this kind of work; her skillset was invaluable in our current context.

Chris's voice, a familiar beacon, drew me back from the edge of my ruminations. "Hey, Karen," he beckoned, his form hunched over as he worked to secure the tent.

"What's up?" I asked, joining him on the ground. My voice carried a mix of curiosity and a faint, underlying hope that perhaps he had stumbled upon something, anything, that hinted at the presence of life in this barren expanse. The silence that enveloped us was oppressive, a dramatic reminder of our isolation. I found myself yearning for even the smallest nuisance, a buzzing fly or the whisper of leaves, as a proof to life's persistence.

Chris handed me the tent peg with a gesture that hinted at something beyond the ordinary. "Take a look at this," he prompted, a trace of intrigue lacing his words. I turned the peg over in my hands, searching for whatever anomaly had caught his attention.

"What am I supposed to be looking at?" I queried, my brows knitting together in confusion. The peg seemed unremarkable, a simple piece of metal, its significance escaping me.

"Try pushing it into the ground," Chris suggested, his voice tinged with a note of discovery. His instruction hinted at an unexpected revelation, something out of the ordinary in our otherwise mundane task.

"You could have told me that to start with," I retorted, my words laced with a playful reprimand as I offered him a smirk.

I pressed the peg into the earth, feeling the initial give of the dust before encountering an abrupt resistance. It was as if the ground itself had solidified, forming an impenetrable layer just beneath the surface. The sensation was unsettling.

"You have to push it harder," Chris encouraged, his eyes sparkling with a mixture of challenge and support. His words, simple as they were, felt like a nudge towards a discovery waiting just beneath the surface.

Confused yet intrigued, I applied more pressure to the peg, expecting it to yield to my efforts. Instead, it stubbornly resisted, moving only marginally deeper. The resistance was unexpected, a silent witness to the unknowns that lay beneath the thin veneer of dust and sand that blanketed everything in Bixbus.

"Hold on a sec," Chris interjected, seeing the futility of my attempts. I paused, stepping back slightly to give him room. Watching Chris dive into the task of uncovering what lay beneath was like watching a child explore the mysteries of a hidden treasure. His hands moved with an energy and purpose that kicked up clouds of dust around us, each motion revealing more of the hard surface that had thwarted my efforts.

I held the peg loosely in my hands, my anticipation building as Chris's digging deepened. There was something about the way he worked, with such focused determination, that transformed the mundane task into an adventure. It struck me then, the stark contrast between the desolation of our surroundings and the vitality of human curiosity. The dust of Bixbus, which had seemed so lifeless and oppressive, now served as the backdrop to a moment of discovery.

The air was thick with the scent of disturbed earth as Chris cleared a small area around the stubborn peg. I leaned forward, driven by a mix of determination and the thrill of the unknown. Positioning the peg once more, I put all my weight behind it, pushing down with a force born of both frustration and hope.

Suddenly, with a sound that resonated with the finality of breaking barriers, the peg cracked through the crust. The resistance gave way so abruptly that I stumbled forward, caught off guard by the ease with which the peg now sank into the ground. The moment was fleeting but filled with a profound sense of achievement and the exhilarating realisation that beneath the harsh exterior of Bixbus, there was room for us to anchor ourselves, however tentatively.

"Holy shit!" Chris's exclamation cut through the air, a blend of shock and wonder that momentarily lifted the weight of our situation. I couldn't help but react, a mix of reprimand and amusement colouring my voice as I regained my footing. "Chris!" His enthusiasm, though at times overwhelming, had a way of piercing the monotony of the daily grind.

"Did you see that?" he continued, undaunted, his hands working feverishly to clear the area around the tent peg.

"No. I was too busy falling on my face, wasn't I?" I retorted, my words dripping with sarcasm. Yet, despite my tone, there was a part of me that was drawn to his excitement.

Chris, oblivious to my sarcasm, picked up a tiny object from the freshly disturbed earth. "Here, look. I think it's a seed," he said, his voice teeming with the thrill of discovery as he handed me the small speck.

Examining it closely, I recognised the shape and texture immediately. "It's a coriander seed," I stated, unable to keep the disappointment from seeping into my voice. In the context of our surroundings, the seed seemed incongruously mundane.

"What the fuck is a coriander seed doing buried under the crust!?" Chris's whisper was filled with awe, as if the seed held the answers to the mysteries of Bixbus. His fascination with the find was both endearing and slightly absurd, considering our circumstances.

"It wasn't," I sighed, the reality of the situation dawning on me. Reaching into my shirt pocket, I retrieved a small ziplock bag filled with coriander seeds. As I opened the bag, a few more coriander seeds spilled out, dotting the soil with reminders of home.

Chris's initial burst of excitement dwindled as quickly as it had surged, his shoulders sagging slightly under the weight of disappointment. "Oh!" he sighed, the sound heavy with the realisation of his mistake. There was a palpable shift in the air, a momentary lull that seemed to mirror his deflated spirits.

"I must have forgotten to give them to Jane," I admitted, the words leaving me with a twinge of foolishness.

"I should have known," Chris mumbled, more to himself than to me, a hint of self-reproach in his tone.

"But I didn't bring those," I said, my focus shifting abruptly as something else caught my eye. It was an unexpected sight that reignited a spark of curiosity within me, cutting through the fog of our earlier disappointment.

"Shit!" Chris couldn't contain his renewed excitement, the word slipping out with an impulsive fervour that was infectious despite the situation.

"Chris! Language!" I couldn't help but chide him, though my heart wasn't in the reprimand. My attention was riveted on the small green shoots that had appeared in the soil, an unexpected green amidst the brown and red of the landscape.

"Are they...?" Chris began, his question trailing off as the same realisation dawned on him.

"Coriander plants," I confirmed, completing his thought. There we were, hunched over these tiny, defiant shoots, a mix of disbelief and awe washing over us. For a moment, the harsh reality of Bixbus faded into the background, replaced by the simple wonder of life asserting itself.

"Did they grow just then?" he wondered aloud, his hands gently cradling the soil around the fledgling plants as if to protect them from the harshness of their environment.

"I'm pretty sure they weren't there before," I responded, my words heavy with sarcasm yet lightened by the undercurrent of shared excitement. "Honestly Chris, sometimes you ask the most stupid questions." But even as I teased him, I couldn't ignore the thrill of discovery, the reminder that, against all odds, growth and life could find a way, even here.

As I tenderly placed another coriander seed into the soil cradled in Chris's hands, the act felt almost ceremonial. The barren landscape of Bixbus, with its unyielding surface and harsh conditions, had offered little in the way of hope or sustenance. Yet here we were, defying those very limitations. Chris's observation, likening our anticipation to watching a kettle boil, was apt yet carried a lightness that contrasted sharply with the gravity of our action.

"Shh!" I couldn't help but silence him, my hand fluttering in the air between us. The moment felt too crucial, too fragile for casual conversation. My heart raced with a mix of nervous excitement and profound concentration. I was desperate to witness this phenomenon again, to confirm that the first time hadn't been a fluke, that life could indeed find a foothold here.

"I don't think either talking or silence is going to make a difference," Chris retorted, a hint of amusement in his voice. Despite his words, he complied, adopting a silence that mirrored my own reverent watchfulness.

As the seconds stretched into minutes, the soil in Chris's hands became a microcosm of anticipation. Then, with a subtlety that belied the enormity of the event, the seed's shell cracked. It was a small, almost imperceptible change at first, but it quickly unfolded into something extraordinary. Roots shyly reached out into the soil, and a slender stalk pushed upward, unfurling tiny leaves that seemed to grasp at the light.

The process, so rapid it bordered on the miraculous, was unlike anything we'd witnessed on Earth. It was as if the seed, and by extension, we, had tapped into something fundamental within the soil of Bixbus, a latent potential for life that we had not dared to hope for.

Witnessing the emergence of the coriander plant from the barren dust was a moment of pure wonder, a beautiful reminder of life's resilience and its capacity to thrive in even the most unlikely places. The experience sent a wave of hope coursing through me. *If a simple coriander seed could take root and flourish with such vigour, what else might be possible in Clivilius?*

❖

Glenda's approach seemed to weave another layer into the tapestry of our small, makeshift community's moment of discovery. "Where the hell did that come from?" Her inquiry, tinged with both astonishment and a thick Swiss accent, perfectly encapsulated the shared sense of bewilderment that enveloped us.

Chris, grounding us once again in the practicalities of our situation, took it upon himself to elucidate. "There's a thick crust beneath all the layers of dust, and there appears to be living soil beneath the crust." His tone was calm, almost reflective, betraying the depth of his wonder at the revelation that beneath the barren exterior of Bixbus lay a layer of fertile promise.

"Fascinating," Glenda echoed, her voice a soft murmur of intrigue as she crouched beside us. Her interest, inherently scientific, was visibly sparked by the phenomenon unfolding before our eyes. "And the plants?" she inquired.

I found myself holding up the small zip-lock bag of coriander seeds, an offering of explanation to the mystery we were all contemplating. "Coriander seeds," I stated, attempting to encapsulate both the ordinariness and the sheer improbability of what we had witnessed. It was a simple truth, yet it held within it the weight of potential breakthroughs in our understanding of Clivilius.

Chris, never one to miss an opportunity for levity, chimed in with a touch of humour. "She's always carrying some sort of seeds…or bugs."

"They're not bugs," I retorted, the irritation in my voice as reflexive as it was mild. It was an old point of contention, trivial in the grand scheme of things, yet in that moment, it felt grounding.

Glenda's interest, sparked by our unusual discovery, was palpable. As she extended her hand, a gesture of both curiosity and a desire to be a part of this small wonder, she asked, "May I?" Her enthusiasm to engage with the experiment added a layer of communal exploration to the moment, amplifying the significance of what we were witnessing.

However, the call from Jamie, slicing through the thick air of anticipation, served as a jarring reminder of our broader predicament. "Glenda, grab the pole!" His voice, laden with urgency, was a tether pulling us back to practical matters.

"Yeah!" Glenda's response, though quick, betrayed a moment of conflict as her attention was torn between the call of duty and the allure of discovery. Yet, her dedication to both our immediate needs and the pursuit of knowledge was evident as she seamlessly transitioned back to our experiment. With a renewed focus, she gently pushed another coriander seed into the soil cradled in Chris's hands.

Her eyes, wide with a mix of scientific intrigue and sheer human wonder, mirrored my own feelings as we observed the seed's rapid transformation. The sight of the seed cracking open, giving way to the sprouting of roots and a small stalk with tiny leaves, was nothing short of miraculous.

Jamie's abrupt query sliced through the air, his annoyance unmistakable and setting a sharp edge to the atmosphere. "What the fuck are you doing?" The question, laced with irritation, and his tone, abrasive as sandpaper, grated on my nerves.

"Come take a look at this," Glenda, undeterred by Jamie's brusqueness, beckoned with a spirit that seemed to light up the dimming surroundings. Her enthusiasm, a beacon in our dusty enclave, was as clear and refreshing as a bell's chime in the quiet of a noisy market.

"What is that?" Jamie's curiosity peeked through his initial annoyance as he leaned in, his gaze locking onto the green shoots that defied the barrenness of our new world.

"They're coriander plants," I found myself repeating, a hint of exasperation bleeding into my voice. Explaining the same thing for the third time, especially to Jamie's seemingly wilful ignorance, tested the limits of my patience.

"Did you bring those plants here?" His direct question, aimed squarely at me, carried an undercurrent of skepticism that felt like a challenge to the marvel we had just witnessed.

"In a manner of speaking, yes I did," I responded, striving for calm.

"In a manner of speaking?" Jamie echoed, his repetition a clear sign of his struggle to connect the dots.

"We found soil below the hard crust that's hidden beneath all the dust and sand. A few seeds accidentally fell out of my pocket and landed in the soil," I explained further, my tone laced with a hope that he would understand the significance of what we had stumbled upon. It was more than just a plant;

it was proof of life's potential in Bixbus, a beacon of possibility in the vast unknown.

"And look what happens," Glenda couldn't contain her excitement, the joy in her voice cutting through the tension. Her action, pushing another seed into Chris's hands, was a testament to the wonder of our discovery, a living demonstration of the miraculous capability for growth in this seemingly inhospitable land.

"My hands are getting a little tired," Chris admitted, his voice carrying a hint of weariness as his hands began to tremble slightly, betraying the strain of holding the soil and seeds so delicately for so long.

"Last time," Glenda promised. In response, I positioned my hands beneath Chris's, offering my support both physically and symbolically.

Jamie, however, remained distinctly unimpressed, his skepticism a sharp contrast to the atmosphere of collaboration and hope that had enveloped the rest of us. "Just because you've planted something, doesn't mean it's going to grow," he retorted sharply, his impatience slicing through the air.

"Just watch. It's incredible," Glenda countered softly, her whisper almost reverent as her focus remained locked on the unfolding miracle in Chris's hands. Her faith in the process, in the evidence of our eyes, offered a counterpoint to Jamie's cynicism, a beacon of hope amidst our collective apprehension.

As we watched, the seed burgeoned into a thriving coriander seedling, its rapid transformation a visible affirmation of life's resilience. Our faces, lit by wide smiles of wonder and shared achievement, reflected the light of a newfound hope—a stark contrast to the desolation that stretched beyond us. This moment of growth, so small in the grand scheme but immense in its implications, symbolised a possibility of renewal and survival against the odds.

"This is great news," Chris observed, his earlier fatigue momentarily forgotten as he took in the vast, empty landscape that surrounded us. His words, imbued with hope, also carried a note of caution—a reminder of the vast challenges that lay ahead. His gaze, sweeping across the horizon, seemed to capture the enormity of our task: to not only understand this new world but to find a way to thrive within it.

"Perhaps this might help explain Joel's condition," Glenda mused, looking thoughtfully at Jamie.

Jamie's skepticism, however, cut through the speculative atmosphere with the sharpness of Occam's razor. "I'm not sure that Joel was buried in the dirt," he quipped, his tone infused with a dryness that bordered on dismissal. Yet, his skepticism was a necessary anchor, a reminder not to leap too swiftly to conclusions without concrete evidence.

Glenda, undeterred, countered with a reflection on the anomalies we'd encountered so far. "Maybe not. First it was the lagoon's water and now the soil. There is definitely something different about this place." Her voice, filled with a blend of wonder and scientific curiosity, underscored the mysterious nature of Bixbus. Her observations served as a beacon, guiding us toward the recognition of this planet's unique ecological characteristics.

Motivated by a blend of excitement and responsibility, I found myself stepping into the conversation with a sense of purpose. "Chris and I will make the study of the soil our priority. It may be possible to get a controlled eco-system up and running," I declared, my mind already racing through the scientific methodologies we could employ. The prospect of creating a self-sustaining environment was more than an academic exercise—it was a beacon of hope, a tangible project that could provide answers and perhaps even a future for us here.

"Hold up. Don't get too ahead of yourselves," Chris cautioned. "We should still apply a great deal of caution. Sure these plants are a great sign, but we still don't know what the conditions here are really like. You and I have been here for less than a day and the others not much longer. We have no idea what dangers we might be yet to face. Cracking the surface could be releasing more than we realise." His caution was not born of cynicism but of a deeply rational respect for the complexities and potential perils of our new environment.

Glenda's words, imbued with a fervent optimism, resonated through the air, her belief in the boundless potential of our discovery evident in her shining eyes. "With miracle soil like this, it can only get better from here," she proclaimed, a statement full of hope and the promise of a brighter future.

As I listened to their back-and-forth, a maelstrom of emotions churned within me. Hope flickered like a delicate flame, fuelled by the undeniable miracle we had witnessed with the coriander plants. Yet, it was shadowed by a pervasive sense of apprehension, a reminder of the complex and often harsh laws that govern survival in the natural world. My background as an entomologist had taught me that life, in its essence, was a delicate balance of give and take. The question that haunted me was, *What will the cost be for us in Bixbus?* The uncertainty of what sacrifices might be required for our survival added a weight to my heart, a silent counterpoint to the optimism that filled the air around us.

Glenda's next words, though meant to inspire, carried a different weight for me. "I'm ready to paint that masterpiece with you, Karen," she declared, her laughter a vibrant note of confidence and shared purpose. Her metaphor, likening our efforts to create a sustainable life in Bixbus to the creation of a masterpiece, was compelling and yet so fraught with unknowns.

Despite the conflict of my thoughts, I offered a casual smile in response, a mask of composure to shield my deeper reservations. I did not wish to quell the burgeoning hope that Glenda's words had inspired in us all. Yet, beneath the surface, my mind was awhirl with the complexities of our situation. Nature, in all its beauty and brutality, did not favour any species unconditionally. The harsh reality was that when an apex predator faces extinction, when the fight for survival becomes dire, sacrifices are often an inevitable part of the equation.

This knowledge, borne of years studying the intricate dance of predator and prey, of ecosystems where every element had its role yet was bound by the unforgiving rule of survival, weighed heavily on me. Here, in Bixbus, we were not just scientists and survivors; we were also unwitting participants in an ecosystem we barely understood. The excitement of potentially creating a self-sustaining environment was tempered by the recognition of the challenges that lay ahead. The balance of life was a complex, often brutal affair, and while we had taken a significant step forward with our discovery, I couldn't shake the feeling that the path ahead would require more from us than we could possibly imagine.

HOLES

4338.208.5

As the ute's wheels churned up dust, I couldn't help but pause and watch the thick plumes that seemed to dance in the sunlit air, a gritty ballet of chaos and departure. Jamie's stride away was more than just a movement; it was a loud, palpable huff that seemed to cut through the tension, leaving a trail of unsaid words and unresolved feelings hanging heavier than the dust in the air.

"What do we do with these plants now?" Glenda's voice pierced through my contemplation, her tone as calm as a serene lake, undisturbed by the ripples of our current turmoil. It was almost enviable, her ability to stay composed when the arrival of the ute and Jamie's abrupt exit had thrown everything else into disarray.

Chris, ever the guardian of all things fragile, didn't miss a beat. "We keep them safe," he declared, his voice carrying a protective edge that seemed to wrap around the seedlings like a shield. I watched as he gently lowered his hands, treating the seedlings with the tenderness of a parent tucking in a child, and planted them in the soil with meticulous care. "The tents should give them a little shade and protection from the sun," he added, a hopeful note in his voice that seemed to counterbalance the uncertainty of our situation.

I sighed softly, a sound lost amidst the symphony of our efforts to salvage what we could. A twinge of concern for the delicate plants gnawed at me, their vulnerability a mirror to our own precarious position. Leaving them exposed, even with the scant protection of the tents, felt akin to leaving a part of ourselves unguarded against the harshness of the world. Yet, in this moment of upheaval, with options as scarce as shade in the desert, it was the best we could do.

The weight of the situation settled on my shoulders, a heavy cloak woven with threads of worry and determination. As I stood there, amidst the dust, the departing backs, and the fragile hope of new growth, I couldn't shake the feeling that we were all, in some way, seedlings fighting for survival in an unpredictable landscape.

"We had better finish putting it up," Glenda said, her voice cutting through the heavy air, filled with the scent of earth and the undercurrent of our shared determination. She got to her feet with a grace that seemed at odds with our rugged surroundings. Extending her hand towards me, a gesture of camaraderie in our little oasis of turmoil, she helped me bridge the gap between the ground and standing once again. Gratefully, I accepted her assistance, my hands, coated in the day's work, gripping hers as she pulled me to my feet with a strength that belied her calm demeanour.

My gaze shifted towards Chris, silently asking, *Are you coming?* It felt almost like a plea, wanting him to join us in our small battle against the elements, hoping he'd set aside his fascination with the earth for a moment to help us secure our shelter. Yet, Chris seemed lost in his own world, his gaze locked onto the ground as if it whispered secrets only he could decipher. It was a side of him that fascinated and frustrated me in equal measure, his ability to become so absorbed in his thoughts that the rest of the world faded into the background.

Slowly, Chris rose to his feet, a figure of contemplation against the backdrop of our makeshift camp. With his hands on his hips and eyes scanning the horizon, he looked every bit the explorer charting unknown territories. "I want to see how far this soil spreads," he mused aloud, his voice tinged with a curiosity that seemed to draw him away from us, towards a quest of his own making.

"Fine," I found myself saying, a shrug lifting my shoulders as I tried to mask my disappointment. It wasn't like I expected him to read my mind, but part of me wished he'd prioritise our immediate needs over his scientific pursuits, just this once. "I'll come and find you when Glenda and I are done with the tent." The words were out before I could weigh them, a declaration of independence tinged with a silent plea for him to notice the effort it took to keep our small world from unravelling at the seams.

Chris's smile, broad and unabashedly grateful, flashed across his face as he collected a tent peg and started towards the river, a lone figure embarking on his own exploration. It was a smile that spoke volumes, a silent acknowledgment of my understanding, and perhaps, an apology for his momentary absence.

Watching him walk away, I half expected him to turn back and return the peg, but he seemed intent on his new mission. "Where are you going with that?" I called out, my voice tinged with frustration.

Chris stopped in his tracks, the peg swinging idly from his fingers as he turned back to face me. His gaze was questioning, feigning a level of ignorance that was almost comical. "With what?" he asked, his voice laced with a pretence of confusion that didn't quite reach his eyes.

"You know what," I shot back, my hands finding their place on my hips as if to anchor my growing irritation. My expression must have been a picture of incredulity mixed with exasperation. It wasn't like Chris to play dumb, but I had come to learn that his single-mindedness often bordered on selective hearing, especially when it came to his scientific explorations.

Realising that his attempt to deflect was failing, Chris raised the peg slightly, as if offering it up in concession. "Well, I'm not going to get too far trying to dig beyond that crust with my bare hands now, am I." There was a logical undercurrent to his words, a soundness to his reasoning that, despite my frustration, I couldn't deny. The soil's crusty layer was indeed a formidable barrier, one that bare hands were ill-equipped to breach.

I let out a sigh, one that carried all the nuances of my frustration and concession. It was moments like these that Chris's rugged determination shone through—a quality that, in different circumstances, I greatly admired. Even when his pursuits led him away from immediate tasks, there was something undeniably compelling about his dedication.

With a nod that felt more like a silent acknowledgment of his victory than I cared to admit, Chris turned back around, resuming his casual stride towards the river. The adventurer in me yearned to join him, to cast aside practical concerns in favour of discovery. I lingered in that thought for a moment, the allure of the unknown tugging at my heartstrings.

But then, a curse from Glenda, sharp and tinged with frustration, snapped me back to reality. I glanced over my shoulder, catching sight of her battling with the tent fabric—a fabric that seemed to have taken on a life of its own, refusing to cooperate with our need for shelter. In that instant, my resolve solidified.

Glenda really does need my help.

❖

As I made my way towards Chris, the gentle hum of the river accompanied my steps, its rhythmic flow a soothing backdrop to the day's warm sun. He was hunched over near its banks, utterly absorbed in his work, the very picture of concentration.

"I've been testing your holes," I announced, drawing near enough for him to hear, my voice laced with a playful note. I couldn't help the smirk that danced on my lips, a silent echo of the mischief I felt.

His reaction was as immediate as it was amusing. His hands, previously steady and sure, flailed momentarily, pressing into the dust as if he sought to anchor himself against an unseen force. It was a moment of pure, unguarded surprise, and I savoured it, a bubble of laughter threatening to escape me.

Chris's composure returned swiftly, his balance regained as he shot me a look that managed to be both exasperated and fond. He glanced past me, his attention shifting back to the task at hand with a dedication that was both admirable and slightly amusing. "We don't want to waste them," he remarked, a note of earnestness in his voice. His eyes, a deep shade of thoughtfulness, scanned the small holes dotting the landscape beside the river, each a cradle for potential life.

"There's plenty to go around," I countered, waving the small seed packet in the air like a flag of reassurance. Peering inside, a flicker of concern crossed my mind as I noticed the dwindling number of seeds. They seemed to disappear faster than I had anticipated. "I'll ask Luke to bring some more," I declared, the resolve in my voice masking the sudden worry that nibbled at my confidence.

Chris's suggestion came from a place of practicality, a trait I had come to both admire and rely upon. "Maybe ask for a broader range of seeds," he said, his voice carrying the weight of experience and foresight.

"Yeah. I will," I agreed, my tone softening as I crouched down beside him. Together, we engaged in the delicate task of planting another seed, a shared moment of hope and anticipation. The earth beneath our fingers felt cool and welcoming, ready to nurture the new life we entrusted to it.

For several silent minutes, we sat together, our gazes fixed on the spot where the seed had been gently placed. Despite having witnessed the miracle of growth countless times before, each new sprout that broke through the soil felt like a marvel, a tiny testament to the resilience and wonder of life. As I watched, a sense of awe enveloped me, a reminder of the simple yet profound beauty of our endeavour. The river flowed on beside us, a timeless witness to the cycle of growth and renewal, and in that moment, I felt an unbreakable connection to the earth, to Chris, and to the endless possibilities that lay dormant in the palm of my hand.

Chris's sudden movement broke the tranquil rhythm of our work beside the river. He stood up abruptly, pressing his hands into his thighs in a gesture that spoke of urgency. "Go move them to the other seedlings near the tent," his command was delivered in a tone that intermingled concern with authority, compelling immediate attention. I felt a flicker of surprise, my eyes narrowing slightly as I sought to understand the shift in his demeanour.

"We can't be certain these tiny plants will survive if we leave them exposed like this," he elaborated, his voice carrying an edge of worry that was uncharacteristic of his usual stoic nature.

As I turned my attention back to the seedling cradled delicately between my fingers, the soil beneath them sent strange tingles through my skin. This sensation, both peculiar and intriguing, seemed to resonate with the very essence of our work—unearthing the mysteries that lay hidden in the fabric of this world. Chris's words, a gentle reminder of the practicality that grounded our experiments, brought a moment of clarity amidst the whirlwind of curiosity.

"We really should be recording the location data if we are going to be experimenting like this," I found myself saying, the thought emerging almost as a whisper. The notion of applying a methodical, scientific approach to our endeavours was not new, but in the face of our discoveries, it felt increasingly crucial. The balance between the thrill of exploration and the discipline of study was a delicate one.

Chris's smile, soft and reassuring, momentarily eased the tension that had begun to build within me. The appearance of a dimple on his cheek, a rare and fleeting glimpse into his lighter side, offered a brief respite from the seriousness of our task. "We can do the experimenting later. Let's just dig a few more holes. Give us an idea whether this is an isolated phenomenon or potentially has much greater spread."

The simplicity of his proposal, coupled with the warmth of his smile, momentarily lifted the veil of uncertainty. Yet, as I stood there, seedling in hand, I found myself caught in a maelstrom of emotions. The desire to delve deeper into the unknown, to push the boundaries of our understanding, was at odds with the methodical, cautious approach that our work demanded. The balance between these two forces, the unquenchable thirst for knowledge and the discipline required to acquire it responsibly, was a tightrope I found myself navigating with increasing concern.

Chris's gaze, laden with concern, pierced through the veil of my hesitation, prompting a shift in our interaction. "What is it?" he inquired.

As my eyes inadvertently caught sight of the rawness marring Chris's hand, a pang of empathy softened my features. My mind raced, urging my mouth to articulate the concern that had momentarily lodged itself in my throat. "We need something better to dig with," I managed to say, my voice a blend of determination and concern. Grasping his arm gently, I coaxed his clenched fist open, revealing the blisters that had begun to form on his palm. The sight triggered a silent sigh within me, a lament for the physical toll this place had exacted on him in less than twenty-four hours.

An unexpected surge of emotion welled up inside me, a yearning to bridge the gap that hardship and time had imposed between us. With deliberate tenderness, I brushed away the tiny grains of dirt adorning his skin, a gesture intimate and caring. Bringing his rough hands to my lips, I kissed them softly, an act that conveyed more than words ever could—a silent promise of support and affection.

"I'll be back soon," I pledged, locking eyes with him. In that gaze, there mingled a spectrum of feelings—concern, affection, and an unspoken understanding that transcended the physical. The connection, fragile yet unyielding, bound us together amidst the uncertainty of our surroundings.

As I turned away, the distance between us seemed to amplify the peculiar tingling sensation in my hands, enhancing the complex tapestry of emotions I was navigating. I rubbed my palms together, as if the friction could erase the unsettling undercurrent of sexual tension that had unexpectedly surfaced. The reality of our physical estrangement, a gap widened by Chris's challenges in intimacy, had been a facet of our relationship I had learned to navigate with grace and acceptance. Yet, here, in this unusual environment, dormant desires and yearnings flickered to life, stirred by an ambiance that seemed to whisper of possibilities and reawakened passions.

"There's something about this place," I murmured to myself, a sense of wonder threading through my voice. As I brushed away the remnants of soil from my hands, the sensation served as a tangible reminder of the day's labours and the inexplicable energy that permeated this land. "Something about this place that feels... different." The words hung in the air, a mysterious allure of our surroundings, hinting at unseen forces at play, weaving their magic into the fabric of our existence, challenging our perceptions and rekindling emotions long subdued. In this moment of solitude, I found myself standing at the threshold of discovery, not just of the land but of the depths within me, awaiting the revelations that this strange new world promised to unveil.

❖

After a futile search for a shovel or any tool that could pass for suitable, I found myself drawn back to the trail of coriander seedlings Chris and I had tenderly placed in the earth. Each little green shoot was a breadcrumb on the path we had created together, leading me back to the last spot where we had worked side by side. As I retraced our steps, a knot of unease tightened in my stomach. The absence of Chris hung heavily in the air, transforming the familiar landscape into a tableau of worry. *Where the hell is Chris?* The question thrummed through my mind, a persistent beat that quickened my pulse.

"Chris!" My call sliced through the silence, laced with a concern that felt thick in my throat. I spun around, my heels churning up clouds of fine dust, eyes darting across the expanse in a desperate attempt to pierce the veil of uncertainty. The riverbank, with its flat and open terrain, offered no hint of his whereabouts. With a sense of purpose, I veered towards the rockier ground, my voice carrying across the landscape, continuously calling his name.

Then, like a mirage materialising from the heat, Chris appeared from behind a rocky outcrop, disturbingly close yet seemingly miles away until this moment. Relief surged through me, a tide that ebbed as swiftly as it had flooded, giving way to a wave of irritation that prickled at my skin.

"Where the hell have you been?" I demanded, my voice sharper than intended, eyes narrowing into slits. The readiness to delve into a litany of worries and admonishments was palpable in my stance, a tension that sought release.

"I had to piss," came Chris's reply, draped in the casual nonchalance that was as much a part of him as the very skin on his bones. His blunt simplicity, a stark contrast to the whirlwind of emotions I had just experienced, left me momentarily speechless.

My brow furrowed deeper, morphing my concern into a scowl that I hoped conveyed more than words could. *You know I don't like that word,* I thought fiercely, hoping my eyes would transmit the disapproval that my voice momentarily couldn't. His choice of words, so casually dispensed, felt like a jarring note in the symphony of our day's endeavours.

"I found a shovel," Chris declared, his voice cutting cleanly through the air, redirecting the current of our conversation away from the eddies of discomfort and irritation.

My initial annoyance evaporated, replaced by a bubbling excitement that rose swiftly to the surface. "Where'd you find that?" I inquired, my curiosity leaping forward, momentarily pushing aside the lingering unease that had taken root in the back of my mind. The prospect of having a proper tool felt like a small victory, a beacon of progress in our struggle to adapt.

Chris's response, however, tempered my enthusiasm with a dose of reality. "I believe I've stumbled across a toilet site," he admitted, his tone threading a delicate balance between humour and resignation.

My eyebrows arched involuntarily, surprise and a dawning realisation intermingling within me. The implications of his discovery unfolded in my mind, painting a vivid picture of the challenges and makeshift solutions that awaited us.

Chuckling at the situation, Chris's next comment carried a light-hearted jest. "Where did you think they were going to go when nature called?" His words echoed a sentiment of acceptance, an acknowledgment of the rudimentary aspects of life.

I couldn't help but cringe slightly, my gaze instinctively sweeping over the expansive landscape that stretched out before us. This was a stark, unadorned reminder of the intricacies of survival in this new world—a world where the conveniences of our previous life were stripped back to reveal the raw and elemental needs of human existence.

Chris drew my attention back to the matter at hand. "Yeah, we'll need to do the same," he stated, his voice imbued with a practicality that grounded me. The simplicity and directness of his statement underscored a truth that, despite its discomfort, was inescapable.

As I exhaled, the air carrying with it a reluctant acceptance, I found myself grappling for the comfort of familiarity. "I suppose it's no different to our camping trips, really," I murmured, the words a feeble attempt to bridge the gap between the confronting reality of our current existence and the cherished memories of past adventures. There was a certain solace in drawing parallels to those simpler times, when the concept of survival was part of a scientific escape, not the all-consuming challenge it would inevitably become here.

"No," Chris echoed, his agreement laced with a hint of reflection. "Well, maybe a little." His words, ambiguous, hung in the air between us, an invitation to delve deeper into the mystery he hinted at.

My gaze lingered on Chris, a silent question forming in the depths of my eyes. His invitation, "Come take a look," was both intriguing and daunting, a call to venture further into the unknown that lay just beyond our current understanding.

Treading behind Chris, my footsteps a mixture of hesitation and curiosity, I navigated the landscape that had become both our home and our challenge. The terrain, marked by large boulders and the omnipresent dust, seemed to shift with each step, a vivid reminder of the unpredictable nature of this place.

When we finally halted, the sight that greeted me was as unexpected as it was unsettling. There, amidst the harsh backdrop of brown rocks and the pervasive red dust, thrived a cluster of small tomato seedlings, their dark green vitality striking a vivid contrast. The realisation of their origin, seeds likely carried here through the most primal of methods, stirred a complex whirlwind of emotions within me. Repulsion and fascination tangled in a tight embrace.

"This isn't a phenomenon we want to adjust to," I found myself saying, an instinctive reaction that made me retract my hand just as it hovered over the verdant leaves of the tomato plants. There was an undeniable allure to the scientific aspects of our discovery, yet the underlying reality of its origins cast a shadow over my curiosity, leaving me feeling unsettled. The juxtaposition of natural wonder against the backdrop of its uncomfortable source created a dichotomy that was hard to reconcile.

"I know," Chris's voice broke through my contemplation, his tone carrying a depth of reflection. "But it gives a good indication of the soil's strength." His words, while acknowledging the complexity of our situation, also hinted at an underlying practicality—a willingness to learn from even the most unorthodox of indicators.

I nodded, silently acknowledging his point. The robust growth of the tomato plants, in contrast to the more delicate coriander seedlings we had planted, spoke volumes about the fertility of the soil—a fertility possibly augmented by the very cycle of life that unsettled me. The notion that something so fundamental as human waste could contribute to the cycle of growth was intellectually captivating, yet it didn't fully alleviate the discomfort that gnawed at me.

Caught in the midst of these reflections, the natural call of my body made itself known, a sudden reminder of the basic biological needs that connected us all to the earth, regardless of the circumstances. "May I?" I asked Chris, a request for privacy veiled in the simplest of terms. My hands moved to unbutton my trousers, an action that felt strangely profound under the gaze of the natural world around us.

"Of course," Chris replied, his voice laced with an understanding that went beyond mere words. He turned away, affording me a semblance of solitude, his presence a respectful sentinel in the vast openness of our surroundings.

Seeking refuge behind a cluster of rocks, I found a spot that promised a measure of privacy. The rocks stood silent and imposing, their rugged surfaces a testament to the untold stories of the land. As I positioned myself, the fleeting thought crossed my mind—*would my own contribution to this patch of earth foster life or disturb the fragile balance we had stumbled upon?* It was a question without an immediate answer, but the urgency of my needs left little room for deliberation.

Squatting down, a wave of relief washed over me, both physical and metaphorical. In this moment, the act felt like a communion with the earth, a humbling reminder of the interconnectedness of all living things. The experience, as primitive as it was, served as a grounding force, a visceral acknowledgment of our place in the natural order. As I rejoined Chris, the complexity of our situation seemed to crystallise further—here, in this uncharted territory, every action and every discovery was a thread in the intricate tapestry of survival, each one weaving together the dualities of discomfort and fascination, repulsion and wonder.

❖

Planting the final coriander seed into the welcoming embrace of the soil, I couldn't help but declare, "Last seed." The words left my lips carrying a blend of emotions—satisfaction at the task completed and a whisper of regret that our supply had dwindled to nothing. I lingered for a moment, observing the spot where the seed vanished into the earth, half-expecting the miraculous sprouting that had become a spectacle in this landscape. The rapid emergence of new life from the soil had turned into a symbol of hope and a constant source of fascination for us, a reminder of the resilience and adaptability of nature.

"I thought you said we had plenty," Chris's voice broke through my reverie, tinged with curiosity and a touch of surprise.

"I did... We did," I found myself responding, my eyes drifting over the trail of green seedlings that marked our passage through this new world. Each tiny plant stood as a testament to our efforts, a verdant thread weaving through the landscape from the river's edge to our makeshift latrine site—a path of life amidst the uncertainty.

Chris's gaze on me was inquisitive, his head tilted in that familiar way that signalled his mind was at work, sifting through the information, seeking clarity. There was a comfort in the predictability of his reactions, a piece of normality in an otherwise unpredictable existence.

Pouting slightly, I felt compelled to clarify, "We planted all of them." It was moments like these that reminded me of the differences in our communication styles—what was obvious to me was sometimes a mystery to Chris.

"All of them?" His repetition carried a hint of disbelief, as if the idea of depleting our entire stock was too surprising to accept without question.

"Yes, Chris. That's what I just said," I retorted, the edges of my patience fraying slightly.

"And they all grew, yeah?" Chris pressed on, his question seeking not just confirmation but perhaps also marvelling at the efficacy of our planting efforts.

"They all sprouted. Whether they continue to grow or not is an entirely different matter," I clarified, my voice carrying a note of cautious realism. It was a small victory to see the seeds break through the soil, yet the uncertainty of their future growth cast a shadow over the moment. The fragile line between initial success and long-term survival in this unfamiliar terrain was ever-present in my mind.

Chris nodded, his expression reflecting a mix of satisfaction and curiosity at my clarification. "How many?" he asked, his interest piqued.

"About thirty. I'd guess we've covered close to three hundred metres. We've still a few hundred metres back to camp," I responded, my mind quickly sifting through the numbers. The distance we had traversed, marked by the trail of sprouting seeds, seemed to stretch even further when quantified.

"Shit!" The word burst from Chris, his usual composure slipping as the magnitude of our discovery hit him. His eyes widened, a clear sign of his surprise and the dawning realisation of the potential significance of what we had found.

I couldn't help but frown at his choice of words, a silent reprimand for the slip in his language. Chris seemed to catch himself, quickly regaining his composure. "I didn't realise we'd gone so far. That's great news if this healthy soil is this widespread," he remarked, his voice now a blend of awe and cautious optimism. His ability to see the silver lining, to grasp at hope in our situation, was both comforting and necessary.

"Healthy soil. That's putting it mildly," I commented, gesturing towards the verdant sprout at our feet. The rapid germination of the seeds was nothing short of miraculous, hinting at the soil's extraordinary fertility and resilience.

Noticing Chris's gaze drifting into the distance, his eyes glazed with a faraway look, concern prickled at the edge of my thoughts. "You alright, Chris?" I asked, my hand finding its way to his shoulder, offering a squeeze meant to ground him back to the moment.

"Yeah," he answered, blinking rapidly as if to clear his mind of whatever thoughts had taken him away. "We're going to be fine." His voice, steadier now, carried a conviction that seemed to anchor him to the present.

As we turned to follow the river back to camp, the gentle rush of water provided a soothing backdrop to our thoughts. Chris's belief in his words, that we were going to be fine, echoed in my mind as a mantra of hope. The contrast between the river's tranquil melody and the silent expanse of the unknown on the other side was stark, a reminder of the balance between beauty and desolation in this new world. Walking back, I couldn't shake off the silent thought that lingered in my heart—*I really hope you're right*. The endless nothingness that stretched out beyond the river seemed less daunting with each step, a horizon of possibility that, despite everything, held the promise of survival and perhaps, in time, a new beginning.

ALLIANCES

4338.208.6

As I settled myself on the roughly-hewn log beside Chris, its surface cool and slightly damp under my fingers, I began to reflect on the day's whirlwind of events. The log's texture was a stark contrast to the smooth, predictable surfaces of my former life. It was barely twenty-four hours ago that I was sitting on the bus with Jane, ensconced in the familiar hum of our daily commute home from work. Those moments, so regular and uneventful, now seemed like fragments from another lifetime. I could never have imagined that answering that phone call from Luke would have completely upended my life forever.

Wrapped in my own thoughts, I felt a peculiar sense of detachment, as if I were observing my life from a distance. Everything still felt so surreal, like a vivid dream that I was yet to awaken from. I was quite certain that the full magnitude of the situation hadn't really sunk in yet. The idea that Chris and I would never be returning to the home we once knew lingered in my mind like a persistent fog. A strong part of me clung to the hope, however unrealistic, that I could simply walk back through the Portal tomorrow and return to my normal life routine. The comfort of that routine, with its predictable challenges and familiar joys, now seemed like a lost treasure.

Luke's sudden arrival, as he materialised seemingly out of nowhere and stepped in front of me, abruptly yanked my wandering thoughts back to the tangible, pulsating present. As he stood there, the flickering flames of the campfire cast a warm, dancing light on his face, accentuating his features and the earnest look in his eyes. It was a reminder that the surreal landscape I found myself in was, in fact, my new reality.

"Chicken tikka?" Luke's voice broke through my reverie, pulling my attention to the plastic container he was extending towards me. It was filled with steaming rice, the aromatic spices mingling with the air, and the sauce overflowed generously, promising a burst of flavour. The sight of it, so unexpectedly luxurious in our makeshift camp, brought a spontaneous and broad smile to my face.

"How did you know?" I asked, the words more of an exclamation than a question, my smile widening. The familiar scent of the dish evoked a fleeting sense of nostalgia, a reminder of countless dinners back in a world that now felt impossibly distant.

"Lucky guess," Luke replied, his voice light, accompanied by a cheeky grin that seemed to light up his whole face.

As Luke moved along, his steps momentarily hesitant, I watched his gaze shift to Chris with a look of focused concentration. It was clear he was weighing his options, considering what might be the best choice for him.

"And for you-" Luke began, his voice trailing off as he turned towards Chris.

"He'll eat anything," I chimed in before Luke could finish, answering for Chris in a playful, teasing tone. It was a little joke between us, a nod to the countless times Chris had proven his easy-going nature when it came to food.

Luke's eyebrows shot up in surprise, clearly taken aback by my interruption. It was a momentary flicker of amusement in his otherwise serious demeanour.

"Anything is fine," Chris confirmed, his voice tinged with a light, reassuring smile.

"Sure," Luke responded, handing Chris the container.

"Lois, sit!" Glenda's voice cut through the evening air, sharp and commanding, as she tried to rein in the exuberance of her excited Retriever. Lois, was a bundle of boundless energy, her tail wagging furiously as she continued to shadow Luke around the circle. Her coat, a rich golden hue, shimmered in the firelight, and her eyes sparkled with a mix of mischief and curiosity.

Watching the playful interaction, I couldn't help but chuckle softly. There was something inherently comforting about the presence of animals, especially in the midst of uncertainty. Their simple, unadulterated joy and lack of awareness of our human complexities always had a way of making me feel instantly at ease, even if it was just an energetic dog chasing after any morsel of food it could get.

"Look, Lois, even Duke has settled," Jamie, sitting across from me, tried to reason with the Retriever, his tone half amused, half exasperated. He reached down and gave Duke a gentle scratch behind the ear. Duke, in stark contrast to Lois, was the picture of calmness, his body relaxed and his demeanour stoic as he basked in Jamie's attention.

"And butter chicken for you," Luke announced, his voice drawing my attention back to him as he handed Jamie the next container of food.

As the food procession continued around the circle, I allowed the chatter and laughter to fade into the background, focusing instead on the meal in front of me. I eagerly pulled off the lid of my container, and immediately, the rich, tantalising aroma of Indian spices wafted up, enveloping my senses. It was a scent that promised warmth and flavour, and my belly responded with a loud, anticipatory grumble.

Carefully balancing the rectangular container on my thighs, I tore off a piece of naan bread, its soft, fluffy texture a perfect accompaniment to the thick, creamy sauces. As I dipped the bread into the mixture, soaking up the delicious, overflowing sauce, I took a moment to savour the sight before taking a bite. The flavours exploded in my mouth – a symphony of spices, perfectly blended, each bite a delightful dance of taste. It was more than just a meal; it was a small piece of normality, a reminder of the world we left behind, and in that moment, it was truly delicious.

The atmosphere around the campfire shifted as Luke finally took a seat, joining our small circle. The group, including myself, settled into a comfortable rhythm of eating, punctuated only by the occasional murmur of appreciation for the food. The glow of the fire cast a warm, flickering light on everyone, creating a cozy, almost intimate setting.

Paul's sudden clearing of his throat, loud and deliberate, instantly drew my attention to him. His expression was serious, his eyes scanning the group as if to gauge our readiness for what he was about to say. "I need everyone to check in at the Drop Zone regularly to see whether Luke has brought any of your belongings. Or perhaps there might be something there that you find you need."

"That sounds reasonable enough," Chris chirped in quickly, his tone light but earnest. It was typical of him to agree so readily, always looking to be helpful.

"Reasonable?" I echoed, my voice tinged with skepticism as I eyed Chris. I couldn't help but wonder where he would find both the time and energy to meander to the Drop Zone, given our current workload. "It's a long way to walk just to check," I found myself voicing my thoughts, my tone laced with a touch of frustration. "I'm too busy to wander over to simply… check."

Chris's face fell slightly, a look of mild betrayal flashing in his eyes. Despite this, I remained firm in my stance, feeling a bit guilty but knowing that practicality had to prevail.

"I'm with Karen on this one," Jamie chimed in, his voice confident and decisive. "Too busy." His agreement was unexpected, but in these circumstances, I wasn't about to object.

"Busy!" Paul's retort was sharp, his frustration palpable. "All you've done is sit in the tent for the past two days!"

Jamie's reaction was immediate and heated. "Fuck off, Paul!" he yelled, his agitation causing a saucy piece of chicken to tumble from his fork and land in his lap.

The tension around the fire grew, but it was an alliance that, given our situation, seemed necessary.

"Didn't you want to be responsible for managing the Drop Zone anyway?" Luke's question to Paul was calm, a contrast to the heated exchange.

Chris, ever the peacemaker, continued his agreeable stance. "I'm happy to wander over. It'll be a nice break and good to see what's there," he said, before quickly stuffing more chicken into his mouth.

I sighed softly, feeling a mix of frustration and resignation.

"You make a good Drop Zone manager," Glenda observed, her tone pragmatic. Her diplomatic approach was a relief, and it seemed she was in agreement with Jamie and me.

"Well, he is shit at building things," Kain's mumbled comment, though almost under his breath, was still audible. His blunt honesty was a bit of comic relief in the midst of the tension.

Glenda continued, turning to Paul. "I think our settlement has more chance of thriving if we each focus on our own strengths," she suggested, her voice reasonable. "With Luke bringing supplies through so quickly now, perhaps it would be best if the Drop Zone had a dedicated manager."

Paul sighed, his body language indicating resignation. "Fine," he agreed. "I'll be responsible for notifying people when things arrive for them and for keeping the Drop Zone in some sort of order."

"Marvellous," I blurted out, a bit too eagerly, glad to have the matter settled. My stomach gave another rumble, reminding me of the more pressing matter at hand – the delicious meal begging to be enjoyed.

"But," Paul began, his tone shifting as he emphasised the word with a hint of urgency. "If I am going to be going back and forth so often, we need to do something about this bloody dust! We need to build a road." His statement hung in the air, heavy with implications.

I mentally face-palmed at Paul's suggestion. It was understandable, yes, but utterly unrealistic. We barely had anything to dig with, let alone the resources to construct a road. It seemed like Paul was reaching for the non-existent Clivilius stars when we were still trying to lay the groundwork.

"That sounds fair enough," Glenda chimed in, her voice calm and supportive as she encouraged Lois to lay down. Her agreement with Paul seemed to come from a place of pragmatism, always looking for solutions to improve our living conditions.

"I can help with that," Chris volunteered, raising his hand in the air with an enthusiasm reminiscent of a young schoolboy eager to participate in a worthy cause. His eagerness was endearing, yet sometimes a tad overzealous.

I sighed inwardly once more. As much as I loved Chris for his unyielding spirit and readiness to help, his penchant for jumping into projects headfirst without considering the practicalities was one of his quirks that I found both charming and exasperating.

"Yeah, I guess we could all pitch in," Kain added, his tone a mix of willingness and hesitation. His eyes scanned the group, seeking validation for his willingness to contribute. When his gaze met mine, I made sure to communicate through my expression that I would be, regrettably, unavailable to participate in this ambitious endeavour.

"I'll help too," Joel chimed in, his voice raspy but determined. The young man's offer of assistance drew my attention, stirring a faint twinge of guilt within me. *But it seems that there are more than enough volunteers for the unachievable project now*, I reasoned with myself, turning my attention back to my food.

❖

"I'll hold the bag open for you," I offered Luke, taking the black garbage bag from his hands and stretching it open. It crinkled loudly as I held it steady. Luke began to drop the empty food containers inside, the hollow sound of plastic hitting plastic echoing slightly.

"You remember the dreams I told you about?" Luke asked, his voice carrying a tone that suggested he already knew the answer. There was a hint of something deeper in his voice, a subtle undercurrent of earnestness that piqued my curiosity.

I chuckled loudly, the memory of those conversations bringing a lightness to my heart. "How could I forget? Jane and I used to make fun of you for them." My laughter was genuine, but there was a tinge of fondness in it too. Those memories of simpler times with Luke and Jane felt like a lifeline to the past.

"You did?" Luke seemed genuinely surprised by my confession, his eyebrows lifting slightly. His reaction was almost comical, and it took me a moment to compose myself.

"Well," I began, not feeling the slightest bit perturbed by his reaction. *He should be used to my brutal honesty by now*, I reasoned to myself. "You were always so serious about them. How could we not find it amusing?" I shrugged lightly, my tone playful yet honest. It was true; his intense seriousness about his dreams had always been a source of gentle teasing among us.

"I guess I shouldn't really be surprised," Luke replied, his voice tinged with a blend of resignation and amusement. There was a lightness to his tone that suggested he wasn't too bothered by our past jests.

"Oh, have you heard the news?" I quickly changed the subject, infused with a sudden burst of excitement. I wanted to steer the conversation away from the past and into something more present, more tangible. I had little patience for dwelling on things we couldn't change, especially in these unpredictable times.

"What news?" Luke asked, his curiosity piqued, his attention now fully on me.

"Follow me," I instructed, dropping the garbage bag and gesturing for him to come along. My voice was laced with an eagerness that I couldn't quite contain. I was already moving away, my steps brisk and purposeful.

Luke followed without hesitation, his trust in my lead apparent. He matched my pace, his steps echoing mine on the barren ground.

"We didn't know what else to do with them, so we've just left them there for now," I explained as we walked. My pace quickened slightly, my words flowing faster with my growing enthusiasm.

"Left what where?" Luke's voice held a trace of frustration.

"The coriander plants," I said over my shoulder, the words almost spilling out of me.

"Huh?" Luke's response was a mix of confusion and curiosity. His steps slowed as he tried to piece together what I was talking about.

I stopped abruptly on the far side of the tent, turning to face him. "Coriander plants," I repeated, pointing at the small, delicate green seedlings that Chris and I had planted near the tent's canvas wall. The plants were tiny, their leaves just beginning to unfurl, a small but significant sign of life and growth.

My excitement was palpable as I gestured towards the plants. It was a small thing, but in our current world, the act of planting something felt like a quiet rebellion against the uncertainty. It was a symbol of hope, of continuity, and of our determination to carve out a semblance of normality in this new life. I watched Luke's expression, eager to see his reaction to our little garden, our tiny patch of green in a world turned upside down.

"How-" Luke began, his voice trailing off in astonishment. His eyes were fixed on the small action I was about to perform. From my pocket, I retrieved a ziplock bag and carefully picked out a single, small coriander seed. Earlier in the day, I had told Chris that we had exhausted all our seeds, but I had found several more lingering in the recesses of my pocket. I had decided to save these for purposeful demonstrations, just like this moment, to show the incredible potential of what we had discovered.

Gently, I pressed the seed into the soil beside the other thriving seedlings. The atmosphere was charged with a palpable sense of anticipation. Within minutes, as if by some kind of magic, the coriander seed cracked open, its tiny roots eagerly reaching into the dirt, and small, delicate green leaves unfurling like a miniature flag of life.

"Impressive," Luke muttered, his voice low and filled with awe. His eyes were captivated by the tiny spectacle unfolding before us.

"But there's a big problem," I informed him, my tone shifting as I addressed a more pressing issue. The frustration I felt about the never-ending dust particles smothering everything resurfaced, tainting the magic of the moment.

Luke crouched down, his movements gentle and respectful, as he ran his fingers lightly across the tiny leaves. "What's that?" he asked, his voice soft and concerned, his attention fully on me now.

"There's too much dust! We need to find a way to clear it," I explained, my voice tinged with exasperation. The dust was a constant, invasive presence, threatening to choke our little oasis of green.

Luke glanced up, his eyes rolling involuntarily, a reaction I wasn't sure he meant for me to see. Regardless, a scowl crept onto my face, a visible sign of my irritation at his seemingly dismissive gesture.

"Any ideas?" Luke quickly redirected, sensing my growing frustration.

"I've tried moving some with a shovel, but in most places that I've checked, it's at least a few feet deep," I responded, my voice heavy with the depth of the challenge we faced. It felt like an insurmountable task, fighting back the relentless tide of dust.

"Hmm," was all Luke could manage. His reply hung in the air, laden with the unspoken acknowledgment of the enormity of the task ahead.

In response, I found myself voicing a bold suggestion, driven by the urgency of our situation. "I think a bit of heavy machinery would be best," I said, the words coming out more confidently than I felt.

To my surprise, Luke's eyes lit up with a spark of possibility. "Leave it with me. I'll sort it," he declared, his voice carrying a newfound determination that caught me off guard.

Sensing that I had successfully nudged Luke back onto the same wavelength as me, I felt emboldened to share more of my burgeoning ideas. "And you know, I was thinking, now that we can grow plants quicker, that we can put a few fences up over there by the river for my ducks. They'd absolutely love it down there with a few reeds and a little duck house," I continued, the words flowing from me with an ease that surprised even myself.

Luke nodded silently, his eyes widening slightly as he absorbed the cascade of ideas I was presenting. It was clear that the scope of what I was proposing was dawning on him.

"And my chickens will need to be relocated," I added without pausing. "Don't forget their henhouse."

"Karen, slow down," Luke interjected, his gaze shifting back to the small coriander seedlings, perhaps seeking a moment of respite from the rapid-fire nature of my suggestions.

But I was undeterred. "Luke, I'm serious. You need to look after my animals until I am ready for you to bring them all here, to me," I stated firmly. The thought of my beloved animals suffering or being neglected in mine and Chris's absence caused a pang of worry in my stomach.

Luke looked up at me then, his expression serious and attentive.

"All of them. I don't want any of them suffering or dying before then," I pressed on, my warning clear and unequivocal.

A hush fell over us, a moment of silence that stretched out as Luke processed my words. Finally, he replied, "I promise."

A wave of relief washed over me, manifesting as a warm smile that spread across my face. Luke's promise, simple yet profound, offered me a sense of reassurance and hope. His commitment to my animals, to this small piece of my past and future, meant more to me than I could express.

❖

Luke and I made our way back to the campfire, where the atmosphere was lively and animated. The chatter and laughter of our companions filled the air, creating a backdrop of warmth and camaraderie. I found my spot beside Chris, feeling a sense of belonging as I settled in beside my husband.

As the sun began its descent behind the distant mountains, painting the sky in hues of orange and pink, the air grew cooler, wrapping us in a gentle chill. It was a beautiful, serene moment, the kind that made me pause and appreciate the simple beauty of our surroundings despite our situation.

Suddenly, a raspy hum of a voice carried on the breeze, breaking through the noise of the campfire. The words were soft yet clear:

"Let us celebrate our story
The words we've yet to write."

I looked around, curious to see who had begun the impromptu performance. To my surprise, it was Joel, the young man who seldom spoke. His voice, though raspy, carried a melody that was both haunting and beautiful.

Joel's presence here had been something of a mystery. The ordeal he had been through in the last few days was the subject of hushed conversations and unspoken questions. His arrival in Clivilius was marked by tragedy, the details of which were never openly shared. In the short time I had been here, I hadn't felt comfortable prying into what clearly seemed a sensitive subject.

From what Chris and I had pieced together, it was believed that Joel was dead, and yet here he was, very much alive. He spent most of his time recovering in his tent, a space where Jamie, who I now realised was his father, often kept him company. The revelation that Jamie had a son was new to me; Luke had never mentioned anything about Jamie's family.

As I listened to Joel sing, there was a sense of vulnerability in his voice that touched something deep within me. It was a reminder of the human stories that wove through our group, each one unique and laden with its own joys and sorrows. Joel's song, simple yet profound, felt like a tribute to our collective journey and the unwritten future that lay ahead of us. In that moment, surrounded by the flickering light of the campfire and the faces of my newfound companions, I felt a profound connection to everyone there, bound together by our shared experience in this strange new world.

Glenda's sudden movement, as she abruptly stood up, broke the enchanting hush that Joel's tune had woven over our small gathering. Instantly, Joel ceased his singing, perhaps startled by the interruption.

"Please, don't stop. You have a beautiful voice," Glenda encouraged him warmly, her voice genuine and supportive. She seemed to recognise the importance of the moment, the vulnerability that Joel was showing.

I personally wouldn't have described Joel's voice as beautiful in the traditional sense, but there was an undeniable rawness and sincerity to it. I considered that without the tragedy that seemed to have affected his throat, his voice might have indeed been quite pleasant. It was touching to see him making such a brave attempt, despite his obvious discomfort.

With a bit of gentle coaxing from Jamie, Joel hesitantly started again. He repeated the tune from the beginning, the same few lines echoing through the air as if they were the only part he knew or felt comfortable sharing.

When Glenda returned to the group, she was carrying a violin, much to my surprise. I had no idea where she had found it – Luke's ability to provide the unexpected was becoming something of a legendary trait among us.

The initial notes from Glenda's violin were a bit rough, a few squeaky chords resonating in the cool air. But it didn't take long for her to find her rhythm, and soon the sound of her violin beautifully complemented Joel's raspy voice. The music they created together was hauntingly soothing, sending a shiver down my spine.

"You know this song?" I asked Glenda, curious. I didn't recognise the melody myself.

"Not until now," she replied, her focus unbroken as she continued to play.

I had never learned to play an instrument or possessed any notable singing talent, but even I could appreciate the simple beauty of the harmony they created. Listening more intently, I found myself captivated by the words Joel sang:

"Let us celebrate our story.
The words we've yet to write.
How we all wound up with glory.
In the world we fought to right."

Another chill ran down my spine as I absorbed the lyrics. They seemed to perfectly encapsulate our current situation, our struggles and the hope that we clung to.

As Joel's voice gradually faded into silence, Glenda played a final stanza on her violin, then slowly lowered the instrument. The last note lingered in the air, a haunting echo of the powerful moment we had just shared.

"To Joel!" Luke suddenly called out, his voice breaking through my captivated trance. His shout was a jubilant acknowledgment of Joel's courage and the unexpected beauty he had shared with us.

"To Joel!" I joined in, echoing Luke's sentiment. My voice mingled with those of the rest of the group as our cheer resonated into the vast quiet beyond our camp. It was a moment of unity and celebration, a collective recognition of both individual and collective contribution to our shared experiences.

❖

As the camp's joviality gradually began to wane, with each person drifting into their own nightly routines, Glenda and I found ourselves engrossed in a deep conversation by the campfire. Our discussion was as intense as the flames that crackled before us, emitting warmth into the cool night air.

Throughout our talk, I couldn't help but notice Chris. He had positioned himself just off to the side, an observer to our interaction. I cast him a sideways glance more times than I could count. His presence was subtly conspicuous - close enough to be aware of our conversation, yet far enough to maintain a semblance of distance. I noticed him shifting his weight from one foot to the other, again and again. It was unlike him to exhibit such nervous energy, and I was certain it had nothing to do with the topic of Glenda's and my discussion.

The curiosity and concern within me reached a tipping point. Unable to hold back any longer, I turned to Chris, my gaze direct and unapologetic. "What the heck is wrong with you tonight, Chris?" I asked, my voice tinged with a mix of frustration and worry. His unusual behaviour was unsettling, and I needed to understand what was causing it.

Glenda, who had been following the exchange with a light-hearted amusement, couldn't help but scoff lightly at my blunt outburst.

Standing there, with the fire's warmth on my face and the night's chill at my back, I waited for Chris's response. The flickering flames seemed to echo the tension of the moment, casting a dancing light over Chris's face, highlighting his every expression. I was keenly aware of Glenda's amused gaze, and the night around us, which seemed to have quieted in anticipation of Chris's answer.

"It's nothing," Chris replied, his voice unconvincing. His unoccupied hand rose to his forehead, wiping away the visible residue of sweat that had accumulated there. The night air wasn't particularly warm, making his nervous perspiration all the more noticeable.

I wasn't buying his dismissive response. "Just spit it out, would you," I pressed, my tone insistent. I knew Chris well enough to understand that whatever was eating at him wouldn't stop until he voiced it out loud.

As Chris bit his lower lip, a telltale sign of his rising anxiety, I speculated that maybe he was hesitant to speak in front of Glenda. Perhaps he preferred a more private setting for this discussion. But I quickly shrugged off the thought. *If Chris wants a private conversation, he needs to be forthright about it.*

Then, quite unexpectedly, Chris withdrew his hand from his trouser pocket. In his palm lay several flat, round objects that resembled medallions. They were unique-looking, with an air of mystery about them. "I found these while we were out digging," he said, his voice a mix of excitement and uncertainty.

Glenda's gasp was sharp, cutting through the air, as she too sensed the significance of Chris's find. I leaned in closer, curiosity piqued. The medallions caught the firelight, their surfaces glinting with an ancient allure. They were unlike anything I had seen before, their designs intricate and seemingly laden with history.

"Fascinating," Glenda whispered, her voice barely audible above the crackling fire. She delicately took one of the artefacts, holding it close to her face for a better look. Her eyes, wide with intrigue, scrutinised every detail, every etching.

"What are they?" I found myself asking, reaching out to take the remaining discovery from Chris. The metal felt cool and heavy in my hand, imbued with a sense of age and mystery.

"I think they might be coins of some sort," Chris responded, his tone one of uncertainty and speculation. "But I'm not really sure."

"Chewbathia," Glenda softly read aloud the inscription on the coin. Her gaze suddenly lifted, meeting Chris's eyes with a startling intensity. "Yes. It's a coin," she stated, her conviction surprising and sudden.

"How do you know for certain?" I questioned, a part of me still clinging to the skepticism born from our earlier conversation. The coin's origins and significance were far from clear.

Glenda's response was a momentary silence, her eyes narrowing as she ran her tongue across her dry lips, seemingly lost in thought. Her silence was becoming frustratingly palpable.

"I think the markings of the twenty cliv make it rather obvious," Chris interjected, breaking the tension. He pointed out the engravings on the coin, drawing my attention to them.

"It means we're not alone," Glenda finally spoke up, her voice carrying a mix of awe and apprehension.

"We don't know that," I countered sharply, my eyes squinting in the dim light as I examined the coin closely. It appeared old, its edges worn from time.

"But it must mean that people have been here before us," Chris said quickly, his words tumbling out in a rush of excitement and realisation. "We're not the first."

The weight of Chris's suggestion settled heavily upon me. The idea that others might have been here before us, that perhaps others were still out there, sent a shiver down my spine. "We should tell Paul," I said decisively, extending my hand for Glenda to hand me the second coin.

"I don't think that is wise," Glenda countered, her fingers wrapping protectively around the coin.

My frustration flared, and I could feel my face tightening, a frown forming. "Why not?" I demanded, more sharply than I intended.

"He is too busy," was Glenda's swift, almost dismissive reply.

Unimpressed and feeling a bit patronised, I huffed loudly. My fingers kept gesturing for her to hand over the artefact, a clear sign of my growing impatience.

"Perhaps Glenda is right," Chris interjected, shrugging nonchalantly as he reached to take the coin from me. "Until we know more about them, there's probably no point saying anything to Paul."

"Yes," Glenda agreed hastily, backing Chris's point. "Paul has enough on his mind with trying to get the settlement up and running."

"And dealing with Luke," Chris added, as if to reinforce the point.

My frown deepened, feeling isolated in my opinion. It was like facing a battle alone. "As our delegated leader, I still think Paul should know," I insisted, more out of stubbornness now than conviction, feeling slightly defeated but unwilling to concede.

Glenda's reaction was abrupt and unexpected. "No!" she snapped, grabbing my coin in a swift snatch.

"Give that back," I demanded, my palm outstretched, my frustration mounting.

"We say nothing to anyone," Glenda stated firmly, tucking the coins into her bra in a swift, almost defiant gesture.

"That's not really your decision to make," I retorted, my hand reaching out towards her, undeterred by her unconventional hiding place for the coins.

"Fuck off, Karen!" Glenda snapped, stepping back from my reach. "I said no."

My eyes must have been bulging with incredulity and anger. Indignantly, I crossed my arms across my chest, and Glenda and I locked in a determined standoff. Our wills clashed silently, an unspoken battle of stubbornness and frustration. Finally, our intense gaze broke, and with a mutual, unspoken agreement to avoid physical confrontation, we each turned and stalked off to our respective tents.

The air crackled with the tension and unresolved anger between us as we parted ways. I retreated to my tent, the implications of the coins and our heated disagreement swirling in my mind.

❖

Back in the safety and solitude of my tent, I let out a deep, weary sigh. A tidal wave of frustration and exhaustion cascaded over me, leaving my thoughts in a dishevelled heap. The encounter with Glenda, the mysterious coins, and the lingering air of unresolved tensions had sent my mind into a relentless spin. I sat there, nestled in the dimness of the tent, my eyes closed, trying to process the evening's tumultuous events.

As I sifted through the whirlwind of thoughts, a soft, almost ethereal voice began to whisper in my mind. It was the voice of Clivilius, an elusive presence that had become an eerie yet familiar part of our new, bewildering reality. Its voice was like a gentle breeze, faint but unmistakable, threading through the fabric of my thoughts. The words it spoke were not loud, yet they resonated with a profound clarity that seemed to pierce through the fog in my mind.

Karen, the voice of Clivilius began, its tone imbued with an ancient wisdom, *in the vast tapestry of existence, every thread has its purpose, its path. The coins you discovered tonight are not just relics of the past; they are keys to understanding deeper truths about this world and your place in it.*

I listened, my heart beating a slow, steady rhythm as the voice continued. *These coins, they are symbols of connection – a link to histories and lives that have woven through the fabric of Clivilius long before your arrival. They whisper of civilisations that once thrived, of people whose stories are etched in the very soil you tread upon.*

The voice took on a more poignant note. *But remember, Karen, while the past holds valuable lessons, it is the present that demands your attention. The challenges you face, the bonds you forge, the decisions you make – these are the true coins of your realm. Treasure them, for they shape the world you are building.*

As the voice of Clivilius faded, a serene calm enveloped me. The message lingered in the air, a profound insight that offered a new perspective. The coins, the tensions, the struggles – they were all part of a larger picture, pieces of a puzzle that stretched beyond my understanding.

I opened my eyes, feeling a newfound sense of clarity and purpose. The voice of Clivilius, with its cryptic yet enlightening message, had given me a glimpse into the intricate web of Clivilius's mysteries. It reminded me that our journey was about more than survival – it was about discovery, connection, and the unwritten chapters of our own story. As I lay back, letting the words sink in, I felt a quiet determination take root within me. We were part of something much bigger, and every step, every decision, was a step towards unravelling the mysteries of Clivilius.

4338.209

(28 July 2018)

SHADOWS

4338.209.1

The sound of loud, panicked voices pierced the stillness outside, jolting me from my light slumber. My heart immediately began to race, its beats echoing in my ears like a thundering drum, reverberating through my entire being. I sat up abruptly in the sleeping bag, the fabric rustling noisily in the otherwise silent tent, adding to the growing sense of unease.

Beside me, Chris stirred, his voice deep and groggy with sleep. "What is it?" he asked, his words muffled by drowsiness. He made no attempt to move, still half-enshrouded in the cocoon of the sleeping bag, his eyes barely open, as if reluctant to face the disturbance.

Outside, the voices grew louder, more panicked, each cry sending a cool shiver of apprehension down my spine, like icy fingers tracing a path of dread. "I don't know," I replied to Chris, my voice laced with a growing anxiety. "I'll go and find out." Determination overrode my initial shock, propelling me to investigate.

Pulling myself out of the sleeping bag, the darkness enveloped me, thick and impenetrable, like a suffocating blanket. It must have been the dead of night, given the absence of any natural light, as if the world had been plunged into an endless abyss. The only faint illumination came from the sporadic, flickering glow of the campfire's flames, casting ghostly shadows around our tent, distorting reality into a nightmarish landscape.

"Karen," Chris whispered sharply, his hand suddenly clasping my arm, his touch firm yet cautious, as if trying to anchor me to safety.

"What?" I turned towards him, squinting in the near darkness, barely able to discern his outline, his features obscured by the oppressive shadows.

"I'm coming with you," he declared, his voice now steadier, more awake.

I nodded in response, aware that he might not see it in the dark, but the gesture was for me more than him - an acknowledgment of our partnership, of not facing the unknown alone.

As I stepped out of the tent, the chilly night air hit me like a slap in the face, carrying with it Kain's spine-tingling cry. "Shit! We're surrounded!" His words were like a bolt of lightning, electrifying the atmosphere with fear and urgency, sending shockwaves through my body.

"What's going on?" I called out, my voice trembling slightly, as a sudden gust of wind whipped fine dust into my face, forcing me to shield my eyes with my hand, the grains stinging my skin like tiny needles.

Chris was instantly at my side, his presence a comforting solidity in the uncertainty, a steadfast anchor in the raging storm of emotions. He placed his hand on my shoulder, a gesture of reassurance that grounded me, his touch a lifeline amidst the growing panic.

Paul's voice cut through the night, trying to rationalise the situation. "I think it's just a dust-" But he stopped mid-sentence, his words swallowed by an awkward silence. The eerie glow of the Portal's bright, rainbow colours momentarily lit up the dunes in the distance, casting a surreal light against the dark sky before disappearing as abruptly as they had appeared, leaving us in a state of disbelief and confusion.

"Is that Luke?" I asked, my voice tinged with apprehension. The strange occurrence made the hairs on my arms stand on end with unease, goosebumps prickling my skin.

"I'm right here," came Luke's response from nearby, his voice strained, as if he too was grappling with the inexplicable.

"If that wasn't Luke, then who?" I muttered under my breath, a shiver of fear running down my spine. The uncertainty of the situation was overwhelming, the darkness around us suddenly feeling more oppressive, more sinister.

Jamie's stern voice broke through the tension. "Duke, stop barking!" he scolded, his words tinged with desperation. He held the dog close to him in front of his tent, trying to control the animal's growing agitation, its barks piercing the night like distress signals.

Lois responded with a guttural growl that seemed to echo the group's collective anxiety, a primal sound that sent shivers down my spine.

Then, a chilling scream shattered the night's uneasy quiet, sending a shockwave of pure terror rippling through the camp, freezing the blood in my veins.

"Lois!" Glenda's voice was a mix of fear and desperation as the Retriever bolted into the darkness, its form swallowed by the inky blackness. I watched, my heart pounding, as Glenda and Paul quickly disappeared after Lois, their figures fading into the night, as if devoured by an unseen predator.

Kain, acting on instinct, grabbed a frying pan from the fire and dashed off in pursuit, his movements hurried and frantic, the pan glinting in the firelight like a makeshift weapon.

"Grab Duke!" Luke barked out an order to Jamie before he, too, followed the others into the darkness, his silhouette merging with the shadows until he vanished from sight.

The rapid succession of events left me reeling, my mind struggling to keep up, my thoughts a jumbled mess of fear and confusion. I felt an almost primal urge to join them, to do something, anything, to quell the rising panic.

"Duke!" Jamie's voice was laced with panic as Duke wriggled free and darted off, a blur of fur and determination. Jamie, head down, chased after the determined dog into the enveloping blackness, their forms swallowed by the night.

I moved to follow, my feet propelling me forward, driven by an instinctive need to act, to confront whatever lurked in the shadows. But Chris's firm grip pulled me back, his fingers digging into my arm, anchoring me in place. "Karen. Don't," he said, his tone serious and unwavering.

Looking into his eyes, I saw the reflection of the fire casting an eerie shadow across his face, mirroring the fear I felt, the uncertainty that gnawed at my core. "I feel like we should be doing something," I said, my voice shaky, my hands trembling with adrenaline, my heart pounding against my ribcage like a caged bird desperate for escape.

"It's pitch-black out there. We'll only get lost too. We need to wait," Chris insisted, his voice steady, trying to impart reason over the panic.

"Okay," I agreed reluctantly, pulling myself closer to Chris, seeking comfort in his warmth, his solid presence a shield against the impenetrable darkness.

The campsite fell into an eerie silence, broken only by the sporadic crackling of the fire and the distant, indistinct shouts of our companions, their voices carried by the wind like ghostly whispers. We were left in a limbo of worry and anticipation, the darkness around us a tangible reminder of our vulnerability in this unfamiliar world, a world where the rules we once knew no longer applied.

Time seemed to stretch into an eternity, each passing second an agonising wait, a torturous dance of hope and fear. The night pressed in on us, a suffocating blanket of uncertainty, its inky tendrils reaching out to ensnare us in its grasp.

❖

Jamie's desperate cry for help tore through the uneasy stillness, a jagged blade cutting the night. "Help me!" His voice, raw with panic, sent icy fingers crawling down my spine as he staggered into the anaemic light of our campfire, Duke cradled in his arms like a broken doll, his face a twisted portrait of anguish and dread.

"Jamie! What's happened?" My words clawed their way out, sharp-edged with worry, straining to be heard over the greedy crackling of the flames. Chris and I lunged forward to meet him, our steps urgent, kicking up phantoms of dust that swirled and eddied in the firelight like restless spectres. The sight of an unfamiliar woman at Jamie's side hit me like a sucker punch, her presence an unsettling enigma. She was a warrior ripped from the pages of a dark fairy tale, a bow in her hand and a quiver of arrows slung across her back with the casual ease of a born hunter.

As Jamie crumpled, his strength devoured by the horrors he'd witnessed, Chris's arms shot out, catching him in a steadying embrace just as his knees gave way. "I've got you," Chris murmured, his voice a solid anchor.

I turned to the woman, my gaze dissecting her, trying to unravel the mystery of her intentions. *Friend or foe?* The question hung in the air like a guillotine blade. As I gathered Duke from Jamie's arms, the warm slick of blood oozed down my skin, soaking into my shirt like a damning prophecy. A sickening dread coiled in my gut, cold and heavy. Duke's small body was a fragile, broken thing in my grasp, his life seeping away with each crimson drop.

"The creature's wounds are serious. He has lost a lot of blood," the warrior woman declared, her voice a dispassionate report tinged with a whisper of sympathy, the firelight dancing in her eyes like mocking imps. Her words fell like hammer blows, confirming the dire reality I desperately wanted to deny.

A strangled gasp tore from my throat as the terrible truth sank its claws into my heart. It was a lead weight in my chest, dragging me down into a black pit of despair.

The woman turned to Jamie, who stood there like a man drowning in his own sorrow, his face a shattered mosaic of grief. "There's nothing you can do for him now." Her words, a brutal mercy, sliced through the night with the finality of a coffin lid slamming shut.

Jamie's anguish was a living, breathing thing, a primal howl that ripped at the very fabric of the world. "Duke," he sobbed, tears etching bitter tracks down his face as he tore free from Chris's grasp, snatching Duke from my arms with the desperation of a man clinging to his last hope. "The lagoon," he rasped, a feverish light flickering in his eyes, a drowning man grasping at straws.

"It's too dangerous," the warrior cautioned, her voice a steel blade wrapped in velvet, the weight of hard-earned wisdom in every syllable. "Whatever is out there will smell the blood and most certainly attack again. I can't protect you out there." Her words were a chilling reminder of the hidden menace lurking in the shadows, waiting to strike.

The situation was a powder keg ready to blow, the fuse lit by Duke's mortal wounds and the unknown shadows prowling the darkness. The arrival of this mysterious warrior only added to the churning maelstrom of uncertainty and danger that threatened to swallow us whole.

Suddenly, a bone-chilling scream ripped through the night like a banshee's wail, coming from the direction of the Portal.

It was a sound that turned my blood to ice in my veins, a sign that the jaws of peril were closing in, ready to devour us all.

"Your friends need help," the warrior declared, her voice urgent yet controlled, a rallying cry that demanded action. In a blur of motion, she vanished into the darkness, an arrow nocked and ready, a fearless hunter stalking her prey.

Jamie, consumed by a desperate need to save his loyal companion, stumbled towards the river, his steps leaden with the weight of his anguish. I followed close behind, my heart a wild thing battering against my ribs, knowing I couldn't abandon him to face the unknown perils alone. The warrior's warning echoed in my mind, a sinister refrain, but leaving Jamie to fend for himself in his broken state was unthinkable.

"Jamie," I pleaded, my hand gripping his shoulder, trying to anchor him to me, to sanity. "There's no time." Urgency and empathy warred in my voice, a tightrope walk between understanding his pain and recognising the deadly reality closing in on us with each passing second.

"The river has healed before. It can heal again," Jamie choked out, his words a broken litany of hope against hope, a desperate invocation for a miracle in the face of crushing despair. He pulled away, staggering towards the riverbank, a man possessed by a single, all-consuming purpose.

Chris fell into step beside Jamie, a makeshift torch blazing in his hand, casting eerie shadows that danced and flickered like demons in the night. "Then I'm coming with you," he said, his voice a steadfast vow, a pledge of unwavering support in the face of the unknown.

After a moment of surprise, I quickly regained my composure and nodded in silent agreement. Together, Chris and I followed Jamie, each step heavy with apprehension, our hearts pounding in sync with the rhythm of our footfalls. The fire torch flickered in Chris's hand, casting long, dancing shadows on the ground as we moved, a mesmerising display of light and darkness. It was a small source of light in the overwhelming darkness, a symbol of our defiance against the shadowy terrors of the night.

The riverbank was a surreal oasis of stillness, the gentle whisper of water against the shore a jarring contrast to the chaos that had shattered our camp. I stood sentinel as Jamie waded into the river, Duke cradled in his arms, the water rippling out in concentric circles like an omen.

"It's okay, Duke," Jamie whispered, his voice a broken rasp as he lowered the small, limp body into the water with the reverence of a sacred ritual. "You'll be okay." His words were a desperate incantation, a plea to the uncaring universe to spare the life of his cherished companion.

The torchlight played across our faces, casting twisted shadows that turned our tears to trails of liquid silver, our grief etched in stark relief against the unforgiving night. It was a tableau of raw, unbridled emotion, a testament to the depths of our shared humanity in the face of unimaginable loss. Jamie's faith in the river's mystic power was a fragile flame in the darkness, and in that moment, I let myself believe, if only to keep that flicker of hope alive.

"I'm so sorry I couldn't protect you, Duke," Jamie wept, his words a broken litany of regret and self-recrimination, each syllable a razor blade across my heart. His sorrow was a tangible thing, a suffocating miasma that hung in the air like a shroud.

I stood there, drowning in my own helplessness, desperate to find a way to ease his pain, to shoulder the burden of his grief. In the guttering torchlight, I watched the water around Jamie bloom red, a macabre blossom that whispered of the fragility of life and the cruelty of fate.

"No, Duke! No!" Jamie's anguished cry shattered the night, his hands cradling Duke's limp form, a futile attempt to call him back from the abyss. It was a primal scream of denial, a sound that would haunt me until my dying day.

The heavy knowledge of Duke's passing settled over me, a leaden weight that crushed the air from my lungs. I met Chris's gaze, seeing my own sorrow mirrored in his eyes, a shared understanding of the magnitude of our loss. He handed me the torch and waded into the water, his hands coming to rest on Jamie's shaking shoulders, a steadying presence in the maelstrom of his grief.

"I'm sorry, Jamie. Duke's gone," I whispered, my voice a hoarse rasp, an inadequate offering of condolence in the face of such profound loss.

Jamie crumpled, his body folding in on itself as he sank beneath the water's surface, as if the weight of his sorrow was dragging him down into the depths of despair. Time seemed to freeze, the very air heavy with the pall of grief.

Chaos exploded as Chris lunged forward, a man possessed by the fierce urgency of now. I hurled the torch aside, plunging into the frigid water, the icy shock stealing the breath from my lungs. My hands groped blindly in the dark depths until they found Duke's sodden form, his fur heavy with the weight of the river's embrace. I dragged him back to shore, my heart a leaden thing in my chest, the burden of his loss an almost physical weight.

Meanwhile, Chris struggled with Jamie, who was limp and unresponsive, his body a dead weight in the water. He managed to drag him out of the water, his movements frantic yet determined, a battle against time and the elements. Chris immediately started CPR, his hands moving with practiced precision, a desperate attempt to bring Jamie back from the brink. Mercifully, it was hardly necessary. Jamie's eyes snapped open, wide with shock, and he coughed violently, expelling mouthfuls of water, his lungs gasping for air.

Jamie, fuelled by a mix of grief and desperation, a man possessed by the need to be with his fallen companion, scrambled over to where I sat with Duke, his movements erratic and frenzied. He almost ripped Duke from my arms, his voice strained with emotion, a raw plea for solitude. "Leave me!" he demanded, his tone leaving no room for argument, a guttural cry of anguish that cut through the night.

I considered protesting, wanting to offer some solace, to provide a shoulder to lean on in this time of profound grief, but I knew it was futile. Jamie was consumed by his grief, a man lost in the depths of his own sorrow, and in that moment, he needed space to mourn, to process the unimaginable loss he had just suffered. I watched him as he sat by the water's edge, his legs dangling into the river, a lone figure enveloped by the night, a silhouette of despair against the inky darkness.

Planting the fire torch near him, Chris and I retreated to a safe distance, pausing near the tents to ensure Jamie didn't re-enter the water, our hearts heavy with concern and empathy. He remained there, a solitary figure in the dark, and I knew that he would likely stay there for the remainder of the night, lost in his sorrow, a man adrift in a sea of grief.

"There's nothing more we can do for him," Chris whispered to me, his voice gentle yet tinged with sadness, a resignation to the inevitable. "We need to get out of these wet clothes."

"You go," I told him, my voice firm, my decision made. "I'm going to stay close and keep an eye on Jamie." I couldn't leave him alone in his grief, not when he was so vulnerable, so consumed by the pain of loss.

"Okay," Chris agreed with a nod, understanding my need to stay, to keep vigil over our grieving comrade. "I'll bring you some dry clothes."

As Chris left to fetch the clothes, I stood there, my gaze fixed on Jamie's hunched figure, a sentinel in the night. My mind drifted, a whirlpool of thoughts and emotions churning inside me, a maelstrom of sadness, fear, and the weight of responsibility.

When Chris returned, he brought a fresh fire torch and dry clothes for me, a small act of kindness that touched my heart. I planted the new torch firmly in the ground and quickly changed, the dry fabric a small comfort against the chill of the night. Then, I sat in the dust, not far from Jamie, keeping watch, a silent guardian in the darkness. The flames of the torch flickered, casting a warm, orange glow that barely penetrated the encompassing darkness, a feeble light against the vast expanse of the unknown.

Sitting there, my eyes on Jamie and the almost silent river, I felt a deep sense of solidarity in our shared vulnerability. In the face the unknown dangers of Clivilius, we were all bound together – by grief, by fear, by the unspoken promise to look out for one another, a pact now sealed in blood and tears.

❖

The camp, which had been eerily silent for a while, was suddenly alive with commotion as people began to return. Their voices, a discordant symphony of relief and lingering unease, shattered the sombre stillness that had settled over us. The night air buzzed with a palpable tension, a current of electricity that set my nerves on edge.

Chris, after a brief, wordless exchange with me, a fleeting meeting of eyes that spoke volumes, left to check on the situation at the camp. His departure was marked by a subtle hesitation, a momentary pause that hung in the air like an unspoken promise to return soon, to not leave me adrift in this sea of uncertainty.

I remained seated, my gaze steadfastly fixed on Jamie, who sat motionless by the river, a ghostly figure etched in shades of grief and despair. He seemed completely detached from the world around him, lost in the labyrinthine maze of his own sorrow, haunted by the spectre of Duke's memory.

As I watched over him, a silent sentinel in the night, I tried my best to drown out the cacophony of noise from the camp. The sounds of people talking, moving, and organising themselves after the night's harrowing events were a distant buzz, a white noise that faded into the background, overshadowed by the leaden weight of the thoughts that churned in my mind like a tempest.

Jamie's pain, raw and visceral, was a tangible presence, a suffocating miasma that hung in the air like a shroud. The uncertainty of what had transpired, the jagged pieces of the puzzle that refused to fit together, gnawed at me like a relentless beast. And beneath it all, the insidious fear of what might still be lurking in the darkness, a malevolent presence that prowled just beyond the feeble circle of flickering torchlight, ready to pounce at any moment.

My eyes, twin mirrors reflecting the exhaustion and emotional toll of the night, began to feel as heavy as my heart, as if weighted down by the burden of the horrors we had witnessed. The flickering flames of the fire torch provided a hypnotic rhythm, a mesmerising dance of light and shadow that lulled me into a state of weary drowsiness, a siren's call to surrender to the blissful oblivion of sleep.

Despite my best efforts to stay alert, to be the steadfast rock that Jamie so desperately needed, my body had other plans, betraying me with its insistent demands for rest. Before I knew it, I was curled up in a tight ball on the ground, my limbs heavy and unresponsive, as if the very earth itself was pulling me into its cool embrace. Exhaustion enveloped me like a thick, suffocating blanket, dragging me down into the welcoming abyss of unconsciousness, a temporary reprieve from the nightmare that had become our reality.

As I drifted off, my mind a hazy blur of half-formed thoughts and fleeting images, the sounds of the camp faded into a distant hum, a muted backdrop to the fractured dreamscape that awaited me. The last thing I saw before my eyes fluttered shut was Jamie's silhouette, a lonely figure illuminated by the ghostly light of the torch, a man forever etched into my memory like a haunting portrait of loss and despair. And then, the world fell away, and I was plunged into a fitful slumber, my dreams a twisted kaleidoscope of dark shadows and eerie whispers, a macabre reflection of the horrors that lurked just beyond the veil of sleep.

❖

The sudden jolt of Chris shaking me awake tore me from the tenuous grasp of a light, yet restless sleep, a jarring return to the waking world. "Come on," he urged, his voice gentle but firm, pulling me from the murky depths of my troubled dreams. "Let's get you back to the tent."

Blinking away the stubborn veil of grogginess, I glanced over at Jamie, who still sat motionless by the river, a ghostly figure carved from the shadows of the night. His stillness tugged at my heart, a silent plea for comfort, but I knew there was nothing more I could do for him tonight, no words that could bridge the yawning chasm of his grief.

"Okay," I agreed, my voice hoarse with fatigue, the syllables scratching against my throat like sandpaper. I rubbed my weary forehead, feeling every bit of the night's toll etched into the lines of my face. Standing up, I felt unsteady, my legs stiff and reluctant to cooperate after having been curled up for so long, as if my body itself was protesting the weight of the burdens we carried.

As Chris and I made our way back to the tent, the camp was draped in an eerie quiet, a noticeable contrast to the earlier commotion, as if the very air itself was holding its breath in anticipation of the next calamity.

The soft whisper of the wind and the distant murmur of voices were the only sounds accompanying our steps, a muted soundtrack to the surreal nightmare we found ourselves in. My mind was a whirlwind of thoughts, a tempest of fear, grief, and uncertainty, but exhaustion blanketed them, muting their intensity, a merciful respite from the relentless onslaught of emotions.

We settled into our sleeping bags, the familiar confines of the tent a small comfort after the night's ordeal, a fragile illusion of safety. Chris began to speak, his words a low murmur that barely penetrated the haze of weariness that enveloped me. Perhaps he sought to debrief the night's happenings, to make sense of the unimaginable that had descended upon us, or perhaps he simply wanted to offer some measure of comfort, a lifeline to cling to in the darkness.

However, I was too spent to engage in any conversation, too raw and exposed to bear the weight of reliving the tragedy we had witnessed. "Chris, I'm exhausted," I said, cutting him off sharply, my voice tinged with an edge of weariness, a plea for silence in the face of the unspeakable. "Let's talk in the morning."

There was a brief silence, a moment of stillness that stretched out like an eternity, and I could sense Chris's understanding, a quiet acknowledgment of my need for rest, for a momentary escape from the relentless grip of reality. The events of the night had drained me, both physically and emotionally. My body ached for sleep, for the sweet oblivion of unconsciousness, and my mind yearned for the respite of nothingness.

HOPE FOR HEALING

4338.209.2

As the first rays of sunshine began to streak through the side window of our tent, I slowly emerged from the restless depths of a slumber haunted by the echoes of the night's turmoil. My eyes, heavy with the weight of exhaustion, felt gritty as I rubbed them, a futile attempt to shake off the lingering spectres of the tragedy we had seen. The pale light of dawn, once a comforting herald of a new day, now seemed to cast an eerie, otherworldly glow, a reminder that the world we had known was gone, replaced by a reality where nightmares walked in the waking world.

Beside me, Chris started to stir, his movements a jarring contrast to the deceptive calmness of the early morning. He opened his eyes wearily, the fatigue etched into the lines of his face like a map of the trials we had endured.

"Good morning," he whispered groggily, his voice rough with the remnants of a sleep that had brought little rest. Despite the exhaustion that clung to him, a playful smile tugged at the corners of his mouth, a valiant attempt at normality in a world that had become anything but.

However, the weight of the previous night's events, the memory of the trauma and the loss, was still too fresh in my mind, a raw wound that refused to be ignored. My logical instincts took control, overriding any pretence of casual conversation.

"Is it?" I replied sharply, my voice tinged with a potent mix of fatigue and lingering stress, the words leaving a bitter taste on my tongue. The thought of facing another day in

Clivilius, with its unknown challenges and lurking dangers, loomed over me like a suffocating shadow, a constant reminder of the precariousness of our survival.

Chris's expression shifted, his brow furrowing as he registered the edge in my voice. He seemed momentarily taken aback, perhaps not fully aware of the extent of the turmoil that still gripped me, the way the events of the night had left a distinct impression on my psyche.

With a sigh, he rolled over, turning his back to me, a silent indicator of his discomfort with the sudden distance that had crept between us.

Just then, Glenda's voice hissed from the tent's entrance. "Psst. Chris. Are you awake yet?" Her words were urgent, laced with a sense of desperation that sent a chill down my spine.

A brief moment of silence followed, heavy with unspoken tension. I glared at Chris's back, my impatience growing with each passing second. I waited for him to respond, to engage with the reality that awaited us outside the flimsy protection of our tent. But he remained motionless, seemingly reluctant to face the day, to confront the challenges that inevitably lay ahead.

"Chris! Get up!" I hissed sharply, nudging his back with my elbow, urging him into action.

As Chris groaned in protest, his reluctance to leave the illusory warmth and safety of his sleeping bag was palpable. "What?" he mumbled, his voice thick with the lingering vestiges of sleep, his eyes barely focusing as he struggled to shake off the clinging tendrils of exhaustion.

I couldn't help but roll my eyes at his slow response, a gesture born of equal parts exasperation and desperation. It was a silent plea for him to hurry, to snap out of the fog of sleep and face the reality that demanded our attention. With a pointed look, I motioned towards Glenda, who was waiting with an urgency that could not be ignored.

Before Chris could voice any further questions or protests, Glenda's voice cut through the morning air again, sharper and more insistent than before. "Chris, I need your urgent help," she insisted, her tone leaving no room for delay.

"Get up, would you," I scolded him, my patience wearing thin. I quickly unzipped my own sleeping bag and clambered out, feeling a rush of cool air hit my skin.

"Oh," Chris exclaimed in surprise, suddenly spurred into action by the urgency in our voices. He fumbled his way out of the sleeping bag, his movements clumsy as he scrambled to find fresh clothes.

Chris hurriedly unzipped the front flap of the tent and poked his head out, still half-dressed. "I need you to help me get Kain to the lagoon. We need to hurry," Glenda informed him, her voice laced with a sense of dire necessity.

"Not this again," I muttered under my breath, my concern growing. The belief some camp members held in the lagoon's healing properties seemed more like desperate hope than anything else. But then, a sudden realisation hit me – Glenda had mentioned Kain, not Duke. My heart skipped a beat at the thought that we might have suffered another loss in the camp.

"Put some blinkin' pants on!" I found myself scolding Chris, as he awkwardly tried to dress himself in a hurry.

"I'll meet you at the medical tent," Glenda called out to Chris before she turned and left.

Realising that Chris had managed to fully dress himself while I still searched in the dim light for a clean shirt, I made a snap decision. "Go. I'll meet you there," I told him.

Once Chris had left, a wave of frustration washed over me. In my haste and agitation, a quiet, "Shit," escaped my lips almost imperceptibly as I hurriedly pulled on the first t-shirt I could lay my hands on.

❖

Making my way to the medical tent, I entered just in time to see Chris and Glenda hovering over Kain, who lay motionless on a mattress. The scene was sobering, the seriousness of Kain's condition evident even from the tent's entrance.

"I'll get Karen," Glenda said to Chris, her back to me, not realising I had already arrived.

"No need," I called out from the entrance, my voice carrying a mix of resolve and concern. "I figured you might need some more help," I added, quickly making my way towards them. "What do you need?" I asked Glenda directly, ready to assist in any way I could.

"We need to carry Kain to the lagoon," Glenda replied, her eyes meeting mine. Her voice dropped to just above a whisper, "He currently has no use of his legs."

My eyes widened in shock at her revelation. The gravity of Kain's condition hit me like a ton of bricks. I hadn't realised there was another injury from last night's ordeal, especially one so serious. I nodded, my mind racing, as I moved to stand beside Chris.

"I'll take the bulk of his weight," Chris said, looking at me. His expression was one of determination, underscored by a hint of worry. "Can you support his waist and legs?"

"Of course," I replied without hesitation, giving his shoulder a reassuring squeeze. The weight of the responsibility was heavy, but there was no room for doubt. We had to act, and quickly.

The task of lifting Kain was more challenging than I had anticipated. As we hoisted him up, grunts and moans escaped our lips, a chorus of exertion and concern. Despite his young age and slight build, Kain's muscular frame added to the difficulty, forcing Chris and me to dig deep into our reserves of strength.

Once we emerged into the clear daylight, we found a steady rhythm in carrying Kain. My attention, however, was repeatedly drawn to his injured leg. Glenda had hastily wrapped the wound in material, but despite her efforts as a doctor, blood continued to seep through, staining the makeshift bandage. The persistent bleeding was an unsettling indicator of the severity of his injury, and it filled me with a deep sense of unease.

As we walked, I grimaced with each step, the weight of Kain's body and the gravity of the situation pressing down on me. Between strained breaths, I managed to ask Glenda what had happened. Her explanation sent chills down my spine. She described how they had ventured into the darkness to chase after Lois and were attacked by a creature that she likened to a black panther – stealthy, vicious, and deadly.

Assuming that Glenda was already aware of Duke's fate, I didn't bring it up, and she didn't mention it. It seemed likely that both Kain and Duke had fallen victim to the same creature. The thought was both terrifying and tragic. Yet, amidst the horror of the attack, a peculiar thought crossed my mind. The existence of such a creature, as frightening as it was, hinted at the possibility of more life beyond our small camp. Maybe, just maybe, there were more people out there, people who could help us survive in this strange and dangerous world.

❖

As we crested the final hill, the weight of Kain's body bearing down on my shoulders, the lagoon finally came into view. The journey had been a gruelling one, every step a struggle against the unforgiving terrain and the relentless sun beating down on us. Sweat poured down my face, stinging my eyes and mixing with the dust that clung to my skin. My muscles screamed in protest, begging for relief from the burden I carried, but I pushed on, driven by the desperate need to find help for Kain.

Despite the exhaustion, I couldn't help but gasp in awe at the sight before me. The lagoon was a marvel, its crystal-clear waters a stark contrast to the barren, lifeless landscape that surrounded it. Hues of brown, red, and orange stretched out as far as the eye could see, painting a picture of desolation. But there, nestled in the midst of this hostile environment, was the lagoon, a shimmering oasis that promised salvation and hope.

As Chris and I carefully lowered Kain onto the bank, the soft sand shifting beneath our feet, I watched Glenda with a mixture of curiosity and skepticism. She approached the water's edge with a reverence that bordered on the mystical, her movements slow and deliberate. Kneeling down, she gently dipped her fingers into the water, her body trembling slightly at the contact as if the lagoon held some profound significance for her. The water rippled around her fingers, creating tiny waves that lapped against the shore, a gentle whisper in the midst of the oppressive silence.

With a determined look in her eyes, Glenda motioned for us to move Kain closer to the water's edge. I hesitated, uncertain about the wisdom of this decision. The lagoon, for all its beauty, seemed to hold an air of mystery and danger, a sense that there was more to it than met the eye. But as I looked at Kain, his face pale and drawn, his breathing shallow and laboured, I knew we had no choice. We had to trust in Glenda's knowledge, in the power of this strange place.

As Glenda guided Kain's legs towards the water, I held my breath, my heart pounding in my chest. The moment his foot touched the surface, a gut-wrenching groan escaped his lips, a sound of pure agony that echoed across the lagoon. His body convulsed, his muscles tensing as if he had been struck by lightning. Chris and I instinctively jerked him back from the water, our faces etched with shock and confusion. *How could something that appeared so serene and inviting cause such intense pain?* Kain's foot, seemingly uninjured apart from its immobility, shouldn't have reacted so violently to a mere touch of water.

"He's fine," Glenda insisted, her grip on Kain's leg firm and unwavering. Her eyes blazed with a fierce determination, a certainty that bordered on the fanatical.

I wasn't convinced. Every fibre of my being screamed at me to protect Kain, to keep him away from the water that had caused him such agony. A tense battle of wills ensued between Glenda and me, our eyes locked in a silent struggle for dominance. But in the end, Glenda's determination prevailed over my doubts. Reluctantly, Chris and I helped her submerge Kain's leg into the water once more, watching as the clear liquid enveloped his skin.

As Kain bit his lower lip, blinking rapidly in a clear sign of his inner turmoil, questions raced through my mind. *What secrets did this place hold? What ancient power lay hidden beneath the surface of the water? Was it truly a source of healing, a miraculous elixir that could mend broken bodies and shattered souls? Or was it something far beyond our understanding? Something more sinister?*

Kain's voice, low and strained, broke through my thoughts. "I want to be alone for a while."

I couldn't suppress a scolding tone in response. "Don't be such an idiot. You can't be alone right now," I told him firmly. The thought of him being alone was unthinkable – not only was he unable to walk, but the threat of the black panther-like creature still loomed over us, a constant, dangerous presence.

Kain turned to Glenda, his eyes filled with a silent plea, seeking her support. But even she shook her head, her expression grim. "Karen's right," she agreed, a hint of regret in her voice. "It's not safe for you to be alone out here."

A sudden pang of fear struck my chest at her words, a cold realisation that sent shivers down my spine. *If Kain, who had already faced the creature once and survived, wasn't safe, then who among us was?* The possibility of encountering the creature was a terrifying prospect. I shuddered at the thought, questioning whether I could even outrun a panther if it came down to it.

"Then take me back…" Kain began to protest, his voice tinged with desperation, but Chris cut him off.

"I'll stay here with him," Chris said decisively, his gaze fixed on Kain. "I can clean his wound."

Kain nodded, seeming to find some comfort in Chris's decision. "I'll be safe with Chris," he insisted, a note of pleading in his voice.

But frustration welled up inside me at Kain's stubbornness, at his insistence on putting himself in danger. *Did he really think now was the time to assert his independence, to prove his strength and resilience?* To me, it felt more like recklessness than bravery, a foolish desire to confront the unknown without regard for the consequences.

Glenda rose to her feet, fixing Chris with a stern gaze. "As long as you make sure his leg gets submerged for a reasonable amount of time," she instructed, her tone brooking no argument. "Regardless of how much he groans about it."

Chris nodded solemnly, the weight of the responsibility he was undertaking etched on his face. I could see the determination in his eyes, the unwavering commitment to Kain's well-being.

Glenda then got to her feet, releasing Kain's leg, and I couldn't help but voice my concern. "Are you sure this is a good idea?" I asked, doubt and worry lacing my words. The thought of leaving Kain and Chris alone, at the mercy of the lagoon and the creatures that lurked in the shadows, filled me with a sense of unease that I couldn't shake.

"We're sure," Kain interjected quickly, his tone a bit too forceful for my liking. It was as if he was trying to convince himself as much as he was trying to convince me.

Glenda crouched down beside him, placing a comforting hand on his shoulder. "You could lose your leg if you don't let the water help you," she reminded him gently yet firmly.

With a tug, Glenda pulled me to my feet, and reluctantly, I followed her away from the lagoon. As we walked, I couldn't help but glance back over my shoulder, watching as Chris and Kain receded into the distance, their forms growing smaller until they were finally out of sight.

❖

As we walked back to the camp through the sand, the early morning air was already beginning to warm up, the sun's rays casting a golden glow across the arid landscape. I could feel small beads of sweat forming across my brow, a reminder of the rising heat and the long day ahead. The sand shifted beneath our feet with each step, its fine grains clinging to our boots and leaving a trail of footprints behind us.

My mind was still reeling from the events at the lagoon, a sense of unease gnawing at the pit of my stomach. The way Kain had reacted to the water, the pain etched on his face, it all seemed so strange and unsettling.

"Did those two seem a little odd to you?" I asked Glenda, my voice laced with concern and curiosity. I glanced over at her, trying to gauge her reaction, wondering whether she would share my doubts and fears.

But Glenda seemed unfazed, her expression calm and collected as she replied, "I'm sure they're just being men." Her tone suggested that she attributed their behaviour to typical masculine bravado, a desire to tough it out and prove their strength.

I wasn't entirely convinced. The image of Kain's leg twitching in agony, the sound of his groans echoing across the lagoon, it all replayed in my mind like a haunting melody. "You don't think maybe there is something weird with the water?" I pressed on, my voice tinged with a growing sense of urgency. "I mean, look what we discovered with the soil."

The soil of Clivilius had already proven to be unlike anything we had encountered before, its strange properties defying explanation. The thought that the water might hold similar secrets, that it might possess powers beyond our understanding, sent a shiver down my spine.

Glenda slowed her pace, her boots kicking up small puffs of dust with each step. She seemed lost in thought for a moment, her brow furrowed in concentration. "I believe the water has some interesting healing properties," she mused, her voice thoughtful. "I suspect the healing process hurts a little."

I couldn't help but scoff at her words, a twinge of cynicism creeping into my voice. "Hence the manly facade," I muttered, rolling my eyes. The idea that pain was just something to be endured with a tough exterior, that it was a sign of strength and resilience, seemed like a simplistic and outdated notion.

But Glenda nodded in agreement, apparently seeing no reason to question their behaviour further. "Exactly!" she exclaimed, a hint of triumph in her voice.

I opened my mouth to argue, to voice my lingering doubts and concerns, but Glenda cut me off abruptly, her hand gripping my arm with a sudden intensity. "I'm sure they'll be fine," she assured me, her eyes locking with mine. "Chris will get us if they have any problems."

I let out a loud sigh, a mix of frustration and resignation washing over me. It seemed like I was the only one perturbed by the whole situation, the only one willing to question the strange and inexplicable events that had unfolded. The feeling of isolation, of being the lone voice of reason in a sea of complacency, weighed heavily on my shoulders.

As Glenda's grip on my arm tightened, her eyes narrowed, scrutinising the three-inch scratch that marred my forearm. The angry red line stood out against my skin, an unfortunate reminder of the previous night's horrors.

"How did you get that scratch?" Glenda asked, her voice laced with concern and suspicion.

The memory of the previous night's events instantly resurfaced, darkening my expression. "Oh," I said, my voice heavy with the weight of those memories. "Duke accidentally scratched me when Chris and I attempted to help Jamie and Duke." The words felt inadequate, failing to capture the sheer magnitude of the trauma we had endured.

Glenda's eyes widened in surprise, her grip on my arm loosening slightly. "Why did Jamie and Duke need help?" she inquired, her voice tentative, as if afraid of the answer.

I was taken aback by her lack of knowledge about the incident. It had consumed my thoughts so entirely, had left such an indelible mark on my psyche, that I had assumed it would be common knowledge among the camp by now. The realisation that Glenda had been blissfully unaware of the night's events surrounding Duke's attack only served to deepen my sense of isolation.

"You haven't heard?" I asked, my voice barely above a whisper, the weight of the news pleading for silence even as the question left my lips.

"Heard what?" Glenda's voice was cautious, her eyes searching mine for answers.

I swallowed hard, bracing myself to relay the devastating news. "Duke-" My voice caught in my throat, the words sticking like shards of glass. I had to clear my throat before continuing, the effort almost physically painful. "Duke was attacked last night too. He didn't make it."

The words hung in the air between us, heavy and suffocating. Glenda gasped, her hand flying to cover her mouth, her eyes glistening with unshed tears. "A Shadow Panther?" she whispered, her voice trembling with a mixture of shock and disbelief.

I nodded, confirming her worst fears. The memory of Duke's lifeless body, his once vibrant eyes now dull and empty, flashed before my eyes, sending a fresh wave of grief crashing over me.

Glenda's expression shifted, a complex mix of emotions playing across her face. "I know Duke and I weren't exactly on the friendliest of terms, but..." Her voice trailed off, lost in a sea of unspoken thoughts and regrets.

I could see the pain etched in her features, the weight of the loss bearing down on her. Despite their differences, despite the tension that had existed between them, the news of Duke's death had clearly struck a chord within her.

Regaining her composure, Glenda looked me directly in the eyes, her gaze intense and searching. "Are Duke and Kain our only losses?" she asked, the question hanging heavily between us.

I felt a surge of tension in my face, my jaw clenching involuntarily. "We haven't lost Kain yet," I replied sharply, a defensive edge creeping into my voice. The thought of losing another member of our group, of having to endure another tragedy so soon after Duke's death, wasn't something that I was willing to entertain.

"Of course not," Glenda quickly corrected herself, her expression softening, a flicker of understanding crossing her face.

"But yes," I continued, my voice gentler now, realising that her question was more about clarity than insensitivity. "I'm pretty sure that Duke and Kain were the only ones injured."

We walked back to the camp in silence, each lost in our thoughts. The camp felt eerily quiet as we approached. Without a word, Glenda suddenly veered off towards Jamie's tent, her steps purposeful and determined. I watched her go, a sense of unease settling in the pit of my stomach.

Moments later, Glenda returned, her face etched with exasperation and fear. "Where are Jamie and Duke?" she asked, her voice tinged with panic, her eyes darting around the camp as if searching for any sign of them.

I shook my head, equally perplexed. "I'm not sure," I admitted, a sense of helplessness washing over me. I hadn't seen them since the previous night.

The sound of rising voices drifted from behind the tents, indicating that Jamie might still be by the river with Duke. The thought of revisiting that scene of sorrow, of having to confront the reality of Duke's death once more, sent a shudder through my body.

I busied myself with the campfire, my hands shaking slightly as I stoked the flames, trying to distract myself from the turmoil raging within me. But my thoughts kept drifting back to Chris and Kain, to the uncertainty of their fate at the lagoon.

The wait for their return was torturous, each passing moment stretching into an eternity. I could feel the tension mounting within me, a blend of hope and apprehension, of fear and desperation. The mysteries of Clivilius, the strange and inexplicable events that had unfolded since our arrival, weighed heavily on my mind, casting a shadow of doubt and unease over everything.

THE LOST

4338.209.3

As I tended to the campfire, lost in my thoughts and anxiously waiting for Chris's return, Paul approached me with an urgency that immediately caught my attention. The look on his face was grave, an unsettling contrast to the usual calm and composed demeanour he typically maintained. His brow was furrowed, his eyes intense and focused, as if he carried the weight of a heavy burden on his shoulders.

"Karen, I need you to go and get Chris and Kain from the lagoon," he said, his voice firm, yet laced with an underlying current of concern. There was a sense of authority in his tone, a commanding presence that demanded immediate action. "We need everyone back at camp and accounted for – it looks like Joel is missing!"

His words hit me like a sudden gust of wind, jolting me out of my contemplative state. The news of Joel's disappearance sent a shockwave through my body, my heart racing with a newfound sense of urgency. The thought of him out there, alone and vulnerable in the unforgiving deserts of Clivilius, filled me with a sickening sense of dread.

Without a moment's hesitation, I nodded in agreement, my voice steady and determined despite the fear that gripped my heart. "I'll go right now," I responded, the implications of Paul's request fuelling my swift reaction. The thought of Joel, alone and possibly in danger, propelled me into action, overriding any sense of hesitation or doubt.

❖

From my vantage point atop the dune that overlooked the lagoon, I called out as loudly as I could, my voice carrying over the vast expanse of shimmering water and sandy shores. "Chris! Kain!" The names left my lips with a sense of urgency, a desperate plea for their attention amidst the tranquil surroundings.

As I waited for a response, my eyes scanned the area below, trying to discern their activities from this distance. Kain seemed to be still lying down, his form motionless on the sandy banks of the lagoon. But Chris, to my surprise and confusion, appeared to be digging in the dirt, his movements purposeful and focused. The sight was baffling – *what could possibly be the reason for him to be digging at a time like this, when our group was in crisis and Joel's whereabouts unknown?*

I quickened my pace, descending the dune with a sense of unease that grew with each step. The soft sand shifted beneath my feet, making the journey more arduous than anticipated. By the time I reached them, I was slightly out of breath, my face flushed from the exertion and the heat of the sun beating down relentlessly.

"Have either of you seen Joel out here?" I asked immediately, my tone laced with urgency as my eyes scanned the shores of the lagoon, searching for any sign of our missing companion.

Chris looked up, his brow furrowed with concern as he shook his head. "No," he replied, his voice tinged with a hint of apprehension. "It's just been Kain and I since you left us earlier."

Kain, still lying on the ground, his face creased with concentration as he tried to recall any recent sightings of Joel. "I don't think I've seen him since dinner last night," he said slowly, his expression turning uneasy as the realisation of Joel's absence sank in. "Is everything okay?"

I hesitated for a moment. The news I had to deliver was not going to be easy, but they deserved to know the truth. "It appears that Joel is missing," I revealed, my voice heavy with worry and concern.

As Kain tried to stand on his injured leg, I instinctively reached out to steady him, noticing the way he stumbled slightly, his face contorting in pain. "How is your leg doing?" I inquired, shifting my attention to his injury, a momentary distraction from the other pressing issue at hand.

"It's still really painful," Kain grimaced, each movement causing him visible discomfort.

I nodded in understanding, my heart aching for the pain he was experiencing. But the urgency of the situation demanded our immediate attention. "Come on," I urged them, my anxiety rising with each passing second. The isolation of the lagoon suddenly felt more threatening, the vast expanse of water and sand seeming to close in on us. "Let's get back to camp. Paul's requested that everyone gather at the campfire."

Chris looked up, confusion etched on his face. "Why the rush?" he asked, his brow furrowed in a mixture of concern and puzzlement.

"Just come on," I insisted, gesturing impatiently for us to start moving. The urgency in my voice was unmistakable. "We need to find Joel."

As we trudged toward the camp, the sun beating down mercilessly on our backs, I couldn't help but notice Kain's discomfort. It was evident in the way he moved – each step a struggle against pain, his face contorted in a constant grimace. The sight of his suffering only added to the growing sense of unease that had taken hold of me.

"Help Kain, would you," I scolded Chris, surprised and a little annoyed at his apparent lack of attention to Kain's plight. Something felt off between the two men, a subtle shift in their dynamics that I couldn't quite decipher. It was as if an invisible wall had been erected between them, a barrier that hindered their camaraderie.

Chris, after a brief hesitation, moved to Kain's side, offering his support. Kain gingerly wrapped his arm around Chris's shoulder, leaning on him heavily as they walked. The way Chris hesitated and Kain's reluctance to accept help spoke volumes of the unspoken tension that had crept into their relationship.

"It's fine," Kain assured me, waving me off as I moved to assist on his other side. His independence, even in the face of pain, was both admirable and a little frustrating. I couldn't help but feel a twinge of concern for his well-being, knowing that his stubbornness could potentially hinder his recovery.

We had barely started climbing the first dune when a loud bark shattered the relative tranquility of our retreat, sending a chill down my spine. My mind raced with fear, the sound triggering a primal instinct of self-preservation. In this unforgiving land, where deadly creatures lurked in the shadows, any unexpected noise could be a harbinger of danger.

I turned toward the sound, my heart pounding in my chest, and there stood Lois at the edge of the lagoon, growling and barking insistently at the water. The sight was unexpected, catching me off guard. "I didn't know Lois was here too," I said, the surprise evident in my voice.

"Me neither," Chris echoed, equally baffled by the dog's presence. It was as if Lois had appeared out of nowhere, a silent guardian watching over the lagoon.

"I wonder what she's found?" I pondered aloud, my curiosity piqued. The way Lois was fixated on the water, her barks filled with a sense of urgency, suggested that there was something amiss, something that demanded our attention.

I took a few tentative steps towards Lois, hoping to discern the cause of her agitation. The sand shifted beneath my feet, making each step an effort.

"I think we should keep moving," Kain interjected, his tone uninterested, perhaps more focused on the pain that wracked his body and the arduous journey that lay ahead.

I glanced back over my shoulder at them, torn between the desire to investigate Lois's behaviour and the pressing need to return to camp. "You two keep moving. I'll go and see what the problem is," I decided, feeling a sense of responsibility to get to the bottom of the disturbance.

"Karen, please be careful. We don't need you going missing too," Chris said, his voice laced with concern.

"I'm sure it's nothing," I tried to sound reassuring, but even as the words left my lips, I couldn't hide the growing unease that had settled in the pit of my stomach. The mysteries of Clivilius seemed to be multiplying with each passing moment, and the disappearance of Joel only added to the mounting sense of dread.

❖

Leaving Chris and Kain to continue their slow journey back to camp, I approached Lois at the lagoon's edge.

"Lois!" I called out, my voice carrying across the tranquil waters, attempting to draw her attention. The sound of my own voice seemed strange and foreign in this isolated corner of Clivilius, a reminder of the eerie silence that hung over the land.

As I neared the water, Lois's barking intensified, her focus fixed on something in the lagoon. The urgency in her voice was palpable, a primal instinct that spoke of danger lurking beneath the surface. It sent a chill down my spine, a sense of foreboding that I couldn't shake.

Cautiously, I edged closer, my feet sinking into the soft sand with each step. My eyes scanned the water's pristine surface, searching for any sign of what had captured Lois's attention. The lagoon, previously serene and crystal clear, now swirled with an unusual phenomenon, a sight that made my breath catch in my throat.

Pockets of water seemed to be swirling in a mesmerising pattern, creating miniature whirlpools that danced across the surface. It was a scene of ethereal beauty, a display of nature's hidden secrets that left me both awestruck and unsettled. The whirlpools moved with a strange rhythm, as if guided by an invisible hand, their movements fluid and hypnotic.

I knelt down beside Lois, my knees sinking into the damp sand, trying to understand what I was seeing. The whirlpools continued their dance, their edges blurring and merging, creating a kaleidoscope of shimmering colours beneath the sun's rays. It was a sight that defied explanation, a mystery that tugged at the corners of my mind.

Lois continued to growl softly, her body tense, as if she too sensed that this phenomenon was out of the ordinary. I reached out to gently pat her, my fingers sinking into her soft fur, trying to calm her, but my eyes remained fixed on the swirling water. The touch of her warmth beneath my hand was a small comfort in the face of the unknown.

In that moment, a myriad of thoughts raced through my mind, each one more perplexing than the last. *Was this another aspect of Clivilius's hidden secrets, a piece of the puzzle that we had yet to uncover? Could this be related to the soil's unusual properties, the way it seemed to defy the laws of nature? Or perhaps it was connected to the lagoon's reputed healing abilities, a power that we had only begun to glimpse.*

The questions mounted, each one adding to the enigma of this place, a web of mysteries that seemed to grow more tangled with each passing experience. I felt a sense of frustration rising within me, a desire to unravel the secrets that lay hidden beneath the surface of this strange land. But I knew that answers would not come easily, that the truth would have to be earned through perseverance and courage.

After a few moments of watching the mesmerising dance of the whirlpools, I realised I couldn't linger any longer. Chris and Kain needed assistance, their journey back to camp hindered by Kain's injury. The mystery of the lagoon would have to wait, a puzzle to be solved another day.

Reluctantly, I stood up, my legs stiff from kneeling in the sand. I gave Lois one final pat. She looked up at me, her eyes filled with a knowing look, as if she understood the weight of the secrets we had witnessed.

As I turned to leave, I made a mental note to keep this discovery to myself, at least for now. The camp was already rife with tensions and mysteries, the disappearance of Joel a heavy burden on everyone's minds. This new phenomenon, as intriguing as it was, could add unnecessary fear or false hope, a distraction from the pressing matters at hand.

We needed to focus on finding Joel, on ensuring the safety and well-being of everyone in our group. The mysteries of Clivilius would have to wait, a challenge to be faced another day. For now, our priority was to stick together.

With a final glance back at the lagoon, I hurried to catch up with Chris and Kain, my mind racing with the implications of what I had witnessed. The image of the dancing whirlpools remained etched in my memory, a taunting allure of the secrets that lay hidden beneath the surface the lagoon's surreal waters.

❖

As I caught up to Chris and Kain, who were almost at the top of the final hill, Lois energetically ran ahead of me, her paws pounding against the soft sand. She was a flurry of motion, her saturated fur sending droplets of water flying in a shimmering arc as she enthusiastically greeted them. Her presence seemed to lighten the mood, even if just for a moment.

I hastened my steps, my legs burning with the effort of climbing the steep incline. The strain of the morning's events was taking its toll on my body, the adrenaline that had fuelled my earlier urgency now fading, leaving behind a bone-deep exhaustion. Each breath felt like a struggle, the air thick and heavy in my lungs, but I pushed forward, driven by the need to reunite with the others.

Chris and Kain paused upon noticing my approach, their faces etched with concern and fatigue. They stood atop the hill, their silhouettes stark against the harsh glare of the sun, waiting for me to catch up. As I drew closer, I could see the weariness in their eyes, the toll that the events of the past few days had taken on them.

"What was the problem?" Chris asked, his voice tinged with concern, as I finally reached them. His brow was furrowed, his gaze searching mine for answers.

I quickly shook my head, dismissing the incident with a wave of my hand. "It was nothing," I replied, my voice steady and reassuring, despite the unease that still lingered in the pit of my stomach. I didn't want to alarm Kain or add to the existing worries that weighed heavily on everyone's minds. The strange phenomenon at the lagoon, as intriguing as it was, would have to remain a mystery for now.

Shooting Chris a stern glare, I silently conveyed that we shouldn't discuss the matter any further. Now wasn't the time for speculation or conjecture, not when we had more pressing matters to attend to. The disappearance of Joel, the safety of our group, those were the things that demanded our immediate attention.

Chris met my gaze, a flicker of understanding passing between us. He gave a slight nod, acknowledging the unspoken message, the need for discretion. We both knew that there would be time for questions and explanations later, when the immediate danger had passed.

"Let's keep moving," Kain urged, his voice strained but determined, cutting through the momentary silence that had fallen over us. His face was pale, the pain of his injury evident in the tightness of his jaw and the sweat that beaded on his brow, but there was a strength in his eyes, a resolve that refused to be broken.

We resumed our journey, making our way back toward the camp in a mostly silent procession, each of us lost in our own thoughts. The only sounds were the crunch of our footsteps on the dust, and the occasional pant from Lois as she trotted alongside us.

My mind was preoccupied with what I had witnessed at the lagoon, the swirling whirlpools that had danced across the surface of the water, the eerie beauty of the scene that had unfolded before me. It was a mystery that tugged at the edges of my consciousness, a puzzle that begged to be solved, but I pushed those thoughts aside, focusing instead on the immediate task at hand – rejoining the others and dealing with the situation of Joel's disappearance.

❖

As we neared the camp, the sense of anticipation intensified, a palpable energy that seemed to crackle in the air around us. Lois bounded ahead of us, her tail wagging with unbridled excitement as she found comfort in Glenda's welcoming arms. The sight of their reunion provided a small moment of normality amidst the tension that hung heavy over the camp, a brief respite from the worries that plagued our minds.

Paul and the warrior woman, who Kain informed me was named Charity, stood nearby, their presence a reminder of the serious nature of the gathering that awaited us. Charity's eyes were keen and alert, scanning the surroundings with a practiced gaze, her stance exuding a quiet strength that seemed to command respect. There was an aura of mystery about her, a sense that she possessed knowledge and skills beyond our comprehension.

As we approached, Kain's voice cut through the silence, a hint of relief in his tone as he announced to Glenda, "The feeling has returned in my good leg."

Glenda's response was immariate, her voice tinged with genuine concern as she rose to her feet, her attention focused solely on Kain. "Well, that's a relief," she said, her eyes searching his face for any sign of discomfort or pain. "And the other leg?" she inquired, her gaze intently focused on the injured limb.

"Seems to be quite the miracle," I interjected, my words an attempt to inject some positivity into the sombre atmosphere.

Kain, ever the stoic, assured Glenda with a mix of gratitude and seriousness, "I'll be sure to give it plenty of rest."

Chris chimed in with an idea, his eyes alight with the prospect of crafting a solution. "We can make you some crutches," he suggested, his mind already racing with the possibilities.

But I quickly dismissed the notion, my voice firm with resolve as I directed my words towards Paul. "Forget making crutches," I said, feeling that efficiency and practicality were key in our current situation. "Just have Luke bring us some real ones."

Glenda nodded in approval, agreeing with my suggestion. "That's a much better idea," she said, her attention suddenly diverted towards the tents, her brow furrowing with concern.

Curious, I followed her gaze and saw Jamie and an unfamiliar woman with long silvery hair emerging from around the canvas walls. I was soon to learn that this young woman was Beatrix Cramer, a friend of Jamie and Luke's, and more surprisingly, our newest Guardian. It had been her screams that had pierced the darkness when the attack began last night.

My heart sank at the sight of Jamie, his face etched with grief, holding a bloodied bundle in his arms. The reality of our situation hit me anew – the dangers of Clivilius were ever-present, and the loss we had already endured was a painful reminder of the fragility of our existence here.

As Paul straightened his posture, there was an air of determination about him that commanded attention, a sense of authority that seemed to radiate from his very being. "Jamie," he began, his voice cracking with a mix of empathy and urgency. "I know things are painful right now, but we need to know when you last saw Joel."

Jamie halted mid-step, a visible shift in his demeanour, his shoulders sagging under the weight of the question. The air seemed to thicken with tension as everyone waited for his response, the silence broken only by the soft rustling of the wind through the fabric of the tents.

When Jamie finally spoke, his voice was laden with sorrow, each word a struggle to form. "It was just before the attack last night," he said, his gaze distant, lost in the painful memories. "He was in bed in the tent when I took off after Duke."

Paul pressed on, his voice firm yet gentle, a delicate balance of authority and compassion. "And when you returned?" he asked, his eyes searching Jamie's face for any glimmer of hope, any clue that might lead us to Joel's whereabouts.

But Jamie remained silent, his expression a canvas of grief and guilt. The silence stretched on, a heavy and oppressive presence.

It was Glenda who finally broke the silence, her arms crossed tightly, her voice carrying a note of finality. "Then it's settled," she said, her tone leaving no room for doubt or debate. "Joel is missing."

At that moment, Charity stepped away from the campfire, her every move exuding confidence and authority, a warrior's grace that commanded respect. "I am certain that Joel has been taken by a Portal Pirate," she announced, her voice unwavering in its conviction. "I will hunt him down and bring Joel back."

My eyes widened in shock, my mind reeling at the revelation. *A Portal Pirate?* The term was unfamiliar, yet it sent a chill down my spine, a sense of foreboding that settled in the pit of my stomach. The situation was escalating into realms I had never imagined, a world of dangers and mysteries that seemed to defy comprehension.

Jamie, driven by a desperate need to act, quickly interjected, his voice thick with determination. "I'm coming with you," he declared, his eyes blazing with a fierce resolve, a clear indication that he was prepared to face whatever dangers lay ahead.

Charity's nod was resolute, her decision made, her gaze unwavering as she met Jamie's eyes. "Prepare your things. We leave immediately."

The look of sheer terror in Jamie's eyes struck a chord in me, a painful reminder of the burden he was carrying. My heart ached for him, for the loss he had already endured.

As Charity approached Jamie, her gesture was both reassuring and commanding. She placed her hand under his chin, lifting his face to meet her gaze, her words direct and blunt. "If you want any chance of finding Joel alive, we must leave immediately."

The scene before me was overwhelming, a whirlwind of emotions and decisions that seemed to swirl around us like a tempest. My gaze shifted away from the tense exchange between Jamie and Charity, seeking solace in the familiar surroundings of the camp.

But what I saw next sent a cold shiver down my spine, a sight that would haunt my dreams for nights to come. There, near the campfire, lay the motionless form of the black panther-like creature, its once sleek fur now matted with dried blood, its lifeless eyes staring blankly into nothingness. It was a chilling reminder of the peril we had faced, the tragic consequences of its attack.

Jamie's voice broke through my shock, his tone quivering with emotion as he spoke. "I need to say farewell to Duke first."

I forced myself to look away from the creature, turning back to Jamie and Charity, my heart heavy with the weight of the decision he faced. The tension in the air was palpable, a suffocating presence that seemed to press down on us all.

Charity's response was unsympathetic, almost harsh in its blatant honesty. "Life is full of decisions and consequences. You need to make a choice, Joel or Duke."

Her words echoed in my mind, a brutal reminder of the cruelty of the situation, the impossible choice that Jamie was being forced to make. A lump formed in my throat, my stomach twisting in distress at the thought of having to choose between mourning and action, between the past and the present.

It was Beatrix who brought a moment of poignant calm to the turbulent emotions swirling around us, her actions tender and understanding as she stepped between Jamie and

Charity. With gentle hands, she took Duke's lifeless form from Jamie's arms. "Duke knows you love him, Jamie. He won't ever forget that," she assured him, her words a comfort in the face of such sorrow.

Jamie's response was heartbreakingly gentle, a whispered apology as he leaned in and placed a tender kiss on Duke's wrapped head. "I'm so sorry, Duke," he whimpered.

Then, with a noticeable effort, he straightened his back and stood taller, as if gathering his strength from some unseen reservoir. "I'll grab my things," he declared, his voice stronger now, but still carrying the weight of his grief.

My eyes began to sting with unshed tears, the scene unfolding before me igniting an intense wave of helplessness within. The honest reality that neither Duke nor Joel could be brought back instantly was a painful truth.

Jamie paused momentarily in his departure, casting a glance over his shoulder, his voice trembling as he made a heartfelt request. "Take good care of Henri for me."

Paul stepped forward, scooping the plump dog into his arms, his voice filled with reassurance and promise. "We'll keep him safe, Jamie. You have my word."

Jamie retreated into his tent without another word, his steps heavy, with Charity following closely behind.

Suddenly, Glenda's scream cut through the silence, a primal sound that sent a jolt of fear through my body. "Clivilius!" she cried, her voice filled with a mixture of agony and revelation.

As she collapsed to her knees, pounding her fists into the ground, her entire being seemed to be consumed by a torrent of emotions, a storm of pain and epiphany that threatened to tear her apart. When she looked up, her face was a canvas of raw emotion, her eyes wide with a newfound understanding.

Paul approached her cautiously, his voice filled with concern as he spoke her name. "Glenda? Are you alright?"

Her response was startling, a declaration that left us all reeling in shock. "My father is alive!" she exclaimed, her hands shooting upwards, her entire demeanour shifting from despair to a sort of elated trance.

It was as if she had been possessed by a sudden surge of euphoria, her revelation leaving her in a state of shock, unresponsive to Chris's attempts to bring her back to reality. The sight of her like this, lost in her own world of revelation and joy, was both alarming and perplexing.

Beatrix, too, broke away from the group, her gaze was distant, fixated on some far-off point beyond our camp. She held Duke in her arms, a symbol of the loss we had all suffered.

Her sudden departure was surprising, a jarring shift in the dynamics of our group. "Beatrix, where are you going?" Paul called out, his voice tinged with confusion and disbelief.

"Home!" she shouted back, her voice strong and resolute, leaving no room for question.

Kain's unexpected announcement made me take an involuntary step back, my heart skipping a beat at the implications of his words. "I'm going with Beatrix," he said, his voice firm, reflecting a decision already made in his mind.

I couldn't help but voice my concern, my words laced with worry as I reached for his arm, trying to convince him to stay. "You need to rest," I countered, my gaze locked onto his, conveying the seriousness of my words.

But Kain was not to be swayed, his determination pushing me away as he retorted, "I need crutches. If Beatrix brings me some crutches, I can go with my uncle."

His belief in Beatrix was unwavering, but I couldn't shake the feeling that he was making a reckless decision. "Don't be so foolish," I rebuked, my voice laced with worry and frustration.

Kain ignored my pleas, his movement laboured and painful as he began to follow Beatrix, his bare feet sinking into the soft dust of the camp with each hobbling step. The sight of him like this, determined yet vulnerable, sent a pang of fear through my heart.

I couldn't just stand there and watch him leave, not without at least trying to protect him. Instinctively, I followed after him, my steps quick and purposeful as I caught up to his side.

If he was determined to be stubborn and go with Beatrix, then he wasn't going to do it alone. He would have to deal with my protective presence, my unwavering determination to try and keep him safe.

LEAVE OF ABSENCE

4338.209.4

As I watched Kain stand forlornly in front of the Portal's transparent screen, a mixture of my practical nature and the poignant feelings of loss from the night's tragic events battled within me. The way he looked, so utterly helpless, tugged at my heart, a painful reminder of the vulnerabilities we all faced in this unforgiving land. Beatrix had disappeared into the Portal before Kain could even reach her, vanishing in a flash of light that left him stranded and bewildered, a lost soul in a world of uncertainty.

Standing shoulder to shoulder with Kain, I couldn't help but feel a sense of helplessness wash over me. The events of the past few hours had taken their toll. The sight of Duke's lifeless body, the anguish on Jamie's face, the revelation of Joel's disappearance - it all swirled in my mind, a kaleidoscope of pain and confusion that was almost overwhelming in its reach.

I stepped up beside him, joining him in his silent vigil at the screen, my presence a quiet offer of support and understanding. The disappointment etched on his face was clear as he stared into the emptiness where Beatrix had been moments before, his eyes searching for answers that seemed to elude him.

But even in the midst of my own turmoil, I couldn't ignore the pressing concern that gnawed at me as I looked at Kain. "Kain, your leg is bleeding," I pointed out, my tone laced with worry, my eyes drawn to the crimson stain that was slowly spreading across the hastily applied bandages.

Kain's glance at his leg was brief but loaded with resignation, a flicker of pain crossing his features before he quickly masked it behind a stoic facade. He limped over to the base of the sandy hill, each step a struggle against the pain that clearly wracked his body, before collapsing onto the ground with a hefty grunt.

I hurried to his side, my heart racing with concern as I tried to help him to his feet, my hands grasping his arms in a desperate attempt to support him. "Come on, Kain. We should head back to camp," I urged, my voice filled with a sense of urgency, a desperate plea for him to see reason and seek proper medical attention.

But Kain was resolute in his refusal, shaking his head and stubbornly remaining where he was, his jaw set in a line of determination that I was getting to know all too well. It was clear that he wasn't going to be moved easily, his stubborn nature asserting itself even in the face of his own well-being.

I sighed in resignation. I knew I couldn't leave him like this, couldn't abandon him to his own devices when he so clearly needed help. "Fine, but I'm going to bring Glenda and some supplies back to look after that wound," I declared, my tone leaving no room for argument, my determination to ensure he received the care he needed overriding any other concerns.

Reluctantly leaving Kain at the base of the hill, I cast one last look over my shoulder at him, my heart heavy with worry and uncertainty. He looked so small and vulnerable, a lone figure against the vast expanse of the desert, the weight of the world seeming to rest on his shoulders. The sight of him like this, broken and defeated, sent a pang of pain through my chest. Yet, I knew that I had to keep moving.

❖

Re-entering the camp, a noticeable hush had settled over the area. The once bustling hub of activity and chatter was now eerily still, as if the morning's events had cast a spell of silence over everyone and everything.

The tents stood like silent sentinels, their canvas walls gently fluttering in the soft breeze. The campfire, usually the heart of our community, was now just a smouldering pile of ashes, with a few weak flames licking the charred wood.

After a quick scan of the area, it was evident that Glenda was nowhere to be seen. I checked each of the tents, peering inside with a growing sense of unease, but none of them revealed her presence. She wasn't anywhere in the small area that was the campsite, and her absence left a palpable void, a gnawing worry that settled in the pit of my stomach.

Turning my attention away from the fruitless search for Glenda, I decided to seek out Paul, hoping that he might have some answers or at least provide a measure of reassurance in this unsettling atmosphere. Paul was remarkably easy to spot, his tall figure easily distinguishable against the backdrop of the surrounding barren sands. He had returned to stand near the campfire, his posture one of deep thought, his gaze fixed on the horizon, as if searching for answers in the vast expanse of Clivilius.

As I approached him, the shifting of the dry dust under my feet seemed to break the quiet spell that had settled over the camp. The sound of my footsteps, usually so insignificant, now seemed almost intrusive in the heavy silence. Paul turned at the sound, his expression changing from contemplation to attentiveness as he noticed my approach. There was a weariness in his eyes, a weight that seemed to have settled on his shoulders since I last saw him.

"Kain's determined to wait at the Portal for Beatrix or Luke to return," I informed him, the concern evident in my voice. I couldn't shake the image of Kain, so vulnerable and stubborn, waiting alone at the Portal, his leg bleeding and his spirits low.

Paul's grunt was soft, almost resigned, as if he had expected this news. "Don't expect them any time soon," he muttered, his gaze drifting away, his voice laced with a weariness that I had never heard before. The lack of his usual optimism, which I often found overly idealistic but nonetheless comforting, was now replaced by a sombreness that was unsettling.

I frowned, the shift in Paul's demeanour making me uneasy. His normally hopeful outlook, although sometimes unrealistic, was a source of comfort in the chaos of Clivilius. It was a constant reminder that no matter how bleak things seemed, there was always a glimmer of hope, a reason to keep pushing forward. To see him so downcast, so devoid of that infectious positivity, was disconcerting.

"Kain's leg has started to bleed again. He can't go far," I explained, hoping to draw Paul's focus back to the immediate issues at hand. Kain's well-being was a pressing concern, and I needed Paul's help to ensure that he received the proper care and attention.

Paul's reaction deepened my concern. His shoulders slumped. "We don't have a doctor anymore," he admitted, his voice tinged with a sense of defeat.

His words sent a wave of panic through me. "What!?" I exclaimed, the possibility of another calamity befalling us so soon almost too much to comprehend. My mind raced with worry, conjuring up scenarios of Glenda injured or worse. *Had something happened to her while I was at the Portal?* The thought of losing another member of our group, especially someone as vital as Glenda, was a gut-wrenching prospect.

Paul's explanation, though, brought more confusion than relief. "Glenda's gone with Jamie and Charity," he said, revealing a piece of the puzzle that I hadn't anticipated. "Something about being determined to find her father."

I stared at Paul, my skepticism clear. Glenda, with her scientific mind and pragmatic approach, succumbing to an emotional quest seemed out of character, almost implausible. The idea that she believed her father was alive and in Clivilius was a stretch, even for this strange world. It didn't align with the Glenda I thought I had figured out, one who relied on facts and evidence, not flights of fancy or emotional impulses.

Paul's next words mirrored my thoughts. "I don't really understand any of it either," he said bluntly, his frustration apparent in the furrow of his brow and the tension in his voice.

As I processed this new information, a mix of confusion and concern swirled within me. Glenda's departure, so sudden and unexplained, left a gaping hole in our group, a void that seemed impossible to fill. Her absence, coupled with Kain's stubbornness at the Portal and now Paul's uncharacteristic pessimism, made it feel like everything was unravelling at an alarming rate, the thin threads of our fragile existence in Clivilius coming undone before our very eyes.

Chris's sudden entry into the conversation momentarily startled me, jolting me out of the troubling thoughts that Paul's revelation had stirred. "The coriander plants are still looking healthy," he chimed in, his tone light and matter-of-fact. "I've just been checking on them," he added, a hint of pride creeping into his voice.

Despite the myriad of concerns and the growing sense of unease in the camp, Chris's mention of the coriander plants was oddly comforting. It was a small piece of success, a reminder of the simpler aspects of our life here in Clivilius. The fact that the plants were thriving, that something as mundane as coriander could still flourish amidst the mayhem, was a glimmer of hope, a tiny beacon of light in the darkness that seemed to be closing in around us.

A half-smile flickered on Paul's lips at Chris's words, a brief moment of levity that lifted some of the weight from his shoulders. It was a fleeting glimpse of the old Paul, the one who could find a reason to smile even in the bleakest of circumstances. It gave me a glimmer of hope that perhaps his usual optimism hadn't completely vanished, that it was still there, buried beneath the layers of worry and uncertainty.

Chris, ever eager to pursue our agricultural experiments, turned his attention to me. "I'm keen for Karen and me to do some more soil exploration," he said, his eyes seeking my approval, a spark of excitement flickering in their depths. It was a reminder of the passion that drove him, the insatiable curiosity that fuelled his desire to learn.

Before I could respond, Paul interjected, his voice firm and resolute. "I'm not sure that I see that as a priority," he stated, his tone indicating that he had other concerns in mind. "We need better protection and storage space first. Putting up the sheds should be our top priority."

I could see Chris was ready to argue, his passion for our scientific pursuits evident in the set of his jaw and the determination in his eyes. He was never one to back down easily, especially when it came to the things he believed in. However, recognising the need to support Paul's newfound assertiveness, I quickly intervened, hoping to diffuse the tension before it escalated.

"No worries, Paul. Chris and I will go and assess the work that's already been done on the concrete bases," I said, aiming to align our efforts with Paul's priorities. It was a delicate balancing act, trying to maintain the fragile equilibrium of our group while still pursuing the goals that we believed were important.

Paul's expression softened at my words, a flicker of relief passing over his features. "Thank you," he said, his voice heavy with gratitude.

I gently tugged on Chris's arm, guiding him away from Paul. Once we were a safe distance away, out of earshot, I gave Chris a serious look, my eyes locking with his. "You start looking at the concrete slabs for the storage shed," I instructed firmly, emphasising the importance of aligning with Paul's plans. "I need to find some fresh bandages for Kain's leg."

Chris nodded, understanding the situation, though I could tell he was reluctant to divert his attention from our agricultural projects. His passion for the soil and the secrets it held was a driving force, a beacon of hope in this strange yet seemingly cruel world. But he also recognised the need for unity, for working together towards a common goal.

"I'll return quickly and help you," I promised, leaving him with a light kiss as a reassurance of my support. It was a small gesture, but one that carried the weight of my love and commitment.

❖

Finding the medical supplies wasn't difficult, thanks to Glenda's meticulous organisation. Despite our limited resources and lack of formal facilities, she had managed to maintain a semblance of order. The clean bandages were neatly stacked, a small reminder of her efficiency and care. It was a comforting sight, a glimmer of normality in a world that seemed to be constantly shifting beneath our feet.

Returning to the Portal, I found Kain just where I had left him, his figure slumped against the base of the sandy hill. His posture reflected a deepening despair, a sense of hopelessness that seemed to emanate from every fibre of his being. It was evident that his brief flicker of hope, the spark that had been ignited by the possibility of Beatrix's return, had diminished even further during my absence.

As I approached, Kain attempted to stand, a valiant effort to maintain some semblance of dignity in the face of his pain and vulnerability. But his injury and the agony it caused forced him to remain seated, his body betraying the strength of his will. "Where's Glenda?" he asked, his voice strained with effort and a tinge of hopelessness.

"Kain," I started, my tone gentle, attempting to mask my own concern and the turmoil that raged inside me. I knew that the news I had to deliver would only add to his burden, but there was no way to soften the blow. "Glenda, Charity, and Jamie have all left the camp. They've gone Portal Pirate hunting."

The impact of my words was immediate, a visible shock that rippled through Kain's already weakened frame. The little colour that was left in his face drained away, leaving him pale and ashen, a ghost of his former self. "Glenda's gone with them?" he asked, his voice shaking with a mix of disbelief and vulnerability, a raw emotion that cut straight to my heart.

I sighed heavily, my fingers absentmindedly playing with the bandages in my hands, a nervous habit that betrayed my own unease. "Paul didn't seem like he had much say in the matter," I said, conveying the helplessness of the situation, the sense that we were all caught up in a current that was beyond our control.

Kain's expression shifted rapidly, a kaleidoscope of emotions that played out across his face. Shock gave way to anger, a flash of hot fury that burned in his eyes, only to be replaced by a profound sense of incredulity. "You mean to tell me that I have a gaping hole in my leg and our only doctor has left us?" His disbelief was palpable, a visceral reaction to the absurdity of our predicament. "Why would she do that?" he asked, the exasperation in his voice echoing the confusion that I also felt, the sense that nothing made sense anymore.

I couldn't meet Kain's searching eyes, feeling overwhelmed by the responsibility that had suddenly been thrust upon us. I looked down at the bandages in my hands, a tangible reminder of the task that lay ahead, the duty that had fallen to me in Glenda's absence. "I don't know," I answered softly, my voice barely above a whisper, a confession of my own uncertainty.

But even as the words left my lips, I knew that I couldn't allow myself to be consumed by the dark thoughts. Shifting my focus, I knelt beside Kain, my movements deliberate and purposeful. "But here," I said, my voice gaining strength, a resolve that surprised even me. "I've brought some fresh bandages. Let's get your leg cleaned up." There was a firmness in my tone, a determination to do what needed to be done, to take control of the situation in whatever small way I could.

Kain nodded reluctantly, his expression a mix of gratitude and resignation, a silent acknowledgment of the necessity of my actions. As I tended to his wound, my movements were quick and efficient. But even as I focused on the task at hand, I made sure that my touch was gentle yet firm, a reassurance that I was there, that he wasn't alone in his suffering.

As I unwrapped the bloodied bandages, a critical thought crossed my mind, a nagging doubt that I couldn't shake. Glenda's stitch work on Kain's wound seemed subpar, far from the quality that I would have expected from a doctor of her caliber. It was especially surprising considering the miraculous recovery that Joel had reportedly made, a feat that had seemed to defy the very laws of nature.

"It's not looking so great," I said aloud, more to myself than to Kain, as I meticulously cleaned the wound, my brow furrowed in concentration. The injury was more severe than I had anticipated, a jagged gash that seemed to mock my meagre attempts at healing. My concern for Kain deepened with each passing moment, a growing sense of dread that settled in the pit of my stomach.

Kain tried to maintain a brave front in the face of his pain. He gulped noticeably, a visible effort to swallow down his discomfort, but managed to speak with a shaky conviction. "I'll be fine," he assured me, though his voice betrayed the depth of his suffering. "Once I get crutches, I'll be able to walk properly."

I found his optimism a bit misplaced, given the severity of his injury. The wound was deep and angry. However, I didn't want to completely dispel his hope, knowing that it was often the only thing that kept us going in the face of overwhelming odds. Gently, my fingers worked to wrap the fresh bandages around the cleaned wound, a delicate dance of precision and care.

Once I finished, I met Kain's gaze, my eyes searching his for some sign of the strength that I knew lay within him. I wanted to offer words of comfort or reassurance, to tell him that everything would be alright, that we would find a way through this nightmare together. But as I looked into his eyes, I found myself at a loss, the words dying on my lips.

"I'll be back soon," I said instead, patting his shoulder in an attempt to offer some small measure of comfort. "I have to get some things done back at camp. Are you sure you'll be okay here by yourself?"

Kain's affirmation came quickly, his nod swift and seemingly confident, a brave facade that I knew was a mask for the pain and fear that lurked beneath the surface. But I didn't push him, knowing that sometimes the illusion of strength was all we had left to cling to.

Standing up, I took one last look at Kain, feeling a twinge of reluctance to leave him there, alone and vulnerable in the shadow of the Portal. However, I knew that I had responsibilities waiting for me back at the camp, duties that couldn't be ignored or postponed. As I began ascending the slope of the hill, the thick dust covering my boots, I reassured myself with the thought that Luke or Beatrix would return soon, that they would bring with them the help and supplies that Kain so desperately needed.

Hopefully, Kain would make a recovery akin to Joel's, a miraculous healing that would defy the odds. This place, it seemed, did have some remarkable properties, after all. Perhaps there was still hope to be found in the midst of the darkness, a glimmer of light that could guide us through the trials and tribulations that lay ahead.

CROSSING LINES

4338.209.5

I had finally returned to Chris, and despite the challenge of taming his enthusiasm for exploring the properties of the fertile soil beneath the Clivilian crust, we had actually made good progress on pouring concrete foundations for the small sheds that Paul wanted to get built as soon as possible. It was a task that required focus and precision, a delicate balance of ingredients and timing that reminded me of the intricate dance of the insect world, each species playing its role in the greater ecosystem.

Our work had been interrupted several times, one of which was when our small camp had yet another new arrival. The young man came into camp with Paul and Kain in a ute, which I presumed to belong to the new man.

From a distance, Chris and I had watched the situation unfold, as Kain pulled himself from the ute, his movements slow and laboured, like a wounded beetle struggling to right itself. The sour look on his face was a testament to the pain and frustration that had become his constant companions. With a determination that belied his condition, Kain slowly managed to find his way past us, his steps measured and deliberate, as he headed in the direction of the lagoon.

After what felt like an eternity of silence, a stillness that hung in the air like the calm before a storm, Paul and the new man emerged from the ute. This new man's appearance was a disruption to the delicate balance of our camp, a new variable introduced into the complex equation of our survival.

Eventually, Paul brought the man over to us. Listening to Paul introduce Nial Triffett, I couldn't help but feel a complex mix of emotions swirling within me, like a kaleidoscope of conflicting thoughts and feelings. On one hand, I felt a deep sense of empathy for the man, a kindred spirit who had been unwittingly and unwillingly dragged into the surreal world of Clivilius, another victim of Luke's unpredictable actions.

I could only imagine the weight of the burden he now carried, the pain of being torn away from his young wife and toddler, the life he had built and the people he loved. It was a sacrifice that no one should have to make, a price too high to pay for the whims of fate or the machinations of someone like Luke.

But as Paul continued to speak, emphasising Nial's background in construction and his ownership of a fencing business in Hobart, I felt a flicker of hope ignite within me, a spark that began to grow and spread like wildfire through my veins. It was as if a colony of ants had discovered a new source of sustenance, a precious resource that could mean the difference between survival and extinction in the harsh and unforgiving landscape of Clivilius.

Nial's arrival, while unfortunate on a personal level, carried with it a strategic value that I couldn't ignore. The potential to procure fencing supplies through his business was a tantalising prospect.

In the natural world, boundaries and barriers are essential for survival, for maintaining the delicate balance of ecosystems and protecting the vulnerable from the predators that lurk in the shadows. And in Clivilius, where the very ground beneath our feet seemed to pulse with an otherworldly energy, the need for such defences was even more acute.

The thought of being able to fortify our camp, to erect a physical barrier against the unknown dangers that threatened us, was a seductive one. It was a chance to exert some measure of control over our fate, to shape our environment in a way that could give us a fighting chance in the battles that lay ahead.

But even as I found myself drawn to the practical benefits of Nial's presence, a nagging sense of unease began to take root in the back of my mind, like a weed that threatened to choke out the fragile bloom of hope. It was a feeling that I couldn't quite shake, a persistent whisper that challenged the very foundations of my moral compass.

Under normal circumstances, the idea of Luke bringing another person into Clivilius against their will would have been unthinkable, a violation of the most basic principles of human decency and autonomy. The fact that Nial was a young father only compounded the injustice of the situation, adding an extra layer of tragedy to an already heartbreaking tale.

And yet, here I was, finding myself not only accepting Luke's actions but actively applauding them, as if the ends could somehow justify the means in this twisted game of survival. It was a realisation that sent a chill down my spine, a cold sweat that beaded on my brow as I confronted the depths of my own moral relativism.

How far was I willing to go to ensure our survival in Clivilius? What lines was I prepared to cross in the name of self-preservation and the greater good? These were questions that I had never thought I would have to ask myself, ethical dilemmas that I had only ever encountered in the abstract realm of philosophical discourse.

But now, faced with the harsh realities of life in this world, I found myself grappling with them on a visceral level, my mind spinning like a butterfly caught in a web of its own making. Each strand of that web represented a moral boundary, a line in the sand that I had once believed to be inviolable.

And yet, as I stood there, watching Paul and Nial interact with Chris, I could feel those lines beginning to blur and shift, the once-solid ground beneath my feet turning to quicksand. It was a terrifying prospect, the idea that my own ethical framework could be so easily compromised by the pressures of survival and the allure of pragmatism.

Like a butterfly emerging from its cocoon, transformed by the crucible of its metamorphosis, I feared that I too might be changed by the trials and tribulations of Clivilius, my moral compass warped and distorted in ways that I could not yet comprehend. It was a thought that filled me with a sense of dread, a deep-seated fear of losing myself in the process of trying to save us all.

But even as these doubts and fears swirled within me, I knew that I could not afford to be paralysed by them. The stakes were too high, the consequences of inaction too dire to contemplate. Like a spider spinning its web, I would have to find a way to navigate the complex moral terrain of Clivilius, to weave a path through the ethical minefields that lay ahead.

Thankfully, Paul had kept the introductions brief, seemingly not wanting to overwhelm the young man, and finding a renewed sense of optimism for establishing our small settlement here. Like a queen bee guiding her hive, Paul ushered the young man back to camp, his presence a stabilising force in the midst of the disruption.

As they walked away, I found myself reflecting on the delicate balance of our existence in Clivilius, the constant push and pull of survival and morality. Like the intricate web of relationships in the natural world, each decision we made had consequences that rippled out into the greater ecosystem of our camp.

And as Chris and I returned to our work, the concrete foundations a tangible reminder of the structures we were trying to build, both physical and emotional, I couldn't shake the feeling that we were on the precipice of something greater, a tipping point that would determine the course of our future.

Like ants building their colony, each task a small but essential part of the greater whole, we worked in silence, our minds filled with the weight of the choices that lay ahead. And as the sun beat down upon us, a relentless force that mirrored the challenges we faced, I found myself lost in the rhythms of the work. With sweat beading on my brow, I could only hope that I would have the strength and wisdom to make the right choices when the time came, to hold fast to my principles even as the ground shifted beneath my feet.

BURNING

4338.209.6

As Nial and I meticulously arranged the smaller fires around the camp's edge in preparation for the inevitable nightfall that would arrive, even if it was yet hours away, the rhythmic crackling of the flames intermingled with our quiet conversation, a symphony of light and sound that seemed to hold the metaphorical and emotional darkness at bay. With each log we placed, each flame we kindled, I couldn't help but draw parallels to my work as an entomologist back in Hobart. Just as these fires provided a barrier against the Shadow Panthers, the intricate defences of certain insect species, like the complex web structures of funnel-web spiders or the chemical secretions of bombardier beetles, served to protect them from predators in the wild.

The task was simple yet undeniably vital — these fires were our first line of defence against the Shadow Panthers that lurked in the darkness, their black eyes and razor-sharp claws a real threat to our fragile existence. I thought back to the countless hours I had spent in the lush forests of Tasmania, studying the delicate balance between predator and prey in the insect world. Now, in this strange land of Clivilius, I found myself a part of that same primal struggle for survival, the stakes higher than any research project I had ever undertaken.

I couldn't help but feel a sense of purpose, a glimmer of hope in the face of the overwhelming odds that seemed to be stacked against us like a house of cards in a hurricane. It was a small victory, a tangible achievement in a world where so much seemed uncertain and beyond our control, like trying to grasp smoke with our bare hands.

"Are we doing the right thing?" Nial asked, his voice laced with a blend of hope and concern as he placed another log onto the small fire we were tending, the question hanging in the air like a fragile soap bubble.

I straightened my back, brushing the dirt from my hands, and looked at him, my eyes searching his face for any sign of the turmoil that I felt churning within my own heart like a tempest. "I hope so. It's the best we can do with what we have," I responded, my words meant to reassure both of us, despite the gnawing doubt in the back of my mind about our dwindling firewood supply, a ticking clock that seemed to mock our efforts.

Nial's gaze swept over the line of fires we had created, a flickering barrier against the encroaching darkness, a valiant but perhaps futile attempt to keep the monsters at bay. "It's unsettling, isn't it? The thought of running out of wood," he echoed my own fears.

I sighed, my eyes lingering on the modest pile of logs we had left, a meagre supply that seemed to dwindle with each passing moment. "It is. We'll have to ration it carefully," I said, the pragmatic side of me already planning how to extend our limited resources, my mind whirring with calculations and contingencies. It reminded me of the resource management strategies employed by eusocial insects like ants and bees, how they carefully allocated food and materials to ensure the survival of their colonies. Perhaps we could learn from their example, find ways to stretch our supplies and make the most of what little we had.

As Nial picked up another log, he hesitated, his question thoughtful and introspective, a momentary reprieve from the weight of our responsibilities. "Do you ever wonder what else is out there, beyond the camp? In Clivilius, I mean," he asked, his eyes searching mine, a flicker of curiosity and apprehension dancing within their depths like a candle flame in the wind.

The question made me pause, my breath catching in my throat as a wave of uncertainty washed over me. It was a thought that had crossed my mind countless times, a nagging presence that refused to be ignored, like a persistent itch that couldn't be scratched. "More than I'd like to," I admitted, my voice barely above a whisper, the words feeling heavy on my tongue. "Clivilius seems to be full of mysteries, a Pandora's box waiting to be opened. Sometimes, I fear what else we might find lurking in the shadows."

I was no stranger to the wonders and horrors that could be found in the natural world. I had seen firsthand the incredible diversity of life, from the breathtaking beauty of iridescent butterfly wings to the grotesque and unsettling forms of parasitic wasps. But Clivilius seemed to operate on a different scale entirely, a realm where the rules of nature as I understood them were bent and twisted into something unrecognisable.

The unknowns of this place had already been both fascinating and terrifying. It was like peering into the depths of the ocean, marvelling at the beauty and diversity of the life that thrived beneath the surface, while simultaneously feeling a sense of dread at the thought of the leviathans that lurked in the abyss, their tentacles reaching out to drag us into the darkness. I couldn't help but wonder what entomological marvels and monstrosities might be waiting to be discovered in the unexplored regions of Clivilius, what new species and adaptations had evolved in this unfamiliar environment.

Nial placed the log onto the fire, and the flames eagerly embraced it, casting a warm glow across his face. "Maybe one day we'll find a way home," he said, a trace of hope in his voice.

His words stirred a longing in me, a deep-seated desire to return to the life I had once known, to the comfort and familiarity of the world beyond the Portal. I thought of my modest lab back in Hobart, the rows of carefully pinned specimens and the stacks of field journals that chronicled my research. It seemed like a lifetime ago, a distant memory that grew fainter with each passing hour. But even as that yearning tugged at my heart, I found myself unable to fully embrace it, the weight of our current circumstances too heavy to allow for such flights of fancy.

The reality of our situation, the challenges and uncertainties of Clivilius, were too pressing, too immediate to be ignored. We were like insects caught in a web, struggling against the sticky strands that held us fast, our only hope of survival lying in our ability to adapt and persevere.

As the fire warmed our faces, the dancing flames casting swirls of smoke into the sky like ethereal dancers, a reflective silence fell between us, a moment of shared contemplation. I found myself thinking of the countless nights I had spent in the Tasmanian wilderness, huddled around a campfire with Chris. Those moments of camaraderie and shared passion seemed so far away now, a distant echo of a life that no longer existed.

Nial and I parted ways, each moving to build a new small fire, our steps heavy with the weight of the task at hand, the burden of survival pressing down on our shoulders like an invisible yoke. The work was repetitive but necessary, a reminder of the importance of the small actions we took to ensure our survival.

As I worked, I couldn't help but feel a sense of solitude amidst the camp, a strange disconnect from the others who moved around me like ghosts, their presence felt but not fully acknowledged. It was as if we were all islands unto ourselves, each grappling with our own fears and doubts, our own hopes and dreams. I thought of the solitary nature of so many insect species, how they went about their lives with singular focus and determination, driven by instinct and the imperatives of survival. In a way, we were not so different, each of us playing our part in the grand tapestry of life, no matter how small or seemingly insignificant.

But even in the midst of that isolation, it was impossible not to notice Paul's active involvement. He moved efficiently from one fire to another, inspecting our work with a keen eye, his brow furrowed in concentration, like a general surveying his troops before battle. I couldn't help but see the parallels to the hierarchical structure of many insect societies, the way that a single queen could orchestrate the actions of an entire colony through a complex system of chemical signals and pheromones.

Paul's leadership was evident, a beacon of stability in a world that seemed to shift and change with each passing moment. And his concern for our safety was palpable, a tangible force that seemed to radiate from his very being. It was a quality that I was coming to admire in him, a strength of character that set him apart from the others and made him the natural choice to guide us through the challenges that lay ahead.

It brought a small smile to my face, thinking about the various roles Paul had taken on in our settlement, the many hats he wore with such optimism and determination, like a juggler keeping multiple plates spinning at once. He was a leader, a protector, a mentor, and a friend, all rolled into one, a multifaceted gem that shone brightly in the darkness.

His adaptability and willingness to shoulder these responsibilities was admirable. And in a strange way, it was also somewhat amusing, a reminder of the absurdity of our situation and the lengths we had to go to just to stay alive. I thought of the elaborate courtship rituals and mating dances of certain insect species, how they could appear almost comical to the human eye, yet served a vital purpose in the grand scheme of things.

With a slight chuckle to myself, I wiped the sweat from my brow and approached Paul, my steps measured and purposeful. "Do you think this will be enough to keep them at bay?" I asked, my voice tinged with a hint of trepidation, a reflection of the fear that still lingered in the back of my mind.

Paul stopped what he was doing and gave my question some serious thought, his brow furrowing as he considered the implications of my words. It was a moment that seemed to stretch on forever. I could almost see the gears turning in his mind, the calculations and contingencies that he was no doubt running through, just as I had done earlier.

"It should help," he finally said, his response initially doing little to quell my anxieties, my heart still racing with the fear of the unknown. "According to Charity, Shadow Panther's eyes are sensitive to light, so they avoid it."

His words brought a measure of relief. But even as I felt that momentary sense of reprieve, I knew that it was a fragile thing. In the insect world, such moments of safety were often fleeting, a brief respite before the next predator came calling.

Paul continued, his voice steady and measured. "But they've evolved to become stealthy apex nighttime predators, so we must remain vigilant."

His addition did nothing to soothe my growing concern, the reality of facing such creatures again, even with our fires, a daunting prospect that sent a shiver down my spine. It was like standing on the edge of a precipice, staring down into the yawning abyss below, knowing that one false step could spell disaster. I thought of the countless insect species that had evolved to become masters of camouflage and stealth, how they could blend seamlessly into their surroundings and strike without warning. The Shadow Panthers, it seemed, had taken those same principles and elevated them to a terrifying new level.

Despite the unease his words caused, I knew it was important to maintain a strong front, to project an air of confidence and determination. Nodding with as much conviction as I could muster, I replied, "We'll keep watch in shifts through the night."

It was a statement that carried the weight of a promise, a vow to do whatever it took to keep our people safe. And in that moment, I knew that it was crucial to keep Paul's leadership and confidence buoyant, to be a source of strength and support for him, even as he shouldered the burden of our collective survival. Just as a queen ant relied on the unwavering loyalty and dedication of her workers, Paul needed us to stand with him, to be the foundation upon which he could build a future for us all.

Nial's arrival with his arms laden with firewood was timely, a welcome interruption to the heavy conversation that had been unfolding between Paul and myself. But even as he approached, his words added another layer of complexity to our already precarious situation.

"We're also more visible now," he said, his voice tinged with caution and concern. "Not just to the Shadow Panthers, but to anything else out there."

His observation struck a chord with me, bringing forth a concern that I hadn't fully considered, a new angle to the multifaceted nature of our predicament. The prospect of attracting unknown dangers was unsettling, a reminder of the vast and unpredictable nature of the world we had found ourselves in. I thought of the bioluminescent insects that used their light as a lure, attracting unsuspecting prey to their doom. Were we, in our attempts to defend ourselves, inadvertently drawing the attention of even greater threats?

I found myself swallowing a dry gulp, my mind racing with the possibilities of what else might be lurking in the darkness, what other horrors might be drawn to the flickering light of our fires like moths to a flame. It was a thought that sent a chill down my spine, a cold sweat breaking out across my brow. In the insect world, such adaptations were a double-edged sword, a delicate balance between defence and vulnerability.

But even as I grappled with the implications of Nial's words, I watched as Paul faced his comment with a calm and assured demeanour, his eyes locking with Nial's in a moment of shared understanding. "I know," he said, his voice steady and unwavering. "But right now, we're dealing with the devils we know. It's a risk, I know, but we have to take it."

His words were a reminder of the difficult choices we faced, the constant balancing act between risk and reward. And as I listened to him speak, I felt a sense of resignation wash over me, a recognition of the hard truths that we had to confront. Just as certain insects had to navigate a gauntlet of predators and environmental hazards just to survive, we too had to make hard choices and take calculated risks if we hoped to see another day.

Internally, I sighed, the weight of our situation pressing down on me. Paul was right, of course. The immediate threat of the Shadow Panthers was a known danger, a tangible enemy that we had already encountered and survived against. To ignore that threat in favour of hypothetical dangers would be foolish, a gamble that we couldn't afford to take.

The choice to light these fires, despite the potential risks it posed, was a calculated decision, a necessary step to protect ourselves from an immediate and pressing threat.

As we stood there, the three of us surrounded by the growing network of fires, our faces warmed by the flickering light, I felt a renewed sense of determination wash over me. Yes, we were potentially exposing ourselves to other dangers, to the unknown horrors that lurked beyond the boundaries of our camp.

But in Clivilius, every decision was a balance between risk and survival, a constant negotiation between the immediate and the long-term. And right now, our priority was to defend ourselves against a known predator, to put up a fight against the darkness that threatened to eliminate us, our journey ended before it had really even begun.

❖

The late afternoon sun cast a serene, ambient glow over our small settlement, enhanced by the flickering lights of the fires we had set around the camp's perimeter. I couldn't help but note how the scene reminded me of the bioluminescent glow of fireflies on a warm summer evening back in Hobart. The comparison brought a fleeting smile to my face, a momentary respite from the constant worry that had become our new normal in Clivilius.

It was a picturesque scene, albeit born out of necessity. Our primary goal now was to maintain these fires, keeping them burning low until dusk to conserve our precious wood supply. We planned to add more firewood only when the cloak of night descended upon us.

I found myself beside one of the nearby fires, my mind partly on the task at hand and partly wandering. As I poked at the hot coals, a thought crossed my mind - *this fire would be perfect for cooking tonight's meal*. The idea of another communal dinner brought a small sense of normality to our camp life. It reminded me of the countless nights I had spent huddled around campfires with my fellow researchers during field expeditions in Tasmania, sharing stories and laughter over simple meals cooked over open flames.

From where I stood, I could see Nial and Paul engaged in a quiet, earnest discussion near the main campfire. Their voices, though audible, were indistinct, the words lost in the soft crackling of the flames. I wondered what they were discussing, but I chose not to intrude. In the insect world, communication was often subtle and complex, relying on pheromones, vibrations, and intricate dances. I couldn't help but draw parallels to the nuanced interactions between my human companions, the unspoken messages that passed between them in glances and gestures.

As I continued to tend to the fire, Kain's return to the camp caught my attention. His arrival seemed to disrupt Paul and Nial's conversation. I watched them from a distance, their chatter louder than before. Kain's voice carried over to me, filled with curiosity. "What's with all the extra fires?" he asked, looking around at our handiwork.

I let my attention drift back to the fire in front of me, letting their conversation become background noise as Paul began explaining our afternoon's efforts. The sound of his voice, steady and reassuring, provided a sense of stability. It was comforting to know that despite the uncertainty and dangers we faced, we were doing everything we could to protect our small community.

As the trio's dull conversation lulled on, I continued to prod the hot coals, preparing them for cooking. Then I noticed from the corner of my eye, Chris in the distance, on his way back from the lagoon.

Chris approached with an unusual sense of urgency in his stride, that caused me with a flutter of concern. Leaving the fire I had been tending, I made my way toward him, curiosity mingling with worry. It wasn't like Chris to be so hurried without good reason. As I drew closer, I noticed a stiffness in his posture, a tension that reminded me of a prey insect trying to avoid detection by a predator.

"What the hell happened to you?" I blurted out as I met him, my eyes immediately drawn to the bruised bump above his brow. It was an alarming sight, and I couldn't hide my concern.

Chris's response was hesitant, his hands fidgeting nervously. He didn't stop moving, but his pace slowed as he spoke. "The rocks around the lagoon are slippery," he said, his voice carrying a hint of something I couldn't quite place.

I narrowed my eyes, studying him carefully. Something about his explanation didn't sit right with me. "And you hit your head?" I pressed, reaching out to gently grab his arm, urging him to pause his hurried march.

He frowned, a simple "Yeah," escaping his lips. His brevity was uncharacteristic, and it only deepened my worry.

"Did you black out? Are you concussed?" I asked, my voice laced with concern as the questions tumbled out rapidly.

Chris shook his head dismissively. "It was just a small cut," he assured me, but his tone lacked conviction.

Leaning closer, I examined the bruise more closely. "It doesn't look cut to me," I observed, my trained eye taking in the details of the injury. "There's no blood. No open wound."

His response was nonchalant. "Perhaps I didn't hit it as hard as I thought," he said, then continued his walk back to camp.

I trailed behind him, his dismissive attitude about the injury leaving me feeling uneasy. There was something he wasn't telling me, and it gnawed at me like a persistent itch.

As we approached the campfire, Paul's gaze fell upon us, his curiosity evident. "The clumsy bugger slipped on the rocks," I quickly explained, hoping to forestall any probing questions. I wasn't sure what Chris was hiding, but I sensed it was best left unexplored for the moment. In the delicate balance of our small community, I knew that sometimes it was necessary to let secrets lie, to avoid disturbing the fragile equilibrium that kept us all functioning.

Yet, as we rejoined the group, my mind couldn't let go of the nagging suspicion that something else had happened at the lagoon – something Chris wasn't ready to share. In Clivilius, every incident seemed to hold deeper implications, and Chris's injury, however minor it might appear, felt like another piece of an ever-growing puzzle.

❖

The bonfire's flickering light cast a warm glow on our small group, but it couldn't dispel the noticeable change in the atmosphere. I was accustomed to observing subtle shifts in behaviour and mood within insect colonies, and the same skills now allowed me to sense the unease that had settled over our camp. The absence of Jamie, Joel, and Glenda hung heavily in the air, their vacant spots around the fire a silent reminder of the events that had unfolded. It was like watching a colony of ants struggling to adapt after the loss of key members, the remaining individuals grappling with the void left behind.

Kain's retreat to his tent without interacting with Chris only added to the evening's subdued mood, fuelling my growing skepticism about what had really happened to Chris at the lagoon. Despite his insistence that his injury was due to a simple accident, I couldn't shake off my disbelief.

We sat around the bonfire, our interactions limited, the usual chatter replaced by a near silence. The unease I felt about Chris's incident cast a shadow over us, and we picked at our food without much appetite or conversation. The meal tonight was a simple affair, requiring minimal preparation. My earlier idea of using one of the smaller fires for cooking was abandoned, mirroring our collective mood of simplicity and reflection.

Across the fire, Paul and Nial sat together, their conversation sparse. What little they did talk about eventually gave way to a persistent silence. It was like watching two ants exchanging chemical signals, their communication brief and purposeful, conveying only the most essential information. I couldn't help but wonder what thoughts were running through their minds, what worries and concerns they were grappling with in the silence.

As I looked around the fire, I couldn't help but feel the weight of the changes that had befallen our small community. The fire's warmth was a stark contrast to the chill of uncertainty that seemed to settle around us. Every absent member was a reminder of the challenges we faced in Clivilius, and every unspoken word around the fire spoke volumes of the concerns and fears that each of us harboured.

4338.210

(29 July 2018)

WASHED CLEAN

4338.210.1

The crisp morning air greeted Chris and me as we emerged from our tent, the first light of dawn casting a soft glow over the camp. The decision to prepare a cooked breakfast over the campfire wasn't just about the food; it was about creating a sense of normality, a comforting reminder of the life we were determined to build here in Clivilius. The aroma of a hearty breakfast seemed like the perfect way to rouse the camp from its slumber and inject some energy into the start of our day.

To our surprise, we weren't the only early risers. As we approached the communal area, we found Paul and Nial already there, engrossed in a conversation that was both hushed and animated. They sat close to the flickering flames of the campfire, their expressions intense yet excited.

"Morning," I greeted them, keeping my voice light, not wanting to intrude on their private conversation.

They both looked up, their conversation pausing as they acknowledged us with nods and brief morning pleasantries. Paul's eyes met mine, a fleeting smile crossing his lips before he turned back to Nial, their voices lowering once again.

Sensing that their discussion was private, Chris and I moved on without probing. We focused on stoking the fire, building it up to a suitable level for cooking. The kindling crackled as the flames took hold, sending a cascade of sparks dancing into the morning sky. I watched, mesmerised, as the sparks rose and fell, their brief lives extinguished as they drifted back to the ground.

Chris busied himself with setting up the griddle over the fire, while I began unpacking the ingredients for breakfast. The sound of sizzling soon filled the air as bacon hit the hot surface, followed by the comforting crackle of eggs. The aroma of the cooking food wafted through the camp, a tantalising invitation for the others to join us.

As the comforting aroma of breakfast cooking over the campfire filled the morning air, I couldn't help but notice a slightly less pleasant scent emanating from both Chris and myself. We had been so caught up in the daily rigours of survival in Clivilius that personal hygiene had taken a bit of a backseat. It was a small, yet smelly reminder of the adjustments we were continuously making in this new environment.

"Are you alright to continue cooking breakfast?" I asked Chris, stepping away from the griddle for a moment.

"Of course," he replied with a warm smile, flipping the bacon with practiced ease. His easy demeanour and the way he seemed to take everything in stride never ceased to amaze me.

"Good," I said, nodding. "I think we need to do some washing today."

Chris pulled his shirt to his nose and took a cautious sniff. His face contorted into a grimace as the full force of the odour hit him. "I think you're right," he agreed, his face scrunching up slightly at the realisation.

I chuckled softly, the corners of my lips curling upward as I observed our makeshift living quarters. Inside the tent, the soft glow of morning light filtered through the canvas, casting a warm, amber hue on everything.

With a determined resolve, I began the arduous task of sifting through our belongings. It was like embarking on an archaeological dig, uncovering relics of our past life. Each item I touched held a memory, a piece of our history that seemed to belong to a different lifetime.

As I dug deeper into the pile, it quickly became apparent that almost everything we owned was either tainted with the smell of sweat or coated in a fine layer of Clivilius' ubiquitous dust. The realisation struck me like a wave of nostalgia for the comforts we once took for granted. Even the simple task of laundry had become a significant chore in this new world.

"Kain," I heard Chris call out firmly, his voice breaking through my contemplative reverie and pulling me back to the present.

I smiled, our plan had worked, and all the settlers seemed to be stirring from their slumber. The sound of rustling fabric and muffled conversations filled the air as people began to emerge from their tents, drawn by the promise of a hearty breakfast.

Glancing at the disarray of clothing I had created, I scooped them up into my arms.

Emerging from the tent with purpose, I called out to Kain, my determined stride carrying me in his direction. "Kain, get me your dirty clothes, and I'll wash them along with ours."

Kain's young eyes widened in surprise, his mouth slightly agape as he processed my request. For a moment, he seemed speechless, his gaze didn't falter as he stared at me, perhaps trying to reconcile the image of me as a leader with the domestic task I had taken upon myself.

"The camp is starting to stink," I explained, my tone resolute. "I think everything around here could do with a good scrub."

"Of course," Kain agreed, finally finding his voice. He hurriedly disappeared back inside his tent to retrieve his laundry.

Chris looked up at me from where he continued to cook food over the open fire. "Are you going to eat before you go?" he asked, concern evident in his eyes.

"Come, give me a few mouthfuls now," I requested, gesturing to my arms laden with clothing. It had taken considerable effort to gather all the clothing without dropping the occasional sock or shirt, and now that I seemed to have everything together, I didn't fancy putting it all back down again.

As Chris approached with a small frying pan, I opened my mouth expectantly.

"Blow on it first," I instructed Chris firmly, a playful smirk dancing on my lips, and I closed my mouth abruptly before he could place a forkful of steaming beans that had come straight from the fire.

Chris blew a little too hard, sending several beans flying through the air and onto the ground. I couldn't help but chuckle at his mishap.

After savouring several successful mouthfuls, I finally relented. "That'll do," I told Chris, licking a trail of sauce from my lips. "I'll eat more when I've finished this washing."

A frown briefly passed over Chris's face. "It'll be stone cold by then."

"You know I'm always happy to eat cold food," I reminded him with a gentle sigh.

"Okay," he said with a hint of resignation, his shoulders relaxing as he returned the pan to the coals.

Kain re-emerged from his tent, his arms piled high with clothing, a precarious tower of fabric threatening to topple at any moment. My eyes widened at the sight of his laundry mountain, and I couldn't help but let out a sigh, somewhat disappointed that I wasn't about to enjoy a moment of personal time to myself. I had been hoping for the opportunity to give myself a much-needed wash as well.

"You're going to have to accompany me," I told him, my voice laced with a hint of resignation. My gaze shifted from the towering stack of clothing to Kain's bewildered expression. "I didn't realise you had so much washing already."

Kain's head poked out from behind the textile monolith. "It's not all mine," he managed to say, his tone a mix of embarrassment and relief.

"Probably just as well," I remarked, turning on my heels and eager to relinquish my burden. The weight of the laundry was becoming increasingly unbearable.

"The river?" Kain asked as he trailed behind me, his steps light and hesitant.

"No," I replied, shaking my head to clear my thoughts. "I thought we'd go to the lagoon. There are more rocks there to help lay clothes out to dry, seeing as we don't exactly have anything to hang them on here." The lagoon seemed like the more practical choice for our laundry venture.

"I'll eat when I get back," I heard Kain tell Chris behind me as he passed him by. "Oh, and feed Henri for me, please?" Kain called out to Chris.

"Sure," Chris answered, his voice filled with reassurance. "I'll make sure he eats something."

The brief conversation between Kain and Chris made me both smile and frown simultaneously. I couldn't help but admire Chris's tender heart and his willingness to help. However, Henri's dwindling energy and lack of appetite had been a growing concern for all of us. I had experienced firsthand how animals could suffer when they lost a close companion, and it lingered in the back of my mind as we set off toward the lagoon.

❖

The morning sun was still low in the sky, casting a warm, golden glow across the smooth waters of the lagoon. It was a deceptive oasis, a serene expanse surrounded by nothing but arid rocks and relentless dust. Yet, as I stood there, my mind began to conjure up vivid images of lush vegetation and vibrant wildlife that might one day thrive in this place. The gentle breeze blowing through my hair teased me with the distant scent of foliage, momentarily transporting me from our harsh reality. However, several strands of my sweaty fringe clung to my cheek, tugging me back to the present and serving as a grim reminder that, despite the arid natural beauty around me, I still stank of sweat and dust.

Approaching the edge of the lagoon, I chose the leftmost area, where the rocks were most abundant. If the clothes were going to get wet, it made sense to keep them as far away from the encroaching dust as possible; otherwise, I'd find myself washing them multiple times.

Satisfied with the location, I lowered the clothes carefully onto the smooth rocks.

"Your leg is bleeding again," I observed, concern in my voice, as I noticed the blood trickling from beneath the bandages and down Kain's leg. I reached out to place a reassuring hand on his shoulder, steadying him as he stumbled.

"It's beginning to throb now," Kain replied, wincing in pain, as he dropped his pile of clothes onto a nearby large rock.

My brow furrowed with worry. After a brief contemplation, I finally spoke. "Look, why don't you go and get your leg cleaned up and get some more river water on it. I can take care of the washing."

Kain's eyes widened in surprise, and he looked at me with a mix of curiosity and suspicion, as if he were trying to uncover some hidden motive. "Not the lagoon water?" he asked, his voice tinged with intrigue.

I rolled my eyes and let out an exasperated sigh. "I can't very well be washing clothes in water that you're polluting with your blood now, can I?" I pointed out, trying to sound reasonable.

The corners of Kain's lips pulled upwards, a hint of amusement playing at his expression. "That is very true," he conceded with a chuckle.

"It's fine. I've got this," I assured him with a nod, my determination unwavering. "But if you could come back later and help me bring the washing back to camp, that'd be really helpful," I added.

"Of course," Kain agreed with a grateful smile.

"Thanks, Kain," I said, my voice softening with gratitude. With that, I turned my attention to the daunting piles of clothing sprawled before me.

❖

Standing on the rocks at the edge of the lagoon, the solitude enveloped me, a rare moment of quietude in the bustling life of our settlement. The water before me was a tranquil mirror, reflecting the vastness of the sky and the verdant fringes of our new world. It's in these moments, alone with my thoughts, that the weight of our situation settled most heavily upon me. I was both a caretaker and a pioneer, navigating the challenges of this unfamiliar environment with every passing hour.

As the first course of action amidst this natural serenity, I set about the task of organising the dirty clothes. Initially, my mind, perhaps clinging to remnants of old habits, prompted me to sort by colour. I started separating the garments, creating little hillocks of fabric on the smooth rocks, a mosaic of our lives through clothing. It was a methodical process, one that momentarily distracted me from the enormity of our circumstances.

However, as I looked at the piles forming, a realisation dawned upon me, halting my actions. Here, by the lagoon, the luxuries of separate washes for colours and whites, the considerations for water temperature and fabric care, were luxuries we did not have. A pang of nostalgia hit me for those easier times, but it quickly gave way to practicality. This was a different world, one where survival trumped all else, and adaptability was our greatest asset.

With this newfound clarity, I revised my strategy, deciding instead to sort the clothes based on ease of washing and drying. Some fabrics, heavier and more cumbersome, would take longer to dry, while others, lighter and more forgiving, could be ready within hours. It was a practical approach, one that spoke to the immediacy of our needs and the resourcefulness we had all been forced to adopt.

As I rearranged the piles, my hands moving rhythmically, I couldn't help but reflect on the journey that had brought us here. Each article of clothing, now waiting to be cleansed by the waters of the lagoon, carried stories of perseverance, loss, and the hope that spurred us forward. In this moment, the task at hand was more than just laundry; it was a reaffirmation of our continued survival, our resilience in the face of adversity.

Grabbing the first item of clothing, one of Chris's shirts, I carefully settled myself on the edge of a rock. The surface was relatively flat and smooth, offering a makeshift seat that seemed almost too perfect for the task. It was low enough to the water that I found comfort in not having to lean too far over the edge to reach the lagoon's surface, minimising my chances of an unfortunate slip. The practicality of this spot, chosen almost by instinct, was a small victory in the grand scheme of things, yet it felt significant.

As I was about to submerge the shirt, a moment of hesitation overcame me. The realisation hit me—I had no washing detergent. The pause was filled with contemplation, wondering if I should trek back to the camp to search for this elusive item. Given our dire lack of supplies, the optimism of finding such a luxury item seemed faint, almost naïve.

Glancing at the water, it struck me how pristine and pure it looked, untouched by the taint of civilisation. The thought of polluting this beautiful, clear lagoon with harsh earthly chemicals felt almost sacrilegious. There was a purity here that seemed to demand respect, a natural balance that we were now a part of. It was a reminder of our intrusiveness in this place, and the responsibility we bore to tread lightly.

With my mind made up, I finally submerged Chris's shirt in the water, committing to the task with a newfound resolve. As the fabric soaked, a surprising sensation caught me off guard—a gentle, invigorating tingle that seemed to seep into every pore of my hands. It was an unexpected moment of connection with the natural world, a tangible reminder that life here was about more than just survival; it was about coexistence.

The sensation sparked a cascade of thoughts and emotions. Here I was, doing laundry in a lagoon in a strange world, and yet, in this moment, I felt a profound sense of belonging. The simplicity of washing a shirt by hand, without the aid of modern conveniences, became a meditative act, a grounding experience that connected me to the essence of our human resilience.

Curious but unfazed by the odd sensation in my hands, I pressed on with my task, each movement deliberate and focused. The act of scrubbing the clothes against the smooth rocks became a rhythmic routine, my hands working tirelessly as I laid each piece of clothing out to dry. The sun bore down, relentless and unyielding, its rays a natural boon for our laundry day. Wiping the sweat from my brow, I acknowledged the labour's intensity—it was demanding, certainly, yet there was an underlying satisfaction in the knowledge that the fierce sun would expedite the drying process.

As the day wore on, I established a rhythm of washing and then periodically turning the clothes. It was important to ensure that both sides of each garment received their fair share of sunlight, a simple strategy to maximise the drying efficiency. This repetition, the constant back and forth, became a dance of sorts, one dictated by necessity and the natural elements at my disposal.

The tingling sensation in my hands, far from fading, seemed to grow more pronounced with each passing moment. It was a curious feeling, not at all uncomfortable. Instead, it brought with it an unexpected tranquility, a serenity that permeated my being at the most unexpected moments. Every so often, as my hands moved through the water, I would be hit by an intense wave of peace, so overwhelming that it caused my body to shudder, teetering on the edge of ecstasy.

These moments of profound peace were disconcerting yet exhilarating. It was as if the very act of washing these clothes, of engaging so directly with the natural world around me, had unlocked a deeper, more primal connection to this world. There was a sense of unity, of being in tune with the environment, that I hadn't anticipated when we first arrived.

The experience was bittersweet. On one hand, it underscored the challenges and dangers of our new home—after all, what was causing this sensation, and what did it signify? Yet, on the other, it highlighted the profound beauty and mystery of this place, offering moments of unexpected joy and wonder amidst the hard work and uncertainty.

Pausing for a much-needed break, I allowed myself a moment to glance over the fruits of my labour thus far. The clothing, now neatly laid out on the rocks to dry, was a testament to the hard work I had put in. There was a distinct sense of satisfaction in seeing them there, transformed from their soiled state to something fresher, cleaner. The sun, still high and unyielding in the sky, promised that they wouldn't remain damp for long. This small victory, the visible progress of my efforts, offered a fleeting sense of accomplishment.

However, as my eyes drifted to the sizeable pile of clothing that remained beside me, a heavy sigh escaped my lips. The realisation that I was only partway through the task settled over me with a weight that was hard to ignore. The satisfaction I had felt moments ago began to ebb away, replaced by the daunting understanding that there was still a long way to go. The pile seemed almost insurmountable now, each garment a reminder of the endless cycle of chores and responsibilities.

Despite the beauty of our surroundings, the tranquil lagoon and the warmth of the sun, a sense of isolation crept in. The task was mine alone, a solitary endeavour in the midst of our communal struggle. It underscored the individual roles we each played in the tapestry of our settlement, each of us wrestling with our own challenges, our own contributions to our collective survival.

Squatting on my chosen rock perch, I reached for another piece of clothing from the pile beside me, the fabric coarse and worn from use. As I leaned down to submerge it in the clear, cool water of the lagoon, a sudden, odd movement in the corner of my eye halted my actions. Instinctively, I knelt on my haunches, my body tense, as I turned my gaze outward, scanning the tranquil surface of the lagoon.

There, further out from where I sat, a small whirlpool was beginning to form. It was an eerie echo of the ones I had observed just yesterday, small yet utterly captivating in its anomaly. The sight of it sent a ripple of unease through me, yet I found myself unable to look away. Within a matter of minutes, several more whirlpools had spawned, each swirling gently, a dance of nature that was both beautiful and foreboding.

These were not any whirlpools that I had seen before. Unlike the turbulent, chaotic whirlpools of Earth's oceans and rivers, these had an otherworldly quality. They shimmered and glistened as they spun, their movement smooth and almost deliberate. The sunlight seemed to catch them just right, occasionally refracting colours into the air, creating brief flashes of iridescence that painted the scene with an ethereal light.

The beauty of it was mesmerising, a stark contrast to the initial jolt of alarm I had felt. It was as if the lagoon was alive, displaying a show of its hidden depths and mysteries. The phenomenon sparked a myriad of questions in my mind. *What caused these whirlpools to form with such regularity? Was it a natural occurrence, or was there something more, something beneath the surface that we had yet to understand?*

As I squinted into the lagoon's depths, my eyes sought any sign of life, any clue that might explain the mesmerising whirlpools before me. The water, so clear and unblemished, seemed like a pane of glass, offering an unobstructed view into the world beneath its surface. Logic dictated that if an animal were responsible for the odd phenomenon, it would be plainly visible in such pristine conditions. Yet, as far as my eyes could tell, there was no creature, no disturbance, nothing to account for the gentle yet rapid swirls multiplying before me.

An unusual and intense desire to understand, to truly experience the mystery of these whirlpools, swept over me. It was a pull stronger than mere curiosity; it felt almost like a call, an invitation from the lagoon itself, as the light they refracted grew brighter, more insistent. The sight was hypnotic, the swirls dancing with colours that seemed to speak directly to some primal part of me.

Mesmerised, I found myself acting on a compulsion I couldn't quite understand. It was as if the boundaries of my usual reserve and caution were being washed away by the spectacle before me. With a sudden clarity of purpose, I began to strip, shedding my clothing piece by piece until I stood fully exposed on the edge of the rocks. The moment my skin met the open air, a fresh breeze caressed me, cool against the warmth of my body. A wave of tingling goosebumps erupted across my skin, a physical reaction to the sudden change but also, perhaps, to the anticipation of what was to come.

This act of vulnerability, of standing naked at the edge of an unknown lagoon, was unlike me. Yet, in that moment, it felt entirely right, as if the lagoon and its mysterious whirlpools had laid bare a part of me that yearned for connection, for understanding beyond the confines of our human experience. The sensation was exhilarating, a mix of apprehension and a profound sense of freedom.

The air around me seemed charged with an electric energy, the light from the whirlpools casting shimmering patterns over my skin. I was acutely aware of the vastness of the sky above, the endless expanse of water before me, and the solid earth beneath my feet. It was a moment of profound connection to the world around me, a reminder of the beauty and mystery of this world we were striving to make our home.

Standing there, on the precipice of the unknown, I felt a deep pull towards the water, an urge to immerse myself in the lagoon's secrets. It was a desire to bridge the gap between the known and the mysterious, to become a part of the swirling dance that had captivated me so completely. The feeling was a potent mixture of fear and fascination, a longing to dive into the depths of the unknown, to surrender to the call of the wild, uncharted world that lay before me.

As I took that first deliberate step into the lagoon, a profound sense of peace enveloped me. It was a feeling so complete and overwhelming that it seemed to wash away all traces of doubt or hesitation that had lingered in my mind. The cool embrace of the water against my skin was invigorating, each step forward intensifying the joy that bubbled up within me. There was a purity in this act, a surrender to the unknown that felt both daring and utterly right.

With each step, the water rose, caressing my skin, its touch both gentle and alive. The further I waded, the closer I got to the heart of the mystery—the whirlpools that danced upon the water's surface. Their gentle yet rapid swirls, which had so captivated me from the shore, now beckoned me closer, an invitation I found impossible to resist.

Approaching the first whirlpool, I found my usual caution abandoned, replaced by a curiosity and a need to understand that drove me forward. The moment I entered the pull of the vortex, a rush unlike anything I'd ever experienced surged through me. The strong pull of the whirlpool was undeniable, a force of nature that demanded respect, yet there was no fear, only a profound exhilaration.

The pressure of the water as it swirled around my body was almost intoxicating. It was as if I could feel the very life-force of the world coursing through me, a tangible energy that pulsed with the rhythm of the natural world. This sensation, so powerful and all-encompassing, was unlike anything I had felt before. It was as though the water itself was alive, its movements imbued with a purpose and a vitality that connected everything it touched.

This moment, within the embrace of the whirlpool, transcended mere physical sensation. It was a communion, a joining of my essence with the essence of this world. The barriers between us seemed to dissolve, leaving a raw, unfiltered connection that was both exhilarating and humbling.

Feeling a deep sense of peace and unthreatened by the whirlpools' mysterious embrace, an idea sparked within me. The experience had imbued me with a sense of daring, a desire to merge the ordinary with the extraordinary. With this newfound exhilaration coursing through me, I waded back to shore, my steps quick and purposeful. There, I gathered the remaining clothes that awaited washing, my arms embracing them as if they were precious treasures about to be offered in some sacred ritual.

Arms full, I made my way back to the swirling eddies, the lagoon calling to me like a siren's song. The water welcomed me back, its surface shimmering with the promise of unseen wonders. Overcome with a sense of jubilation, a giggle escaped me, reminiscent of a schoolgirl's carefree laughter. It was a sound so pure, so full of joy, it seemed to echo against the vastness of the surrounding desert sands.

In a moment of whimsy, I threw the clothes into the air above the whirlpools. Time seemed to pause, the world holding its breath as the garments hung suspended in the moment. The sunlight, playing off the whirlpools, caught the fabric, transforming it. The colours of the clothes were enhanced, imbued with a vibrancy that was almost otherworldly. It was as if the very essence of the lagoon's magic had woven itself into the fibres, illuminating them with an inner light that was both mesmerising and surreal.

As the gentle breeze whispered secrets only the wild knew, the clothes began their slow descent, swirling around me in a dance orchestrated by the elements themselves. It was a spectacle of harmony and beauty, the garments moving as though they were alive, in tune with the waters that caressed my skin and the air that played through my hair. This melody, this symphony of nature and fabric, resonated with every fibre of my being, a chorus that sang of unity, of connection to the world around me.

Standing there, amidst the swirling clothes and the enchanting eddies, I felt a profound connection to Clivilius, a sense of being part of a greater whole. The lagoon, with its mysterious whirlpools, had offered me a glimpse into the wonders it held, blurring the lines between the mundane and the magical. This moment, this interaction with the natural world, was a reminder of the beauty that exists when we open ourselves to the possibilities of the unknown, when we allow ourselves to be carried away by the joy and wonder of discovery.

Embracing the unparalleled freedom that surged through me, I found myself utterly hypnotised by the refracting colours that multiplied and complexified in the sky above. It was as if the heavens themselves were putting on a show, just for me, painting the canvas of the sky with hues that defied description. The spectacle was a symphony of light, each ray bending and weaving through the air, creating patterns that seemed almost alive, pulsing with an energy that resonated deep within my soul.

Compelled by a joy that felt both ancient and new, I began to turn in circles, my movements spontaneous and unrestrained. With each turn, I flung up water into the air, sending droplets flying like diamonds catching the sunlight.

The water, cool against my skin, became an extension of the dance, each splash a note in the melody that played around me. It was a celebration of life, of connection, of being part of something vast and beautiful.

As the clothes finally descended, joining me in my reverie, they too were caught by the swirling embrace of the whirlpools. They danced around me, animated by the currents, as if they too felt the joy of the moment. The sight of them, swirling in the water, carried by forces unseen, was both surreal and grounding. They moved with a grace that belied their inanimate nature, each piece a partner in this unexpected dance.

This dance, this moment of uninhibited freedom, was a stark contrast to the structured life we had left behind. Here, in this foreign landscape, I was discovering parts of myself I had never known, facets of my being that craved the wildness and the unpredictability of this place. The refracting colours in the sky, the dance of the clothes in the whirlpools, the cool embrace of the water—all of it was a reminder that beauty and wonder can be found in the most unexpected of places, if only we are open to experiencing them.

❖

As the surge of elation that had filled me began to ebb, the spectacle of the whirlpools followed suit, dissipating almost as rapidly as they had first appeared. The lagoon, which moments ago had been a canvas of swirling colours and movement, now lay remarkably still, its surface smooth and undisturbed, as if the dance had never happened. The transition was startling, a reminder of the fleeting nature of beauty and chaos alike.

With the water's return to stillness, the clothes that had accompanied me in my impromptu dance floated gently to the surface. I moved through the water, my movements now slower, more reflective, as I began to gather them. Each piece felt transformed, not just by the water but by the experience itself. They smelled fresh, a clean and natural scent that seemed to carry the essence of the lagoon itself. They felt clean, mirroring the sense of renewal that I felt washing over me, both inside and out. It was as if the lagoon had imbued them, and by extension me, with a purity that went beyond the physical.

Gathering all the clothes in my arms, I started my way back to the shore, the fabric damp against my skin. The journey back felt different, almost meditative. The water lapped gently at my legs, a soothing contrast to the earlier excitement. It was a moment of transition, from the exhilaration of connection and discovery back to the reality of our daily survival. Yet, I carried with me a sense of calm, a profound cleanliness that felt like a balm to the soul.

"Enjoy your little swim?" Chris's voice reached me, a casual teasing in his tone, my head snapped up, my attention abruptly pulled from the serene aftermath of my lagoon experience. He was making his way down the dusty hill, his figure becoming clearer with each step towards me. A wave of embarrassment instantly washed over me, hotter and more engulfing than the sun that had warmed my skin moments before. I could feel the flush spread across my face, a telltale sign of my inner turmoil.

"How long have you been watching me for?" The question came out more defensively than I had intended, my voice tinged with vulnerability. Chris's smile, coy and knowing, did little to ease the sudden self-consciousness that tightened around me like a vice.

"Not long," he replied, but the nonchalance in his voice didn't convince me. His eyes held a glimmer of amusement that suggested his timing might have been just too perfect, yet I struggled to decipher whether he was simply enjoying the moment or if there was a hint of teasing at my expense.

Chris quickly shifted the topic, perhaps sensing my discomfort or choosing to spare me further embarrassment. "I thought I'd come and help you with the washing," he said, his tone becoming more earnest. "I've left Kain's ute just over the hill for us," he added, pointing back in the direction from which he had come.

"Thanks," I managed to say, the word simple yet laden with a mix of gratitude and lingering awkwardness. I hastily threw the wet pile of clothing onto the rocks, eager to pull myself together, both physically and emotionally, as I emerged from the lagoon. Despite the fact that Chris was my husband and there was an inherent comfort in our shared experiences and years together, the suddenness of his appearance and the thought that it could have easily been someone else stumbling upon this scene urged me to quickly don my clothes. The fabric clung uncomfortably to my damp skin, but the need for modesty outweighed the discomfort.

The rapid shift from a moment of solitary connection with nature to the abrupt intrusion of reality left me feeling exposed in more ways than one. It was a necessary reminder of the fine line between personal freedom and the communal life we led in this new world. As I adjusted my clothing, attempting to regain my composure, I couldn't help but reflect on the complexities of our existence here—how the vastness of this world could make one feel so infinitely small and yet so vividly alive in the same breath.

As Chris began to methodically collect the wet washing, spreading it along the rocks to catch the full brunt of the sun's rays, a pang of guilt washed over me. My earlier distraction with the whirlpools, though a moment of personal revelation, had left the task incomplete. "Sorry I'm not finished yet," I found myself apologising, the words heavy with an unexpected guilt for having momentarily abandoned our shared responsibilities for a dive into self-discovery.

"It's fine," Chris replied, his voice light, infused with a chuckle that seemed to dance on the warm air between us. "There's no rush." His casual dismissal of my apology, the easygoing acceptance of the situation, was a balm to my sudden self-reproach. It was a reminder of Chris's unwavering support, his understanding of the occasional need to step away from the mundane and connect with the world around us.

While Chris took over the task of laying out the wet clothes, I busied myself with those already basking in the sun's embrace. I flipped them over, ensuring each side received its fair share of warmth, and began to gather those that had dried completely. Without bothering to sort them by owner, I started a folded pile on a large rock situated away from the water's edge, a makeshift collection of our communal life here.

With our immediate tasks winding down, Chris and I found ourselves with nothing left to do but wait for the remaining clothes to dry. We settled on the rocks, the hard surface surprisingly comforting as we found our spots. Nestling comfortably into Chris, I felt a resurgence of the subtle peace that had enveloped me in the lagoon's waters. The turmoil and guilt of earlier moments melted away, replaced by a serene contentment as we sat in silence.

Our gaze was drawn outward, across the expanse of the lagoon, its surface now calm, reflecting the sky above with perfect clarity. In this moment, the lagoon was a mirror, not just of the world above but of the tranquility that had settled over us. It was as if the water, the rocks, and the sky were all complicit in offering us a moment of reprieve, a chance to simply be, together yet each lost in our thoughts.

As we sat there, the world around us seemed to pause, acknowledging the journey we had embarked upon, the sacrifices made, and the victories, however small, that we had celebrated. This moment, simple yet profound, was a reminder of what we had, what we were building, and the promise of what was yet to come.

CARAVAN

4338.210.2

Realising the challenge that lay ahead, the prospect of navigating the ute over the rolling sandy hills seemed daunting, a test of endurance for both the vehicle and us. The thick layer of dust that blanketed the terrain whispered tales of struggles past, of engines labouring and wheels spinning fruitlessly against the soft, shifting ground. It was a scenario I was keen to avoid, my mind working through the logistics, searching for an alternative that promised less resistance, more grace in our passage.

Then, it struck me—the river. Its course, a natural guide through the landscape, offered a flatter path, one less marred by the relentless sands and their dusty veil. I had noticed earlier, during brief moments of respite, that the dust layer thinned as one neared the river, as if the water's presence held back the desert's eager advance. "Let's try and follow the river," I suggested, my voice carrying a hint of optimism, a belief in the simplicity and wisdom of this natural path.

Chris's agreement came swift. His readiness to embrace the suggestion spoke volumes, a mutual respect for each other's insights shaping our decisions.

The task of folding and collecting the dried washing that lay strewn across the rocks at the lagoon became a dance of efficiency and care. Each piece of fabric, kissed by the sun and caressed by the breeze, held the scent of the outdoors, a tangible memory of the place that had given me momentary reprieve. As we piled them into the ute, there was a sense of closure, of leaving behind a fragment of my journey, secured within the confines of the vehicle.

Setting off on our adventure back to camp, we followed the curve of the river, allowing it to guide us through the landscape. The ute, with renewed vigour, seemed to embrace this path, its wheels finding purchase on firmer ground, the engine's hum a contented purr against the backdrop of the flowing water. The dust we kicked up, though still present, seemed less hostile, carried away by a gentle breeze that whispered through the air, a serene companion on our journey.

As Chris took the helm, guiding the ute with a steady hand, my role shifted to that of an observer, my eyes drawn inexorably to the world outside. The river, a constant companion on our journey, unfurled beside us, its breadth more generous than I had previously realised. It carved a path through the landscape, a natural divide between our fledgling settlement and the vast expanse beyond. That other side, mirroring our own in its emptiness, stretched out, a canvas void of life, yet brimming with silent potential.

Leaning against the window, the glass cool against my skin, I found myself lost in thought, my imagination taking flight. The landscape that lay across the river, so similar to our own, sparked a curiosity within me. *What if, beneath its seemingly barren surface, lay soil as rich and promising as the one we had discovered back at camp?* The possibility of such a discovery ignited a spark of excitement, a vision of transformation that was both daunting and exhilarating.

In my mind's eye, I envisioned us crossing the river, our hands and tools at the ready, to break through the crust that shielded the hidden bounty beneath. The idea of turning that desolate expanse into a thriving oasis, much like we had begun to do with our own settlement, filled me with a sense of purpose. I imagined rows of greenery taking root, a testament to our determination and resilience, a bridge between two once lifeless shores brought to life through our efforts.

Yet, as these thoughts danced through my mind, a twinge of reality tugged at the edges of my daydream. The challenges of such an endeavour loomed large, the uncertainty of what lay beneath that crust, the resources and time such a transformation would demand. It was a reminder of the balance between dreams and practicality, the fine line we walked in our quest to forge a life in this untamed wilderness.

Despite the daunting nature of the task, the idea lingered, a seed planted in the fertile ground of my imagination. It was a vision that spoke not just of the transformation of the land, but of us, of what we could achieve when driven by hope and the desire to create something lasting. As the river flowed beside us, a symbol of both division and connection, I found myself grappling with the possibilities, the challenges, and the promise of what lay on the other side.

The sudden stop of the ute jerked me back to reality, the abrupt motion a jarring contrast to the gentle flow of my thoughts. For a moment, the transition was disorienting, the physical lurch mirroring the mental leap from what could be to what was. Chris turned towards me, his expression a mix of amusement and curiosity, a smile that seemed to bridge the gap between our shared reality and my solitary reverie.

"You seemed to be deep in contemplation, there," he observed, his voice carrying a warmth that softened the edges of my abrupt return to the present. It was a gentle nudge, an invitation to share the vistas of my mind.

My brow furrowed from the effort to hold onto the fleeting images that had seemed so vivid moments before. "I was," I admitted, the words accompanied by a sigh that felt like a farewell to the lush landscapes of my imagination. The reality of our situation, stark in its infancy of development, was a grounding force. Our modest achievements, embodied by the few coriander plants that marked our tentative steps towards cultivation, stood in sharp contrast to the rich tapestry of life I had envisioned. The chasm between dream and reality was wide, a reminder of the long journey ahead.

"Care to share?" Chris's inquiry was genuine, a bridge extended in the hope of understanding, of connection. Yet, in that moment, the prospect of articulating my daydream felt too heavy, too fraught with the weight of unfulfilled potential.

I shook my head, a gesture of deferral rather than dismissal. "Perhaps later tonight," I suggested, the promise of future sharing a compromise between my need to process and his offer of companionship in contemplation. "We have clean washing to get put away," I added, a pivot to the immediate tasks that awaited us. The mundane, yet necessary, chores served as anchors, pulling us back to the tangible demands of our daily survival.

Unbuckling my seatbelt, I stepped out of the vehicle, the act a physical crossing of the threshold from the realm of what might be to the world of what was. The ground beneath my feet, solid and unyielding, was a reminder of the present, of the reality we were working to shape with our own hands.

As Chris and I divided the spoils of our laundry day between us, the precarious tower of clothes he had assembled in his arms drew a line of concern across my forehead. "Don't drop it!" The words tumbled out, edged with a half-hearted attempt at sternness. My frown deepened slightly, a silent testament to the hours I had spent washing, drying, and now, finally, retrieving the clothes. The thought of them scattered in the dust, undoing all my hard work, was enough to tighten my grip on my own bundle.

"I've got it," Chris countered, his tone brimming with the confidence of a tightrope walker. The folded clothes in his arms wobbled, a visual contradiction to his assurance. It was a sight that both amused and exasperated me, a balancing act that seemed to defy the laws of physics and common sense in equal measure.

Despite my initial reaction, a chuckle escaped me as I watched him, my eyes rolling in a blend of fondness and disbelief. His enthusiasm, often bordering on reckless optimism, was a trait that, in moments like these, I couldn't help but appreciate. After all, his willingness to help, to come and collect me from the lagoon with his characteristic zeal, had not only saved me from the tedious back-and-forth trips but also injected an element of light-heartedness into the task.

The lagoon, with its tranquil waters and serene ambiance, had been a brief respite from our daily toil, a momentary escape that had rejuvenated both body and spirit. Yet, the return to reality, marked by the logistics of handling our laundry, was a reminder of the endless cycle of chores that underpinned our existence in this wilderness. In this context, Chris's gesture, however haphazardly executed, was a beacon of solidarity. It underscored the unspoken pact between us: to share the burden, to lighten the load not just with our hands but with our hearts.

As we made our way back, the warmth of the sun on my back and the slight breeze that danced through the air served as gentle reminders of the beauty that framed our struggles. The landscape, with its rugged charm and untamed spirit, was a constant backdrop to our endeavours, a silent witness to the moments of connection and camaraderie that punctuated our journey.

"Hey, Chris. Look!" The words burst from me with an uncontainable excitement, a spark of curiosity igniting at the sight that unfolded before my eyes. In my eagerness, I nearly let the bundle of laundry I was cradling escape my grasp, a precarious juggle as I attempted to gesture. "There's several caravans." The sight was unexpected, several caravans on the outskirts of camp, an anomaly in the vast expanse of emptiness that surrounded us.

Chris, caught up in my sudden enthusiasm, strained to see where I pointed, his attention divided between the balancing act of his own laundry load and the direction of my gaze. It was a comical scene, his arms laden with clothes that teetered on the edge of collapse, a testament to his determination to carry on despite the odds.

Just then, as if on cue, Nial appeared, materialising with the timely intervention of a guardian angel. His arrival was both dramatic and fortuitous, saving Chris from an imminent avalanche of freshly laundered clothes. With a laugh that echoed in the open air, a sound rich with mirth, Nial relieved Chris of part of his burden.

"Where do you want these?" Nial's question, simple yet laden with the willingness to assist, pulled me from my momentary distraction.

I hesitated, the logistical part of my brain taking over as I considered the best course of action. "We may as well take them all to our tent. I need to sort them all anyway." The words were practical, a decision born of necessity as much as convenience.

Nial's raised eyebrow was a silent query, a request for clarification that I met with an explanation. "There's a bit of everyone's clothes here," I said, hoping to convey the communal nature of our laundry expedition.

Understanding dawned on Nial's face, his nod an acknowledgment of the communal effort and shared responsibilities. "Understood. The tent it is."

As we approached our tent, the air was thick with the day's heat and the faint smell of dust kicked up by activity. With a sense of purpose, I carefully placed my pile of clothes on the floor, arranging them with a neatness born of habit and a desire for some semblance of order.

"Chris!" The word flew from my lips, a reflexive scold as I watched him carelessly drop his bundle onto the floor. The clothes, moments ago neatly folded, now lay in a dishevelled heap. My admonishment, however, was a beat too slow, as Nial, perhaps taking Chris's action as a cue, let his own load fall beside Chris's unruly pile.

The immediate flush that coloured Nial's cheeks was bright and undeniable, a visible sign of his embarrassment. "Sorry," he muttered, his apology tinged with genuine remorse. The sight of his discomfort, so raw and unguarded, silenced any further reprimand I might have had. Instead, I let out a heavy sigh, a non-verbal expression of my frustration and resignation, a sound that seemed to echo off the tent walls.

"My wife is always telling me off for this sort of thing too." Nial's attempt at lightening the mood, a comment about his wife's similar grievances, carried a bittersweet undertone. For a fleeting moment, his chuckle broke through the tension, a shared moment of human connection in our far-from-ordinary circumstances. Yet, as quickly as it appeared, the lightness in his expression vanished, replaced by a shadow of something deeper, more poignant.

The sudden shift in Nial's demeanour struck a chord within me, a twinge of guilt for the harshness of my initial reaction. The realisation of his situation, of all our situations, was a sobering thought. Nial, torn from the familiarity and comfort of his family, was here with us, in this distant landscape that offered no promise of return. The constant reminders of what he had left behind, in moments as mundane as being chided for a mess, underscored the profound sense of loss and displacement we all felt, in varying degrees.

Turning my gaze to Chris, I was overcome with a wave of gratitude. Despite the challenges, the uncertainties, and the myriad of small irritations that marked our daily life, we had each other. This shared experience, this journey into the unknown, had bound us together, offering a semblance of comfort and companionship in a place that was relentlessly indifferent to our struggles.

In that moment, standing in the dim light of our tent, surrounded by the scattered remains of our laundry, I was acutely aware of the delicate balance we maintained. Each of us, in our own way, navigated the complexities of this new existence, clinging to the fragments of our past lives, even as we sought to forge a path forward, together.

The shift in conversation, brought on by Chris's question, sliced through the previous tension like a knife through still air. "Who are those caravans for?" His curiosity, so typical of his nature, momentarily redirected our collective focus.

"Chris!" The rebuke slipped from my lips before I could temper it, a knee-jerk reaction to what I perceived as his lack of tact. The topic felt loaded, given our current circumstances, and his bluntness caught me off guard.

Nial's reaction, however, was unexpected. His face transformed with a sudden brightness, a welcome contrast to the sombre mood that had momentarily settled over us. "One of them is actually yours," he announced, a broad smile breaking across his face, dispersing the lingering shadows of our previous conversation.

"Are you sure?" My response was automatic, tinged with a mix of disbelief and hope. The idea of having a caravan at our disposal seemed too good to be true, especially in the context of our makeshift existence. "You're not just saying that because of Chris?" I pressed, seeking assurance, unwilling to let my hopes soar on a whim.

Nial's laughter, light and genuine, was reassuring. "Of course not," he assured us, his amusement evident. "That Beatrix woman has been bringing us caravans. Apparently she's going to bring enough for all of us over the next few days." The news was unexpected, a beacon of progress in our ongoing struggle to establish some semblance of normality in this place.

"That's brilliant," Chris's enthusiasm mirrored my own burgeoning sense of relief and excitement. The prospect of moving from a tent to a caravan represented a significant improvement in our living conditions.

Nial continued. "Paul asked me to let you know."

There was a brief pause as Chris and I absorbed the significance of Nial's announcement. The possibility of transitioning to a caravan, with its promise of greater security and comfort, was a welcome development. Despite the rustic charm of tent living, the allure of a more stable, enclosed space was undeniable.

"Come," Nial's invitation was both a command and a gesture of inclusion. "Let me show you." His enthusiasm was infectious, a shared excitement for this new chapter in our journey.

Chris and I exchanged a glance, a silent agreement passing between us, before we both nodded in eager assent. The prospect of seeing our new accommodation, of stepping into a space that would soon become our own, was invigorating.

As we followed Nial, I couldn't help but feel a surge of gratitude for this unexpected gift. The caravan, a simple structure to some, represented so much more to us: a home, a haven, and a stepping stone towards building a new life.

The caravan door let out a familiar squeak as Chris pushed it open, a sound that had quickly become a part of our new routine. "I think that's everything," he announced, stepping into the cramped but welcoming space that was now our caravan home. His voice carried a note of finality, marking the end of one phase and the beginning of another in our ever-evolving journey.

I followed him inside, a sigh of relief escaping my lips. The transition from our makeshift tent to the caravan hadn't been without its challenges. While the prospect of moving into a more stable and comfortable living situation was undoubtedly a positive change, the sheer amount of effort required to make it happen had taken me by surprise. I wasn't ungrateful for the upgrade—it was a significant improvement from our previous arrangement—but the physical and emotional toll of relocating our lives under such extraordinary circumstances was more than I had bargained for.

Looking around, I was struck by how quickly we had managed to accumulate belongings in such a short span of time. Our possessions, a mix of essentials and personal items, had been scattered between the tent and the Drop Zone—a place where Luke had been depositing items brought through the Portal, unbeknownst to Chris and me. The realisation that pieces of our old lives had been quietly waiting for us at the Drop Zone added a layer of complexity to our adjustment process. It was as if fragments of who we were before were slowly being reintegrated into our new reality.

Gathering everything into the caravan felt like a small victory. The relief of having all our belongings in one place was palpable. It wasn't just about the physical consolidation of our possessions; it was a symbolic gathering of the scattered pieces of our lives.

Among the myriad of items that had made their way to us through the Drop Zone, I stumbled upon a stack of my nature and science magazines and journals. The sight of them, nestled amidst the essentials and the unexpected, struck me as profoundly curious. Of all the items Luke could have selected from the remnants of our previous life, he chose these. It made me wonder about the criteria behind his choices—was it a nod to normality, a gesture towards preserving a slice of who I was, or simply a random selection in a hurried attempt to bring us pieces of home?

Chris, meanwhile, had taken to the task of organising the magazines with a focus that bordered on meditative. He sat at the cramped table in our caravan, shuffling through the pages, arranging them into what I could only describe as an organised chaos—a system that, I suspected, only he could decipher. Given our limited space, his method seemed almost quixotic. *Where did he plan to store them?* The practical side of me couldn't help but anticipate that, despite his efforts, they would end up in a single stack, tucked away in a corner or perhaps serving as a makeshift table base.

Turning away from the sight of Chris engrossed in his sorting, I directed my attention to the more mundane task of dealing with our laundry. The clothes, originally dumped haphazardly at our tent by Chris and Nial, had been transported to our caravan in much the same chaotic state. Now, each piece demanded my attention—sorting, folding, organising.

As I sifted through the pile, separating our clothes from those belonging to others in our group, I decided to shoulder the responsibility for all of it. It was easier, somehow, to take on the task entirely, planning to return the items that weren't ours to their rightful owners later. This decision, a small act of communal living, felt right. It was a way of maintaining connections, of acknowledging our shared situation, and of offering help in the small ways that were available to us.

❖

The sharp, insistent knocking on the caravan door jolted me from my thoughts, echoing loudly in the compact space. It was quickly followed by a familiar voice, deep and slightly anxious, "Hey, Karen, Chris, it's Paul. Can I come in?"

I moved towards the door, feeling a mix of curiosity and slight irritation at the interruption. I opened the door with a practiced, welcoming smile, masking my initial annoyance. "Hi Paul, come on in," I said, my voice steady and friendly. I stepped aside, making room for Paul to enter our cramped living space.

As Paul stepped inside, dwarfing the doorway with his broad shoulders, I noticed the subtle lines of worry etched on his forehead. I couldn't help but return to the task of folding the washing, my hands automatically smoothing out a crumpled t-shirt.

"Just got the third caravan from Beatrix," Paul announced, his voice betraying a mix of nervousness and forced confidence. "She also brought some power generators. I'm planning to allocate one to each caravan, but, honestly, I have no clue about setting these things up." His gaze flickered around the caravan, avoiding direct eye contact.

Chris, who had been engrossed in a lump of soil, looked up at this, a spark of interest igniting in his eyes. "I can help with that," he offered, his tone infused with an unexpected note of reassurance. "I'll make sure that all the caravans get connected." His words seemed to lift a weight off Paul's shoulders.

"That'd be great, Chris. Thank you," Paul replied, his relief palpable in the slight easing of his shoulders.

Pausing mid-fold of a t-shirt, I chimed in, feeling a wave of optimism wash over me. "It's amazing how quickly things are coming together," I noted, my voice laced with genuine wonder. Despite the newness of our situation, there was something exhilarating about building something from the ground up.

Paul nodded, a trace of a smile flickering across his face. "I was planning to check in on Kain. I'll take the generator to him myself," he said, his tone adopting a sense of newfound purpose.

"Sure thing, I'll handle the rest," Chris confirmed, his response light and pleasant.

As Paul bid farewell and stepped out of the caravan, grunting under the weight of one of the generators, I watched him for a moment. His figure, silhouetted against the bright sunlight, seemed to embody the resilience and determination we all longed for. After waiting a few moments to make sure that Paul hadn't forgotten anything and wouldn't suddenly turn back, I gently closed the door, sealing us back into our own little world.

SANCTUARY

4338.210.3

The sight of Paul arriving at the camp with two additional people instantly piqued my curiosity. My gaze quickly identified the young man as Grant Ironbach, someone I recognised as the Director of the Bonorong Wildlife Sanctuary. The woman with him, I assumed, was his sister, Sarah, known to me as the Assistant Director of the same sanctuary. The realisation that they were here, in Clivilius, stirred a mix of surprise and confusion within me. *What are they doing here, so far from their usual environment?*

Compelled by my curiosity, I began to approach the trio, eager to greet them and perhaps understand the reason behind their unexpected presence. But before I could get too close, Paul was by my side, intercepting my path with an urgency that was uncharacteristic of him.

He leaned in close, and his whispered words sent an unsettling shiver through me. "Don't mention anything about them not being able to leave," he cautioned in a hushed tone.

The implication of his words struck me. The Ironbach siblings were unaware of the true nature of Clivilius - that once here, leaving was not an option. I softly gasped at the gravity of their situation, a situation they were, apparently, blissfully ignorant of.

I gave Paul a brief nod, acknowledging his request. The thought of breaking such life-altering news to them was daunting, and I wasn't ready to witness or handle the emotional turmoil that would inevitably follow. It was an unfortunate reality for Grant and Sarah, but at that moment,

I was grateful that the responsibility of revealing the truth did not fall on me.

"Karen, this is-" Paul began the introductions. But I quickly interrupted him. "I'm well aware of who they are, thank you, Paul," I said, my voice tinged with a concern that was rapidly growing within me.

Grant extended his hand, his greeting casual yet warm. "Karen, what a surprise to see you here," he said, offering a firm handshake.

"Yeah, small world," I responded, attempting to maintain a semblance of normality. I managed a smile, though it felt forced under the circumstances. Inside, a whirlwind of questions and apprehensions was swirling.

Paul, seemingly aware of the tension or perhaps eager to avoid lingering questions, quickly interjected. "Let's find you a place to settle in for now," he suggested, decisively cutting short any further conversation.

He promptly led Grant and Sarah away from me, heading towards Nial's caravan. I watched them go, my gaze lingering on their retreating figures. My mind raced with questions about their unexpected arrival. *How did they ended up in Clivilius? And why is Paul so keen to usher them into Nial's caravan so swiftly?*

The situation was perplexing. I stood there for a moment longer, contemplating the implications of their presence and what it meant for our already complex situation.

Turning back to the campfire, I resolved to focus on the immediate needs of the camp. Yet, the puzzle of Grant and Sarah Ironbach's arrival in Clivilius lingered persistently in the back of my mind. How could a pair of wildlife enthusiasts, known for their expertise in a field so far removed from our current predicament, be of any help here? We were in a world where our primary concerns revolved around survival, dealing with mysterious threats like Shadow

Panthers, and managing the scarce resources of our camp amidst never-ending dust. The skills and knowledge that Grant and Sarah possessed seemed so disconnected from the realities we faced daily.

There was no doubt in my mind that this was another doing of Luke's, but for the life of me, I couldn't begin to understand his logic. Not this time.

❖

Walking towards the river, my thoughts were absorbed in the recent turn of events at the camp. The serene environment around the river offered a momentary escape from the complexities back at the camp. The gentle flow of the water was soothing, allowing me a chance to reflect.

I was so deep in thought that I almost didn't notice Paul calling out to me. "Karen!" his voice broke through my reverie.

Startled, I turned to see him approaching. My expression shifted from a distant gaze to mild surprise. "Oh, Paul! Didn't hear you coming," I admitted, feeling a bit disoriented for a moment.

Paul fell into step beside me, matching my slow, contemplative pace. The peaceful ambiance of the river, with its soft murmurings, contrasted sharply with the undercurrent of unease back at the camp.

"You're familiar with the Ironbachs, aren't you?" Paul inquired, his tone carrying an unmistakable hint of enthusiasm.

His question sent a wave of apprehension through me, leaving me to wonder where he might steer the conversation. "Ah, the Ironbachs. Yes, our paths crossed in the world of conservation. Smart and committed, both of them," I responded, choosing my words carefully. I wanted to acknowledge their expertise without revealing too much of my own knowledge or concerns about their unexpected presence in Clivilius. "They'll undoubtedly be great assets here," I added, maintaining an optimistic tone, albeit cautiously.

The visible easing of tension in Paul's demeanour was palpable. "Would you mind meeting with them then? To help them integrate more fully into our community and understand our work?" Paul asked, his tone suggesting he was almost certain of my acquiescence.

I paused for a moment, letting my eyes wander over the tranquil river. Its gentle flow seemed to mirror the calm I needed to approach this situation. The Ironbachs had appeared content enough when I first saw them, but their unexpected arrival still puzzled me. *Was there more to their presence here than met the eye?* "Yes, I can do that," I finally responded, breaking my contemplative silence. "Their sudden arrival did surprise me a little. What role are they expected to play here?"

Paul seemed to ponder my question, choosing his words with care. "Well, that's where things get a bit murky. Luke seems to think they've been involved with another Guardian group. They're here for the Wildlife Sanctuary project," he revealed, handing me the set of folders that he was carrying. "These plans outline the initial concept."

It was a lot to take in at once. *Another Guardian group? A Wildlife Sanctuary here in Bixbus?* The ideas swirled around my brain as my fingers began to flip through the pages, and with each turn, my interest deepened. Diagrams, plans, and notes filled the pages, outlining a vision that seemed almost too ambitious for our current situation. "This is intriguing," I commented, my eyes absorbing the details of the documents.

Paul shifted uneasily beside me, indicating there was more to the story. "There's one more thing," he said with caution in his voice. "I don't believe Grant and Sarah are aware that this trip to Clivilius is a one-way journey. They still think they'll return to Bonorong."

My brow furrowed in concern. The confirmation that the Ironbachs were unaware of their permanent relocation to Clivilius added a layer of complexity to the situation. It meant handling their integration with care and tact. "I see. That's delicate," I acknowledged. I was acutely aware of how sensitive this information was and the potential shock it could cause. "I'll approach this carefully."

Paul expressed his gratitude, his relief evident. "Thank you, Karen. This means a lot."

I managed a somewhat curt smile. The folders in my hands, filled with the plans for a wildlife sanctuary, were undeniably captivating. They presented an opportunity to contribute something meaningful to our new world. Yet, my enthusiasm was tempered by the knowledge of the Ironbachs' situation. "I'll speak with them shortly," I assured Paul, my gaze drifting to the river, imagining the possibilities that lay within the vast emptiness of Clivilius.

Paul's response was respectful. "Whenever you're ready," he said, understanding the delicacy of his request.

As Paul walked away, I stood there for a moment longer, the river's gentle flow providing a calming backdrop. The conversation ahead was not going to be easy. Breaking the news to the Ironbachs about the permanence of their stay in Clivilius required a thoughtful and sensitive approach. But for now, my mind was also filled with visions of what the Wildlife Sanctuary could become, a project that could bring a sense of purpose and hope to our community. It was a balance of challenges and opportunities, much like everything else in Clivilius.

❖

Finding a quiet place to sit along the riverbank, I felt the world around me fall into a hush, the gentle murmur of the water blending with the distant sounds of our camp. My hands, betraying a mix of anticipation and nervousness, trembled slightly as they grasped the first folder.

As I opened the folder, the pages before me unveiled a project that was as audacious as it was visionary—a wildlife sanctuary designed specifically for the unique and diverse ecosystems of Clivilius. Unlike anything on Earth, this sanctuary was intended to bridge the gap between our human presence and the alien landscape that now surrounded us. The pages were densely packed with detailed plans, drawings that leapt off the page with vibrant life, notes scrawled in margins, diagrams that mapped out habitats and ecosystems. Each element contributed to a vision that was both grandiose in its scope and meticulously planned in its execution.

My journey through the detailed plans of the Wildlife Sanctuary unfolded before me like a story, each page, each chapter revealing the sanctuary's evolution from its conception to its advanced stages of development. It was akin to watching the birth and growth of a living, breathing entity, each stage meticulously planned and executed with a vision that extended far beyond the immediate future.

Initially, I found myself captivated by the simplicity and ingenuity of the early plans. They spoke of humble beginnings, where ambition met the raw realities of our new world. The pages detailed the first steps: soil preparation, the establishment of a reliable water source, and the construction of rudimentary shelters designed to house the sanctuary's first animal inhabitants. These efforts, marked by a striking resourcefulness, reflected a deep understanding of the need to start small, to build from the ground up—literally. The materials chosen were portable and lightweight, specifically selected for their ease of transport through the portal, underscoring the logistical challenges we faced.

The focus on securing a sustainable water supply and creating fertile ground was not just practical; it was symbolic of the sanctuary's broader mission—to create life from the barren, to encourage growth in a land that was not our own. As I pored over the notes, I could see the roles of the initial team members come to life: horticulturists labouring over soil composition, hydrologists mapping out water flow and sustainability, carpenters shaping the shelters that would protect the first inhabitants, and animal care specialists planning for the well-being of species not yet arrived. Each individual's contribution was crucial, a piece of a larger puzzle that, when assembled, would form the backbone of the sanctuary.

As I delved deeper into the sanctuary's evolving plans, the scope of the vision seemed to unfurl before me, broadening with every page. The introduction of diverse flora and fauna was not just a list but a testament to the meticulous consideration given to each species' new home in Clivilius. The enclosures, detailed with precision in the plans, were designed not merely as spaces but as ecosystems, each reflecting a deepening understanding and respect for Clivilius's unique environment.

The phased approach to introducing Earth's wildlife captivated me. It began with resilient species, those deemed most capable of adapting to the foreign conditions of Clivilius. This strategy was both pragmatic and visionary, acknowledging the challenges of transplantation while embracing the potential for new beginnings. The plans outlined a gradual progression towards more complex ecosystems, indicating a future where the sanctuary would not just survive but thrive, expanding in complexity and diversity.

I was particularly struck by the thoughtfulness behind each habitat's design. It was evident that every enclosure, every space allocated for the animals, was crafted with an intention to mimic their natural environments as closely as possible. This wasn't about containment but about creating a semblance of home, a space where the animals could exhibit natural behaviours and thrive under the unfamiliar sky of Clivilius.

Moving forward, I uncovered plans for integrating technology and sustainability into the sanctuary's operations. Solar panels, rainwater harvesting systems, and composting methods were outlined, showcasing a commitment to minimising the environmental impact. The sanctuary would expand to incorporate educational centres and interactive exhibits, leveraging augmented reality and other technologies to enhance visitor experiences. I was impressed by the sanctuary's dual focus on conservation and education, aiming to inspire a deep respect for nature among its visitors.

The designs went beyond mere physical structures; they encompassed the sensory experiences of the inhabitants— visual cues, scents, sounds, and textures all considered to provide a semblance of the Earthly wilds. It was a bold attempt to weave together the familiar and the foreign, creating a tapestry of life that honoured both origins.

As I absorbed the details of each proposed habitat, I couldn't help but feel a mix of awe and humility. The sanctuary was a reflection of determined ambition to bridge worlds, to create a space where life from Earth could find a foothold in the vast unknown of Clivilius. Yet, it also underscored the enormity of responsibility. Each decision, each species selected for introduction, carried with it the weight of ethical considerations—of ensuring not just survival but well-being.

The sanctuary, as it stood on these pages, was a dream being woven into reality, a delicate balance of science, ethics, and vision. The thoughtfulness behind the habitat designs was a ray of hope but also a reminder of the challenges ahead. It was stepping into uncharted territory, attempting to create harmony in a place where the rules of Earth did not apply.

The later stages of the sanctuary's development unfolded before me, revealing plans that stretched far beyond the initial visions of habitat and preservation. These pages detailed ambitious plans for global collaboration and conservation efforts that were both inspiring and daunting. As I read about the advanced breeding programs, genetic research initiatives, and partnerships with international wildlife organisations, I couldn't help but feel a mixture of pride and trepidation. The sanctuary was evolving into a centre for conservation science, poised to contribute valuable research to inter-world efforts to preserve endangered species.

This evolution spoke of a future where Clivilius was not just a new home for humanity and Earth's wildlife but a beacon of hope for conservation on an inter-planetary scale. The thought was exhilarating—this work could potentially save species from extinction, offering them a new beginning on another world. Yet, the complexity and ethical considerations of such endeavours weighed heavily on me. Genetic research and breeding programs were fraught with challenges, requiring a delicate balance between intervention and the natural order of life.

The plans didn't stop at conservation. The introduction of eco-friendly lodging and gourmet restaurants catering to visitors marked a significant transformation of the sanctuary into a world-class attraction and research facility. This aspect introduced a new layer of complexity, blending the sanctuary's core mission with the need for public engagement and financial sustainability. The idea of attracting visitors from across the wide expanse of Clivilius underscored the sanctuary's potential to educate and inspire, to showcase the beauty of Clivilius and its inhabitants, and to highlight the importance of conservation.

Yet, this vision of a bustling destination, with its eco-lodges and restaurants, sparked a flicker of concern. Balancing the sanctuary's role as a centre for science and conservation with its public-facing aspects would be crucial. There was a fine line between raising awareness and commercialisation, between inspiring visitors and impacting the very ecosystems we sought to protect.

As I pondered these plans, I realised the sanctuary's transformation into a world-class attraction and research facility represented a microcosm of our broader journey in Clivilius. It embodied the potential for incredible achievements and the myriad challenges that accompanied great ambitions. The sanctuary, in its envisioned future, was a testament to human ingenuity and desire to make a positive impact on worlds.

In the final documents, reflections on the sanctuary's impact unfurled before me, painting a picture of its influence not just on Clivilius but on Earth as well. The words resonated with me, stirring a profound emotional response. The sanctuary had transcended its physical boundaries to become a symbol of hope, a testament to the power of collaboration across worlds. It stood as a living legacy of humanity's commitment to conservation and the exploration of new frontiers, a beacon that illuminated the potential for harmony between the known and the unknown.

My exploration of the sanctuary's plans had transformed my initial curiosity into a deep sense of purpose. I no longer saw myself as merely an observer of this grand project but as an integral part of its unfolding story. The sanctuary's journey mirrored my own—a path of discovery, learning, and a growing commitment to make a difference in this new world. The realisation that I could play a role in this ambitious endeavour filled me with a sense of responsibility and excitement.

Closing the last folder, I felt a surge of inspiration and resolve. The Wildlife Sanctuary, in my eyes, represented more than just a project; it was a profound expression of hope, innovation, and the enduring spirit of conservation across the cosmos. I envisioned myself working alongside the dedicated team, contributing my expertise to meet the sanctuary's evolving needs. This wasn't just about joining a project; it was about becoming part of a legacy that bridged worlds, a legacy that promised a future where the natural beauty and diversity of life could flourish, unbounded by the confines of a single planet.

With my head spinning, saturated with information and visions of grandeur that seemed almost too vast to contain, I sought refuge in the simplicity of the natural world around me. I let myself sink into the dust, feeling its fine grains against my skin, a grounding contrast to the lofty dreams that danced through my thoughts. Slowly, I closed my eyes, allowing the gentle flow of the river nearby to wash over me in waves of sound, its rhythmic babbling a soothing balm to my overstimulated mind.

As I lay there, the images of the grand sanctuary flooded my mind with relentless force. Each plan, each drawing, each note I had poured over earlier now came to life in the darkness behind my closed eyelids. I saw the habitats, vibrant and teeming with life, the flora and fauna of Earth coexisting with the landscape of Clivilius in a harmony that was both daring and delicate.

I embraced these visions fully, letting them wrap around me like a cocoon. The sanctuary, with its promise of conservation and collaboration, its potential to bridge worlds and species, filled me with a sense of purpose that was both exhilarating and overwhelming. It was as if, in those moments of quiet contemplation, I could feel the pulse of the sanctuary's future heartbeat, a rhythm that was inextricably linked to my own.

The sanctuary was more than a project; it was a dream of what could be—a place where the beauty and diversity of Earth's wildlife could thrive amidst the stars, where the challenges of conservation were met with innovation and hope. It represented a leap into the unknown, a testament to the resilience of life in all its forms.

Yet, as I lay there, embraced by the visions of what we hoped to achieve, a shadow of apprehension crept in. The grandeur of our plans, the scale of our ambition, was daunting. The sanctuary, for all its beauty and promise, was a monumental undertaking that would require more than just passion and vision—it would demand sacrifice, perseverance, and a willingness to face the unknown.

In the quiet of my contemplation, the sanctuary became a mirror, reflecting not just the future of Clivilius and Earth's wildlife, but also my own journey. The sanctuary's potential to change the world was clear, but so too was the challenge it represented. It was a challenge I was willing to meet, but not without acknowledging the weight of the responsibility it carried.

Slowly, I let the sound of the river anchor me back to the present, the images of the sanctuary still vivid in my mind but now tempered with a newfound resolve. As I embraced the grand visions and the daunting challenges alike, I knew that the path ahead would be as much about discovery as it was about creation. The sanctuary, in all its envisioned grandeur, was not just a destination but a journey—one that I felt I was now irrevocably a part of.

❖

My eyes snapped open, startled from a doze I hadn't intended to take. The light had shifted, casting long shadows and bathing everything in the warm, golden hues of late afternoon. A flicker of annoyance at myself flared up for having lost track of time. I had promised Paul I would visit Grant and Sarah, and now the day was slipping away from me.

With my pulse quickening in a mix of frustration and urgency, I scrambled to gather the folders that had been my companions in vision and thought just moments before. Clutching them to my chest, I made my way back to the camp, the dust kicking up under my feet as a reminder of the haste I felt.

As the familiar sights of our small settlement came into view, my heart sank. I was too late. Grant and Sarah were already there, standing near the campfire, deeply engaged in conversation with the settlers who had begun to gather for our ritual communal dinner. The scene was one of warmth and camaraderie, the kind of moment that had become a cornerstone of our daily life here, yet I felt a wave of defeat wash over me for not having made good on my commitment.

With a heavy sigh of defeat echoing quietly in the cooling air, I paused momentarily, allowing myself a brief moment to collect my thoughts. The warmth of the campfire ahead, with its welcoming glow and the sound of familiar voices, offered a stark contrast to the flurry of emotions swirling within me.

It was then, amidst this tangle of feelings, that a sudden thought struck me with clarity. Instead of making a grand entrance at the campfire with the wildlife sanctuary plans tucked under my arm—a gesture that might have seemed out of place given the casual, communal nature of our gathering—I decided on a more subtle approach. With a newfound resolve, I opted to quietly and discreetly sneak off to my caravan, a plan forming in my mind. The folders, brimming with the ambitious visions of the sanctuary, deserved a second, more thorough perusal, one that the serene solitude of my caravan could provide.

Slipping away from the gathering, unnoticed, felt strangely liberating. The short walk to my caravan was a journey in introspection, each step a reminder of the fine balance between individual pursuits and communal responsibilities. Once inside, I placed the folders on the small table that had become my makeshift desk. The promise of diving back into those plans later, with fresh eyes and a calmer mind, was a comforting thought.

Leaving the sanctuary of my caravan, I returned to the campfire. The air was filled with the aroma of cooking food and the sounds of laughter and conversation. As I approached, the initial feelings of defeat and frustration that had weighed on me began to dissipate, replaced by a sense of belonging and purpose.

Joining my fellow settlers at the campfire, I was greeted with smiles and nods, an unspoken acknowledgment of my return. Settling in among friends and colleagues, the plans for the wildlife sanctuary momentarily set aside, I allowed myself to be fully present in the moment.

The warmth of the fire, the shared stories, and the collective anticipation of the meal ahead served as a gentle reminder of the importance of these gatherings. They were not just a means to an end but an essential part of our journey in Clivilius, a way to forge bonds and build a community that could withstand the challenges ahead.

DREAM OF A WORLD REBORN

4338.210.4

As the sun dipped below the horizon, painting the sky in hues of deep orange and purple, our small group of settlers gathered around the bonfire. The energy around the camp was notably more lively than it had been earlier in the day. The presence of our newly acquired camping gear, the comfort of caravans, and the convenience of small portable power generators, all thanks to our Guardians, had infused a sense of normality and cheer into our evening.

The aroma of a hearty chilli simmering in a large pot over the fire filled the air. The scent of tender beef and beans stewed in a rich tomato sauce mingled with the rustic charm of crusty bread, tantalising our senses. Preparing and sharing a meal like this reminded me of the many outdoor camping trips Chris and I had enjoyed in the remote areas of the Tasmanian wilderness. It was a simple yet comforting reminder of a life once lived, a small touch of homeliness in our otherwise challenging existence in Clivilius.

Sitting close to the fire, I watched the flames dance and crackle, the warmth reaching out to us. The settlers' conversations buzzed around me, a mixture of laughter and stories filling the air. Despite the constant vigilance we had to maintain, there was a sense of community and togetherness that couldn't be dampened.

Sharing a meal like this, under the open sky with the flickering fire as our centrepiece, felt like a moment of respite. It was a reminder of the resilience and adaptability of our group. As we broke bread together, sharing the chilli that had been lovingly prepared, I couldn't help but feel a sense of gratitude. In Clivilius, amidst the uncertainty and dangers, we had found ways to create moments of joy and camaraderie.

I glanced at Chris, noticing the contentment in his eyes. These moments, though simple, were a testament to our human capacity to find light in the midst of darkness. As we ate, laughed, and shared stories, I felt a renewed sense of hope. Together, we were more than just survivors; we were a community building a new life in a strange world, finding comfort in the small joys and the company we kept.

❖

My gaze drifted across the loose clusters of settlers, picking out Grant and Sarah engaged in animated conversation with Paul and Beatrix. Even from my vantage point some distance away, Paul's taut body language broadcasted waves of unease, like a prey animal sensing a predator's approach. Beatrix seemed oblivious as she steered their conversation along, her voice carrying on the gentle breeze like a persistent honeybee.

Downing the last swallow of my drink, the amber liquid burning a warm path down my throat, I rose and began making my way over, every protective instinct sharpening my senses like a knife's edge. Grant and Sarah may have happily walked straight through the Portal, their steps light and carefree, but they still remained blissfully unaware of the true captivity of their situation, like birds in a gilded cage.

As I drew near, Beatrix's eager tones drifted over the ambient crackles of the campfire, her words hanging in the air like a tantalising lure. "...you have?"

Sarah caught my approach out of the corner of her eye, flashing a warm if momentarily distracted smile in greeting, her face glowing in the flickering firelight. "Oh, hey Karen!"

"We're only here for a week or two," she continued airily, giving a small dismissive wave of her hand in Beatrix's direction as I arrived properly, her gesture as light as a butterfly's wing.

Beatrix's eyes fairly danced with the glint of someone zeroing in on an intriguing new line of query, like a cat spotting a mouse. "And after that?"

I could practically feel the waves of tension emanating from poor Paul as Beatrix pressed on, heedless of his subtle attempts to redirect the conversation, like a ship trying to steer clear of rocky shores. Shooting him a conspiratorial wink, a silent promise of support, I pounced on the opening with a bright countenance.

"A simply lovely evening, isn't it?" I chimed in, catching Sarah's gaze fully and returning her smile with interest, my voice as smooth as honey. "I was just admiring those incredible twilight hues bathing the whole camp in that ethereal glow, like a painting come to life."

Predictably, Sarah's face lit up at the subject change, those keen conservationist's eyes instinctively swivelling to drink in the view I'd highlighted, her appreciation for nature's beauty as deep as the ocean. "Oh! Oh yes, it's quite magical. The way those indigo highlights bleed into the oranges and reds, like a symphony of colours..."

"Bonorong won't manage itself forever," Grant answered Beatrix's question with a chuckle that sent my gut lurching, like a sudden drop on a rollercoaster. They really did have no idea that they would never be returning to Earth, or their beloved sanctuary, their home and heart.

The fleeting tension seemed to dissipate as naturally as the fractal swirls of smoke rising from the crackling fire pit, the moment passing like a cloud across the sun. Sarah was off, eagerly filling the silence with updates about their various animals back at the Bonorong sanctuary, her love for the creatures shining through every word.

Casting a sidelong look at the suddenly crestfallen Beatrix, I could practically hear the gears turning behind her brow, like a clockwork mechanism in need of oiling. Something in Grant's phrasing must have rung discordant against whatever assumptions or theories she'd begun formulating, like a false note in a symphony.

A gentle hand on Beatrix's arm caused her to break off abruptly, her train of thought derailed by the unexpected touch. Paul urged Beatrix away from our small group with the slightest of tugs, his grip as firm as his resolve.

Beatrix opened her mouth, features creasing in obvious protest, like a child denied a treat, but seemed to think better of it under Paul's steady imploring gaze, his eyes speaking volumes without a word. With one final lingering look over her shoulder at Grant and Sarah, she allowed herself to be drawn away towards the fringes of the firelight, her curiosity left unsatisfied.

Once they'd moved out of easy earshot, the crackle of the fire filling the void, I turned back to find Grant and Sarah watching me with open amusement, their eyes twinkling with mirth. Sarah was the first to crack, her melodious laughter ringing out like a bell, pure and joyful.

"You're in fine form tonight, you old charmer," she teased, leaning over to give my arm an affectionate squeeze, her touch as warm as her smile. "Poor Beatrix wouldn't have had a chance if you and Paul hadn't intervened, like knights in shining armour."

The distant chuckles from Chris and Kain punctuated her mirth, their laughter carrying on the night air like a soothing balm. Grant shook his head ruefully, his expression a mix of exasperation and fondness.

"Is she always that... persistent?" he asked once Sarah had caught her breath again, his tone as dry as the desert air.

I considered the question carefully for a long moment, absently toying with the fabric of my shawl, the soft texture a comfort beneath my fingers. In the end, I could only meet them with a small, tight smile that didn't reach my eyes, my true feelings hidden behind a carefully constructed mask.

"You've no idea..." I murmured at last, resisting the urge to glance back in the direction Beatrix had been led away.

For now, the cat remained firmly trapped within its bag, so to speak, the truth of their situation still hidden from view. Grant and Sarah remained insulated from the tragic truth by whatever thin veil of comforting assumption they still cloaked themselves in, like a blanket shielding them from the cold reality.

But part of me couldn't help wondering just how much longer that blissful illusion could persist before Paul or one of the others inevitably fumbled or faltered, like a juggler dropping a ball... and the weight of their permanent exile fully materialised before their eyes, like a ghost taking form.

It was a burden too cruel to wish upon anyone any sooner than was strictly necessary.

Shaking off the morose reverie, I plastered on a fresh smile, quirking an inquisitive eyebrow in Sarah's direction, my expression as bright as the flames before us.

"Now then... where were we? You were saying something about Humphrey the emu still giving your attendants nightmares back home, like a mischievous poltergeist?"

Sarah's expression morphed instantly from one of gentle amusement to playful exasperation at the mere mention of Humphrey's name, her eyes rolling heavenward. I couldn't stifle a small grin as she launched into a colourful retelling of the latest exploits from Bonorong's most obstinate and mischievous emu resident, her words painting a vivid picture.

"That overstuffed featherduster is going to send poor Tilney into early retirement, I swear!" she exclaimed, eyes alight with conservationist affection even as her words carried a teasing edge, like a parent discussing a beloved but troublesome child. "Just last week, we had to completely reinforce the damned night enclosure after he managed to dismantle a section of the outer fencing... again! It was like he was playing a game of Jenga with the posts!"

Grant issued a snort, seemingly unsurprised by the tale, his expression one of long-suffering familiarity. "So much for our vaunted eucalyptus log barriers, eh? Leave it to Humphrey to reduce a construction crew's workweek into a pile of splinters and shame, like a tornado in a lumberyard."

The siblings exchanged a look loaded with familiar commiseration, an entire saga's worth of unspoken context and inside jokes passing between them in that moment, like a secret language only they understood. Despite the alien environs in which we found ourselves, these two clearly remained anchored by a lifetime's accumulated experiences and battles with their furry, feathered, and scaled wards, a bond unbroken by distance or circumstance.

In a strange way, it was almost comforting to realise some pillars of normality remained adamantine and unbowed, even here in this far-flung exile, like a lighthouse in a storm. The thought tugged at something deep in my psyche, prompting me to pose a question that had been lingering with increasing insistence, like an itch begging to be scratched.

"So tell me something - and grant me an old friend's brutal honesty here," I began, unconsciously lowering my voice as if to imbue the words with greater gravity, my tone as serious as a judge's gavel. "How are you both... really handling all of this?"

I swept one hand out in an all-encompassing gesture, letting the vague implication soak in, like ink spreading through water. For despite the nightly reveries and campfire banter, the truth remained inescapable - they had essentially been transported across the universe to a place of permanent isolation, like castaways on a desert island.

For several long heartbeats, the only response was the crackle and snap of fresh branches being consumed by the flames, the sound as loud as gunshots in the sudden silence. Grant and Sarah's expressions had sobered considerably, the familiar sibling shorthand of speaking looks and minute micro-expressions clearly conveying an internal flux of emotions and considerations, like a silent conversation only they could hear.

Finally, Sarah exhaled a measured breath, shoulders rising and falling in a shrug I suspected was more performative nonchalance than genuine insouciance, like an actor playing a role.

"It's not been... easy, I'll admit that much," she said carefully, her words as delicate as eggshells. Her jade eyes seemed to glaze over briefly, no doubt reflexively reviewing the litany of sacrifices and resignations they'd each needed to make, like a mental checklist of losses. "Letting go of the life we knew, the work, the home and community, even if only momentarily..."

A tremor of emotion caused her voice to hitch for a moment, until Grant's rough palm came to rest over her hand - a gesture of silent support and grounding affection.

"But we've stayed true to the most important aspects," he continued, dipping his chin soberly, his voice as steady as a mountain. "The passions, the treasured wards under our care, that binds us to the natural world, like roots to the earth. As long as that endures, we can still find fulfilment and higher purpose, even worlds away, like a compass pointing true north."

Sarah seemed to steady herself through his stalwart proclamation, some of the earlier light rekindling behind her eyes, like a flame reigniting. One corner of her full lips tugged upwards in a rueful half-smile, a hint of her indomitable spirit shining through.

"Yes... yes, Grant's right. It's not been simple, but the core of who we are transcends mere physical location in the end, like a soul untethered by earthly bonds."

She held my gaze levelly, though I fancied I detected the faintest of watery sheens glistening in her eyes when she next spoke.

"But enough of such dismal thoughts for now. We're here, in one piece, and surrounded by new vistas and possibilities just waiting to be explored, yes? With friends like you at our side, I suspect this will yet prove the grandest adventure of them all!"

The quiet strength and conviction in her tone rang out far louder than her words alone, penetrating straight to the empathetic well of emotion resonating within me, like a tuning fork struck in perfect pitch. Sarah had voiced the very mantra I myself had adopted to stay centred and resolute amidst the vast existential desolation we found ourselves within.

As my gaze roved first to Grant's stoic features, then took in the broader vista of our fire lit outpost, a profound sense of connectedness and shared purpose washed over me, like a wave cresting on the shore.

Thinking back on the detailed sanctuary and conservation plans that I perused merely hours earlier, a serene calmness settled over my breast as the enormity of our ambitious role asserted itself. Yes... for all their unspoken private anguishes and sacrifices, Grant and Sarah clearly perceived the same overarching truth that energised me.

With a renewed sense of conviction solidifying in my soul, I turned back to my compatriots with a look loaded by fresh epiphany, my eyes shining with determination.

"Then let's stop squandering this glorious hearth and get back to the real business at hand, shall we? We've got a proper ecosystem resurrection to plan out, like architects of a new Eden!"

And with that I led Grant and Sarah to my caravan, my steps as purposeful as a general leading troops into battle. Chris wasn't far behind, his presence a comforting constant at my side. Together, the four of us would talk long into the night, discussing the grandiose plans that the siblings had brought with them, our voices rising and falling like the tides as we mapped out a vision for the future, a dream of a world reborn.

And as the night wore on, the embers of the fire slowly fading to ash, I felt a renewed sense of hope blossoming in my chest, like a flower pushing through the snow. For the first time since our arrival in Clivilius, the future seemed not just possible, but vibrant with promise, a canvas waiting to be painted in bold strokes of green and gold.

⁂

Finally bidding Grant and Sarah goodnight, my mind still buzzing with plans and possibilities, I couldn't help but feel a sense of gratitude for their presence, for the reminder that even in the darkest of times, the human spirit could find a way to thrive, to create beauty and meaning in the face of adversity.

And as I lay my head down to rest, the memory of snarling dogs and lurking Shadow Panthers a haunting lullaby, I felt a sense of peace settle over me, like a warm blanket on a cold night. For all the challenges and uncertainties that lay ahead, I knew that we would face them together, united by a common purpose and an unbreakable bond of friendship—even if Grant and Sarah didn't quite realise the full picture, just yet.

4338.211

(30 July 2018)

SPIDERLINGS

4338.211.1

The monotonous task of stacking bags of firewood felt like a heavy burden in the otherworldly environment of Clivilius. Each laboured breath drew in air thick with a hazy dust that coated my throat. The sun blazed relentlessly from the sky, its searing rays turning every menial chore into a battle against the draining forces of the new world. As I hefted another bag onto the towering pile, beads of sweat trickled down my face, stinging my eyes.

My thoughts drifted, seeking refuge in memories of the vibrant, teeming ecosystems I had studied back on Earth. Lush rainforests pulsing with life. Coral reefs awash in a kaleidoscope of colours. Such richness and diversity seemed like a distant dream compared to the desolate, dun-coloured wasteland stretching endlessly in all directions.

A subtle motion amidst the static backdrop snapped my attention away from the endless expanse. I froze, eyes straining to locate the source of the furtive movement. There - near the bottom of the woodpile, trapped behind the clear plastic, an elongated dark form scurried with an unsettling quickness. Leaning in closer, I could discern the distinctive shape of a huntsman spider.

My heart skipped a beat, a rush of exhilaration tempered by a twinge of melancholy. This hardy species, a fellow traveller from Earth now making its home on this desolate world, filled me with wonder. In the face of Clivilius' barren hostility, life still clutched tenaciously, adapted and endured - even if embodied by this solitary arachnid refugee.

Seeing that unmistakable outline reminded me that we were not alone in our struggle. Other stowaways had hitched a ride through the cosmos, just like us, to eke out an existence against all odds on the driest, most inhospitable rock in the universe. A sobering realisation, but one that also kindled a slender glimmer of hope. Where there is life, however small, the spark of tenacity flickers on.

Observing the spider's plight, confined within that thin plastic prison, made one thing abundantly clear - left exposed on the surface, its chances of seeking out a solitary existence were next to nil. The unrelenting environmental onslaught of baking heat, desiccating winds, and lack of any sustainable food source would quickly snuff out that fragile spark. My heart constricted at the thought of such a hardy survivor being consigned to an agonisingly slow demise after making the astronomical journey between worlds. No living thing deserved that cruel fate, not on my watch.

Driven by a fierce protective instinct, I sprang into action, making a beeline for the ramshackle assortment of supplies and improvised tools we called the Drop Zone. Upended boxes, dismantled machinery, and random fragments of Earthly technology lay strewn about in entropic piles. But among that disorganised heap, I knew I'd find something suitable. My urgency grew as I rifled through the hodgepodge until - there! Nestled between a battered multitool and a tangle of wiring, several large repurposed jars of thick polycarbonate caught my eye. Snatching them up, I could already envision their new purpose as life-saving arks.

I hurried back to the woodpile, cradling the jars protectively against my body like precious cargo. With trembling hands, I grasped the edge of the plastic bag and carefully tore it open, bracing myself to rescue the solitary survivor trapped within. But as the rent widened, releasing a small puff of dust, I stumbled back in shock. It wasn't just a single huntsman spider after all.

There, nestled among the desiccated logs and bark, huddled an entire fragile nursery teeming with newly-hatched spiderlings. Dozens of minuscule dark bodies scurried in all directions, each one more tiny and vulnerable than the last. Their lives, just mere threads in the tapestry of Clivilius' harsh existence, now rested unexpectedly in my hands.

A profound sense of responsibility washed over me, even as a tendril of doubt snaked through my consciousness. *Could I really save something so delicate, so fleeting?* My mind raced - these infinitesimal beings required resources and environs so incredibly specialised. *Could I possibly recreate what eons of adaptation had optimised?* But as I watched them scatter, using their miraculous instincts to seek out whatever meagre shelter they could, I knew I had to try.

Time was quickly becoming the enemy, as the spiderlings' frenetic movements dispersed them further into the unforgiving environment. I had to work quickly. With an almost revered delicacy, I began carefully scooping them up one by one, cradling each impossibly tiny life in my cupped palms. My movements were guided by a silent litany, a pleading mantra to the uncaring cosmos that I might be able to offer these fragile beings safe harbour, however fleeting.

With each minuscule form gently transferred into the transparent jars, I felt the weight of responsibility like a lingering presence. These weren't just wards randomly assigned to my care - they were representatives of life's inevitable resilience, unexpected nomads that had beaten the odds to find refuge, however precarious, on this fresh frontier.

As their numbers gradually swelled within the makeshift terrariums, I studied the trapped spiderlings through the curved transparency. Though limited by the narrow confines, their bustling, purposeful movements channeled eons of ancestral coding, indomitable imperatives to explore, persist, multiply. My role was now also coded, an endless cycle as ancient as life itself - to nurture and safeguard this unseen spark as gently as a candle flame against the vacuum of oblivion.

With the jars now brimming with their fragile living cargo, I cradled them close, using my body to shield the vulnerable spiderlings from Clivilius' punishing sunlight. Every step towards the temporary shelter of my caravan had to be measured and deliberate. One jarring movement, one unlucky tumble, could potentially undo all my carefully orchestrated efforts and snuff out these tenacious pioneers before they had a chance.

The caravan loomed ahead, a welcome oasis of human ingenuity amid this starkly inhospitable landscape. Its durable alloy skin deflected the worst of the solar bombardment, while its self-contained life support systems maintained a micro-scaled replica of Earth's nurturing environs. This wouldn't just be my ephemeral home - it would become an ark to ensure this tiny detachment of life's expeditionary force could survive transit across the cosmic void.

As the armoured portal hissed open, clutching my fragile burdens tightly, I crossed the threshold into a sanctuary infinitely more hospitable than the scorched wasteland outside. For these unexpected creatures, the caravan's hermetically sealed confines would become the sole cradle nurturing their tentative toehold on this utterly foreign world.

Once inside the caravan's protective embrace, I carefully arranged the jars along the starboard windowsill. Through the reinforced transparencies, filtered rays of Clivilius' sunlight could reach the fragile spiderling nurseries without subjecting them to the full brunt of the blazing exterior conditions. With a tiny hand-bore tool, I meticulously punctured the lids to allow an ingress of the recycled but life-sustaining air.

As I stepped back, my gaze lingered on the minuscule forms scurrying about, already instinctively seeking to map and inhabit their new constrained universe. Though little more than specks, mere motes in this inhospitable void, they embodied life's deepest, most profound imperative - the universal directive to explore, spread, persist against whatever life threw in their path.

Here, in a human-made sanctuary, who knows how far away from the nurturing cradle that spawned our ancestors, these unlikely pioneers staked their claim alongside my own expedition. We were fellow nomads, outcasts by cosmic circumstance, striving to gain toeholds of existence wherever meagre purchase could be found. Watching their frenetic movements, I marvelled at the resiliency of that singular driving force, an eternal flame that burned undimmed even against the interstellar vacuum's inhospitable depths.

I stood transfixed, watching the flurry of activity as the spiderlings instinctively began establishing their replica habitat within the jar's enclosed micro-cosmos. What I had initially undertaken as a simple act of preservation was gradually revealing itself as something profoundly more symbolic. These tiny beings were more than just random lives plucked from the maw of oblivion. They were emissaries, unwitting heralds representing life's inexorable cosmic vanguard.

As I absorbed this realisation, my own role's significance surfaced with resounding clarity. We humans were not merely pioneering survivors, clinging to existence on this harsh new frontier. We were custodians, tasked with the sacred responsibility of nurturing and seeding new footholds for the miracle of life wherever fleeting opportunity availed itself. Just as Earth had cradled and proliferated life's embryonic spark over eons into the dazzling biospheric kaleidoscope, so too did any viable crucible - even one as marginal as Clivilius - demand the same nurturing stewardship.

Watching the spiderlings' struggle to gain purchase and propagate despite the limitations, I felt an overpowering sense of spiritual kinship. These tiny sojourners and I were partners in life's perpetual journey, merely two branches reaching along divergent paths in pursuit of the same immutable objective - to flourish, populate, and diffuse our shared spark into the deepest recesses of the cosmos. In that reverent moment, their fragile tremors became reminders of the awesome privilege bestowed upon me - to uphold the unbroken chain of life's perpetuation as both survivor and midwife across this utterly bewildering landscape.

MENAGERIE DELIGHTS

4338.211.2

The sudden arrival of Paul, his energy almost palpable as he rushed into our camp, immediately drew my attention away from the comfort of the bonfire. "Karen!" he called out, his voice carrying a sense of urgency that made me sit up straight, my senses instantly on high alert. "I need a favour."

"Sure, Paul. What's up?" I asked, my curiosity piqued by the somewhat excited tone in his voice, like a child with a secret to share.

"We've got some new residents," he began, the corners of his mouth curling into an odd smirk that momentarily filled me with unease. "A goat named Vincent and a bunch of hens from Yunta," he clarified, his words hanging in the air like a punchline waiting for a response.

For a moment, I was taken aback, my mind struggling to process the unexpected information, like a computer trying to decipher a foreign code. "You're kidding!" I couldn't help but blurt out, my voice tinged with both surprise and a hint of amusement.

Paul's response was accompanied by a wry smile that seemed to dance in his eyes. "I wish I was. Beatrix just brought them in. We need to get them settled somewhere," he said, his tone a mix of exasperation and amusement, like a parent dealing with a precocious child.

A soft chuckle escaped me as I carefully set my mug down on the table beside me, the ceramic making a gentle clink against the wood. The thought of welcoming a goat and a bunch of hens to our camp was both amusing and strangely endearing. For a brief second, my mind wandered to the drink I was leaving behind, considering the insects that might take the opportunity to dive into it, like tiny swimmers in a pool. But then I remembered - Clivilius, with all its oddities, seemed to be devoid of such small pests. No ants to march into my mug, no flies to hover over our meal, like a land frozen in time.

Energised by the task at hand, I rose from my seat by the bonfire, my muscles protesting slightly from the sudden movement. "Alright, let's do this," I declared, though a practical concern immediately came to mind. "But where do we put them? We don't exactly have any secure enclosures."

Paul's eyes sparkled with sudden inspiration, a characteristic I was gradually getting used to, like a magician always ready with a new trick up his sleeve. He was full of surprises, his enthusiasm seemingly boundless. "How about Glenda's BMW?" he suggested with a hint of excitement. "It's secure, and it's not like she's using it right now."

Under normal circumstances, the idea of using a luxury car as a makeshift animal enclosure would have seemed absurd, like using a Picasso as a placemat. But in the context of Clivilius, with its unending surprises, it somehow made sense. It was a surreal dream that followed its own logic. I couldn't help but laugh, a genuine chuckle at the oddity of our situation and Paul's earnest suggestion. "A BMW coop? Why not!" I agreed, amused by the practicality of his idea. "It's the safest place for them tonight, especially with no fences up yet."

Together, Paul and I headed towards Glenda's car, our steps falling into sync. As we drove the vehicle over to the Drop Zone, the engine humming beneath us like a contented cat, curiosity got the better of me. "So, how did we end up with a goat and chickens?"

Paul launched into an animated recount of Beatrix's unexpected rescue operation and the ensuing chaos that followed, his words painting a vivid picture in my mind's eye. I listened intently, shaking my head in disbelief as I tried to comprehend the bizarre turn of events.

If Beatrix is going to rescue every animal she comes across, we're going to need more than just the help of Grant and Sarah, I remarked to myself, half-jokingly. *We'll be needing an entire wildlife team before long!*

❖

Arriving at the Drop Zone, the sight that greeted us was almost comical. Vincent the goat meandered about, appearing quite content with his new surroundings, his hooves kicking up small puffs of dust with each leisurely step. The hens, on the other hand, pecked at the dusty ground, seemingly exploring every inch of their newfound freedom, their feathers ruffling in the gentle breeze.

The scene at the Drop Zone quickly escalated into a farcical display that would have given any seasoned comedian a run for their money. As Paul swung open the back of Glenda's BMW, converting the luxury vehicle into an impromptu chicken coop, I couldn't help but marvel at the absurdity of our situation. The juxtaposition of the sleek, high-end car and the decidedly rustic purpose it was now serving was a sight to behold, like a fine china tea set being used to serve a hearty stew.

The hens, sensing their impending relocation, seemed to have conspired to make our task as difficult as possible. Each time we thought we had one cornered, it would dart away with a surprising burst of speed, leaving us grasping at thin air and a cloud of dust.

"Got any experience with chicken catching, Paul?" I asked, my words laced with humour as I watched him lunge awkwardly at a hen, only to stumble forward as it nimbly sidestepped him, like a matador dodging a charging bull.

"Not exactly part of my skillset," Paul responded, a hint of amusement in his panting voice, his brow glistening with sweat. "But how hard can it be?"

The chickens, however, seemed to take his words as a personal challenge, their beady eyes glinting with a mischievous spark. One particularly spry hen led Paul on a merry chase, darting between his legs, doubling back, and at one point even perching atop his head, leaving Paul spinning in circles, like a dog chasing its own tail. The sight was so hilarious that I had to bite my lip to stifle a laugh, the absurdity of the moment threatening to overwhelm my composure.

Not one to be outdone, I threw myself into the fray, determined to show off my hen-wrangling skills honed on my own land. But these hens were not the docile creatures I was accustomed to, their wiry frames belying a surprising agility and cunning. They zigzagged across the Drop Zone with the agility of seasoned athletes, dodging every attempt at capture with an almost cheeky flair, their feathers flying in the wake of their evasive manoeuvres.

At one point, I managed to corner a hen against the car, my arms outstretched like a goalkeeper ready to make a save. But just as I thought I had it, the hen leaped over my outstretched hands with a flap of its wings, ruffled its feathers, and strutted away, leaving me sprawled on the ground, my dignity as ruffled as the hen's feathers.

Paul and I exchanged looks of exasperation and disbelief, our efforts descending into fits of laughter, the absurdity of the situation finally getting the better of us. We must have been quite the sight, two grown adults engaged in a comedic battle of wits with a flock of hens, our clothes dusty and our hair dishevelled from the chase.

"Wait," I said, stopping abruptly, a new idea of my own arriving like a bolt of lightning. "What if we lure them in with some food?" I suggested, my eyes widening with the realisation that sometimes the simplest solutions were the best.

Paul nodded, his expression a mix of relief and admiration at my sudden stroke of genius.

The brief walk back to camp was almost a relief, a chance to catch my breath and regroup. It gave me a moment to gather my thoughts and a much-needed break from the comedic chaos, like a intermission in a particularly lively play. I scavenged for seeds and leftover food scraps, gathering an assortment that I hoped would be irresistible to our feathered escape artists, like a gourmet buffet designed to tempt even the most discerning of palates.

Additionally, I grabbed a makeshift fire torch, acutely aware that our prolonged efforts might extend into dusk, and the last thing we needed was to be caught in the dark with a flock of uncooperative hens, like a horror movie gone terribly wrong, where the hunters would suddenly become the hunted.

Returning to the Drop Zone, I laid out a tempting trail of food leading straight into the back of Glenda's BMW, the seeds and scraps forming a path like breadcrumbs in a fairy tale. Paul and I then stepped back, crossing our fingers that our plan would work, our breath held in anticipation.

To our delight and slight amusement, the hens, ever curious and perpetually hungry, began to take notice of the food, their heads cocking to the side as they eyed the offering with interest. One by one, they pecked their way towards the car, lured by the promise of an easy meal, their steps growing more confident with each morsel they gobbled up. Their heads bobbed inquisitively as they approached the car, and then, almost tentatively, they hopped inside, their feathers brushing against the plush leather seats in a bizarre juxtaposition of the wild and the luxurious.

Paul's comment, delivered with his usual good-natured grin, brought a smile to my face, the tension of the moment finally broken. "Looks like we've found our chicken whisperer," he said, looking at our accomplished task with a sense of pride, his eyes twinkling with mirth.

I watched as the last hen cautiously made its way into the luxury coop, its tail feathers disappearing into the depths of the car, the strange reality of the situation not lost on me. We carefully shut the doors of the BMW, taking extra care to leave the windows cracked open just enough to ensure good air circulation, yet narrow enough to safeguard our feathered guests from any potential predators lurking in the night, like a protective cocoon shielding them from the dangers of the outside world.

"This has got to be the most expensive chicken coop in history," I joked, my laughter echoing our shared amusement over the absurdity of housing chickens in a high-end vehicle, the irony of the situation not lost on either of us.

Paul's smile faltered slightly, a hint of concern creeping into his expression. "I hope Glenda has a sense of humour," he mused thoughtfully, his brow furrowing slightly at the thought of her reaction to our unorthodox use of her prized possession.

"We'll clean it up before she finds out," I assured him, though a part of me couldn't shake off the uneasy feeling that Glenda's absence might extend longer than any of us anticipated. As much as I tried to maintain a light-hearted approach to our situation, the reality of our predicament in Clivilius often loomed in the back of my mind, lingering like a dark cloud on the horizon.

Deciding to end our chicken adventure on a high note, I added with a chuckle, "Let's just hope the chickens don't go for a joyride." The image of chickens behind the wheel of Glenda's BMW, cruising around Bixbus, was amusing enough to momentarily distract from the more serious undertones of our conversation.

❖

The sudden appearance of a car emerging from the Portal instantly drew Paul's attention away from our previous conversation, his head snapping towards the sound like a compass needle pulled by a magnet. "Beatrix!" he shouted as soon as she stepped out of the vehicle, his voice filled with a mix of relief and urgency. Without a second thought, he dashed towards her, his feet kicking up small clouds of dust in his wake.

Grabbing the fire torch, I trailed behind Paul, my curiosity piqued by his sudden excitement. "And hopefully it's not more hens," I murmured to myself, only half-joking given our recent escapade. The sweat from chasing those feathered rascals was still fresh on my forehead, yet it had been a comedic interlude in the otherwise serious business of survival.

Reaching Beatrix, Paul wasted no time, his words tumbling out in a rush. "Did you find her?" he asked, his voice filled with hopeful anticipation, his eyes searching her face for any sign of good news.

Beatrix's response, however, was a shake of her head accompanied by a sombre, "Sorry, Paul. I couldn't find her." Her words hung in the air like a heavy fog, dampening the spark of hope that had briefly ignited in Paul's eyes.

Standing next to Paul, I felt somewhat disconnected from their conversation, like an outsider peering in through a foggy window. I wondered who 'her' referred to and why Paul seemed so invested in Beatrix's search, my mind spinning with possibilities and theories.

Paul's reaction was one of immediate disappointment, his shoulders slumping. "Really?" he said, his voice deflating like a punctured balloon, the hope draining from his face.

It was then that Beatrix noticed me, her gaze shifting from Paul to meet my own. "Is everything okay here?" she asked, her brow furrowed with concern.

"We've been chasing those blinkin' chickens of yours," I said to Beatrix, a hint of humour in my voice but underscored with a serious undertone, like a melody with a discordant note. While I tried to keep the mood light, I couldn't mask my feelings of frustration about the situation she had inadvertently created.

Beatrix's decision to bring a goat and chickens to Clivilius, although well-intentioned, seemed to lack practical forethought, like a child bringing home a stray puppy without considering the long-term consequences. She had introduced these animals into our already complex environment without considering the essential resources they would need for their safety and sustenance.

I glanced at Beatrix, hoping she would understand that while her heart was in the right place, her actions had consequences that affected all of us, like ripples in a pond spreading outward from a single pebble. In Clivilius, every decision, no matter how small, could have significant implications.

A look of confusion spread across Beatrix's face, her eyebrows knitting together like tangled threads. For a moment, I questioned whether Paul had confused Beatrix with Luke, the two names swirling in my mind like leaves caught in a whirlwind. But before I could voice my thoughts, Paul stepped in.

"You gave me an idea earlier. I was going to wait for your return, but then I figured that they'd probably be better in separate cars anyway," he explained, his hands gesturing as if trying to paint a picture in the air.

However, Beatrix remained blank, her expression as uncomprehending as a student faced with an incomprehensible math problem.

"The chickens," Paul reiterated, his voice tinged with a hint of exasperation, as if explaining the obvious to a child.

"Yeah, I got that part," Beatrix replied sourly, her words as sharp as a lemon's bite. "What about the chickens?"

I groaned loudly at the over complicated turn of the conversation, my patience wearing thin.

"I've taken Glenda's car..." Paul began, his words trailing off.

"You mean we," I interjected, not letting Paul take all the credit for cleaning up Beatrix's mess.

"Of course," Paul corrected himself, his cheeks flushing slightly with embarrassment. "We've taken Glenda's car to the Drop Zone and decided to turn it into a hen house."

"You've put the chickens in a BMW?" Beatrix exclaimed, her voice echoing her disbelief, her eyes widening like saucers.

I couldn't help but chuckle, even as I recognised the ridiculousness of it all. "I take that back," I said with a smirk, turning to Paul, my eyes twinkling with mischief. "The idea was all yours, Paul."

Paul, for his part, seemed a little defensive, his hackles rising like a cornered animal. "It's not as though we really had many options," he protested, his voice rising slightly in pitch. "We can't very well leave them running freely around camp. They're a threat to all of us."

I nodded in agreement with Paul, my expression growing serious once more. "He's not wrong," I added.

"We can't risk them attracting more wild creatures," Paul reiterated, trying to justify our unconventional decision.

Beatrix's frown deepened, her displeasure as evident as a storm cloud on the horizon. "So, you'd rather sentence them to a torturous death out here... alone?" she questioned, her tone laced with accusation.

I felt a wave of frustration wash over me, my patience finally snapping like a twig underfoot. "Beatrix, don't be so foolish," I retorted sharply, my eyes meeting hers with a stare that underscored the potential consequences of her actions. "You know as well as I do that we can't let our love for the preservation of nature surpass the logical faculties that the universe has bestowed upon us."

For a moment, both Paul and Beatrix just stared at me, as if trying to process my words, their expressions as blank as freshly fallen snow. The silence was suddenly broken by the synchronised rumbling of our stomachs.

"I'm so hungry. I don't think I've eaten today," I admitted, surprised at myself for having overlooked such a basic necessity, my hand automatically going to my stomach as if to quell the growling beast within. The day's events had been so consuming that eating had slipped to the back of my mind, like a forgotten chore.

"You're in Broken Hill now, aren't you, Beatrix?" Paul asked, his eyes lighting up with the mention of food, his earlier disappointment momentarily forgotten in the face of potential sustenance.

"Yeah," Beatrix responded, her reluctance fading as the topic shifted away from chickens and toward something more mundane, her shoulders relaxing slightly.

Paul's enthusiasm for food was almost infectious, his face breaking into a grin as wide as the Cheshire Cat's. "I think there is some food being prepared back at camp, but..." he trailed off, his expression turning dreamy as he thought about the culinary delights of Broken Hill, his eyes glazing over with anticipation. "You must get us some Rags chips. They are simply divine," he said, almost moaning at the thought, his hand clutching at his heart as if overcome with emotion.

"Rags?" Beatrix echoed, her confusion as evident as my own, her head tilting to the side like a curious puppy. The name didn't seem to ring a bell with her.

"They're on Oxide Street. Simply the best chips you've ever tasted!" Paul declared with a fervour that made me chuckle. His passion for food was a pleasant distraction from our usual discussions about survival and logistics.

"Sure," Beatrix finally acquiesced, perhaps more to appease Paul's enthusiasm than out of any real interest in the chips, her shoulders shrugging in resignation.

❖

As we waited for Beatrix's return, Paul and I found ourselves engrossed in conversation about the day's events, our words flowing as easily as water down a stream. The topics meandered from the chickens and their luxury coop to more pressing matters we faced daily in Clivilius, our thoughts intertwining like vines in a dense jungle.

It was a peculiar, yet comforting, bonding experience, like sharing secrets with a close friend. Sharing our thoughts and reflections on the day's adventures, absurdities, and challenges had a way of bringing us closer. It was moments like these that underscored our shared human experience in this strange new world – a world where each day was as unpredictable as the last, yet filled with moments of camaraderie that made it all bearable.

As we sat there, the fire torch flickering beside us like a friendly companion, I couldn't help but feel a sense of gratitude for Paul's presence, for the way he could find humour and hope even in the most trying of circumstances. It was a quality that I admired, a resilience that seemed to flow through his veins like lifeblood.

❖

As Beatrix approached, the enticing aroma of freshly cooked chips wafted towards us, carried on the gentle breeze like a fragrant herald of culinary delights. The scent was a tantalising promise, instantly making my mouth water and my stomach rumble with renewed vigour, like a beast awakened from slumber.

But it wasn't just the chips that caught my attention, my eyes widening with curiosity as I noticed Beatrix carrying a container brimming with something unfamiliar.

"This," Beatrix announced, her voice tinged with excitement, her eyes sparkling with anticipation, "is cheeseslaw. Apparently it's a game-changer." She held out the container like a precious offering, a culinary treasure waiting to be discovered.

I watched as Paul eagerly reached for the cheeseslaw, his fingers already grasping for a taste of this intriguing new creation. Curiosity getting the better of me, I grabbed a chip and scooped up a generous portion of the cheeseslaw, the creamy mixture clinging to the crisp edges like a delectable embrace.

The moment the combination touched my taste buds, I was pleasantly surprised, my eyes widening with delight as a burst of flavours danced across my tongue. The cheeseslaw, a delightful twist on traditional coleslaw, but with an added cheesy richness, complemented the salty crispness of the chips perfectly, like a symphony of taste and texture.

The unique flavours melded together in a way that was both satisfying and unexpectedly delightful. The creaminess of the cheese, the crunch of the carrot, and the tang of the dressing all combined to create a taste sensation that was nothing short of remarkable, like a culinary masterpiece crafted by a skilled artisan.

"Wow, this is amazing!" I couldn't help but exclaim, my initial skepticism vanishing with each bite, replaced by a growing sense of appreciation and wonder. The chips were indeed divine, just as Paul had promised, their golden hue and perfect crispness a testament to the skill of the Rags chefs. And the cheeseslaw, oh the cheeseslaw, it was an excellent addition, elevating the humble chips to new heights of deliciousness.

As I savoured each mouthful, I couldn't help but marvel at the simple pleasure of enjoying a simple meal. It was a moment of pure indulgence, a brief respite from the constant demands and uncertainties of life in Clivilius.

Paul, still enjoying his mouthful of food, asked between bites, his words muffled by the delectable combination of chips and cheeseslaw, "Should we share this with the rest of the camp?" His question hung in the air for a moment, a suggestion that was both generous and slightly reluctant, like a child hesitant to share a favourite toy.

I considered his question for a moment, my mind weighing the pros and cons of sharing this rare treat with the others. On one hand, the idea of spreading this culinary joy to the rest of the camp was appealing, a way to boost morale and bring a smile to the faces of our fellow settlers.

But as we both reached for more chips and cheeseslaw, our actions spoke louder than words, our hands moving in unison like a choreographed dance. We continued to indulge in this rare treat, our collective silence confirming that, for now, this was our little moment to enjoy, a secret shared between friends.

4338.212

(31 July 2018)

VINCENT & MAGGIE

4338.212.1

The midday sun was relentless, beating down on the camp like a merciless tyrant, its scorching rays turning the air into a shimmering haze of heat. I wiped the sweat from my brow, the salty droplets stinging my eyes as I squinted against the harsh glare. I had just finished restocking our food supplies, a task that had left me drained and parched, when I heard hurried footsteps approaching, the sound of urgency cutting through the oppressive stillness.

"Karen! Have you moved the coriander plants?" Chris called out, his face flushed with exertion and worry, sweat beading on his balding head.

I furrowed my brow, confusion etched across my features like a question mark. "No, why would I have done that?" The idea of moving the plants seemed absurd, a notion that had never even crossed my mind.

Chris rested his hands on his hips, as if trying to grasp at some semblance of control. "They're gone. All of them. I went to check on them this morning and the entire planter bed is empty."

A sinking feeling settled in my gut, a cold dread that spread through my veins like ice water. After painstakingly cultivating those plants, coaxing them to life in this unforgiving environment, nurturing them with a tender hand and a determined spirit, the thought of losing them was devastating. It was like watching a cherished dream wither and die, a piece of our hope for the future snatched away in the blink of an eye.

"Let me see," I said, my voice barely above a whisper, as if speaking too loudly might make the terrible truth more real. I followed Chris to the area beside the tent, where the coriander plants should have remained.

Sure enough, the ground lay barren, returned to a desolate wasteland of upturned soil, without even a single stray leaf to hint at the lush crop that had once thrived there. It was a sight that made my heart ache.

I crouched down, examining the area closely, my eyes scanning the disturbed earth for any clues that might reveal the fate of our precious plants. That's when I noticed it - telltale impressions in the dirt, bearing the unmistakable marks of a nose and hooves.

"They were eaten," I murmured, the realisation dawning on me like a cold, hard truth, a bitter pill that stuck in my throat and refused to be swallowed.

Chris let out a frustrated groan, his hands balling into fists at his sides as if he wanted to pummel the very earth that had betrayed us. "Those damn chickens! I knew we shouldn't have expected them to stay at the Drop Zone without an enclosure." His words were laced with anger and self-recrimination.

I shook my head slowly, my mind racing with the implications of what I had discovered. "No, these markings are too large for the chickens."

A memory resurfaced, a fleeting image of a certain four-legged troublemaker that had been the bane of my existence since his arrival. A new suspicion took hold, a gnawing doubt that ate away at the edges of my mind like a persistent rodent.

I straightened up, scanning our camp with narrowed eyes, my gaze sweeping over the scattered tents and makeshift structures that stood as a testament to our tenuous grip on survival. "Where's Vincent?" The question hung in the air like an accusation, a damning indictment of our own negligence.

Chris matched my gaze, his eyes widening with a sudden realisation as he noticed the conspicuous absence of our resident goat. "You don't think..."

We exchanged a loaded look, a silent communication that spoke volumes about the depth of our shared exasperation and dread. Then, without another word, we set off in search of the wayward creature, our steps heavy with purpose and determination.

Our camp wasn't huge, a small oasis of civilisation in the vast expanse of the desert wilderness, but it seemed that Vincent had a talent for getting himself into all sorts of nooks and crannies, his insatiable curiosity and mischievous nature, despite his old age, leading him into every corner and crevice.

"Vincent!" I called out sternly, my voice echoing across the camp like a thunderclap, a warning shot fired across the bow of the recalcitrant goat's bow. "Vincent, you woolly menace, you better not have-"

A sudden commotion from the direction of the supply tent cut me off, a cacophony of shouts and crashes that shattered the oppressive stillness like a hammer through glass. Nial's unmistakable voice rang out, a combination of surprise and strangled frustration that spoke volumes about the chaos that had erupted.

"What the...? No, no! Shoo! Get out of there!" His words were punctuated by the sound of clattering metal and the frantic scuffling of hooves on canvas, a discordant symphony of drama and mayhem.

Chris and I broke into a jog, our feet pounding against the compact dust as we entered the supply tent to find Nial engaged in a bizarre standoff, a scene that would have been comical if not for the seriousness of the situation. Vincent had somehow made his way into the supply tent, a feat of acrobatic prowess that defied all logic and reason.

From the looks of the upturned supplies and scattered food packages, the goat had gotten his fill… and then some. It was a scene of utter devastation, a post-apocalyptic wasteland of ruined rations and shattered boxes.

"You blasted beast!" Nial growled, his face contorted with rage and frustration as he tried in vain to shoo the intruder from the tent. But Vincent, ever the unflappable agent of chaos, regarded him with casual indifference from atop the mattress, idly cud-chewing as if he hadn't a care in the world.

Despite my exasperation, I couldn't stifle an amused snort at the absurd scene playing out before my eyes, a moment of levity in the midst of the unrelenting hardship. Nial, flustered and at his wits' end while Vincent carried on as if he were the rightful ruler of this makeshift kingdom.

"Having trouble, Nial?" I couldn't resist the gentle prod, a teasing lilt in my voice that belied the seriousness of the situation.

He wheeled on me, his eyes wild with desperation as he gestured helplessly at the recalcitrant goat, his hands flailing in the air like a drowning man grasping for a lifeline. "This… this animal broke in and has turned the supply tent upside down! I've tried every blasted thing to get him to leave, but he just digs in further." His words were punctuated by a series of colourful expletives that would have made a sailor blush.

Vincent chose that moment to issue a defiant bleat, a sound that seemed to echo through the camp like a battle cry, firmly staking his claim on the tent and all that lay within. It was a declaration of war, a gauntlet thrown down at the feet of all who dared to challenge his supremacy.

I sighed, equal parts annoyed and endeared by the obstinate creature's antics. Moving forward with a sense of grim determination, I fixed Vincent with a stern look, my eyes narrowing into slits of barely contained fury.

"All right, you lawnmower of the expedition, let's go. You've caused enough trouble for one day." My words were clipped and harsh, a verbal lashing that would have sent lesser creatures scurrying for cover.

Ignoring Nial's indignant sputtering, his face turning an alarming shade of purple as he tried in vain to maintain some semblance of dignity, I reached out and grabbed Vincent by the scruff, hauling his bulky frame off the mattress amid a chorus of bleating protests. He twisted and stamped his hooves, a whirling dervish of fur and fury, but I held firm, my grip as unyielding as the iron will that had brought me this far.

"I'll get this escaped convict secured back at the Drop Zone," I assured Nial and Chris, my voice heavy with the weight of responsibility. "You two see if you can't salvage what's left of the supplies." It was a forlorn hope, a desperate attempt to find some shred of order in the tragedy that had descended upon us like a plague.

With a resigned sigh, I began hauling the ornery goat back towards the Drop Zone, my steps heavy with the burden of our collective misfortune. As I walked, my mind raced with thoughts of all the extra fortifications we'd need to make it Vincent-proof, a task that seemed to stretch out before me like an endless road.

Even as I felt equal parts amused and irritated by the troublesome creature's antics, a strange sense of affection welled up within me, a grudging admiration for the indomitable spirit that seemed to embody the very essence of our struggle for survival. In a world where every day was a battle, where the very ground beneath our feet seemed to shift and change with each passing moment, there was something almost comforting in the stubborn persistence of this old humble goat.

❖

Tugging firmly on Vincent's lead, I guided the stubborn goat through the makeshift gate into the Drop Zone area, my muscles straining against his resistance. He bleated in protest, his voice echoing across the barren landscape like a disgruntled chorus, clearly unhappy about being relegated back to the impromptu pen.

"Oh hush, you. This is what happens when you can't behave yourself," I chided the creature, my voice tinged with a mix of exasperation and grudging affection.

As I set about tethering him to a grounded stake to ensure he couldn't pull off another escape, my hands working deftly to secure the knots, movement in my peripheral vision caught my eye. Beatrix was aimlessly wandering about the Drop Zone, her brow furrowed in apparent distraction, her movements erratic and unfocused like a sailor lost at sea.

"Everything alright over there, Beatrix?" I called out, my voice carrying across the dusty expanse, a note of concern colouring my words.

She started slightly, as if jolted from a deep reverie, then waved a dismissive hand, her fingers fluttering like a bird's wings. "Yes, yes... I'm fine. Just... looking for something." Her words were vague and evasive, a verbal smoke screen that did little to allay my growing unease.

Eyeing the array of boxes, equipment, and assorted supplies strewn about the area, a veritable maze of discarded artefacts and forgotten treasures, I arched an eyebrow, my skepticism as plain as the sweat on my brow. "Need a hand? This place is a labyrinth," I offered, my tone a mix of sarcasm and genuine concern. In a world where resources were scarce and every scrap of material precious, the idea of Beatrix rummaging aimlessly through the detritus of our former lives seemed almost sacrilegious.

"No, no. I'll find it," she replied absently, already refocusing her search. Her dismissal stung, a sharp reminder of the walls that still existed between us, the secrets and fears that we each carried.

With a small shrug, I returned my attention to corralling Vincent, my hands working to secure his lead with a renewed sense of purpose. A few minutes passed in relative quiet, the silence broken only by Vincent's indignant bleating, before Beatrix spoke up again.

"What exactly are you doing over there?"

I paused mid-knot to throw her a look of disbelief, my eyebrows raised in a silent challenge. "Seriously? I'm securing this woolly menace after he rampaged through camp and made a meal of the coriander crop," I replied, my voice dripping with sarcasm, the frustration of the day's events bleeding into my words like poison.

Beatrix's eyes widened in sudden panic, a look of pure terror flashing across her face like a lightning bolt. "You're going to leave Vincent here? Karen, I really don't think that's wise..." she trailed off, her words hanging in the air like a dark cloud, a portent of some unseen danger lurking just out of sight.

Her uncharacteristic fretfulness piqued my curiosity, a sudden spark of interest flaring to life in my chest like a match struck against stone. "What's going on, Beatrix? You're acting even odder than usual," I pressed, my voice tinged with a mix of concern and suspicion. In a place like Clivilius, where trust was a precious commodity and secrets could be deadly, any hint of deception was a red flag, a warning sign that something was amiss.

She worried her lower lip, her teeth digging into the soft flesh like a nervous tic, her gaze flickering about the Drop Zone like a hunted animal searching for escape. Finally, she seemed to come to a decision, her shoulders slumping in defeat as she let out a heavy sigh.

"I... may have misplaced Maggie," she admitted, her voice barely above a whisper, as if the words themselves were too terrible to speak aloud.

My eyes narrowed suspiciously, my mind racing with the implications of her confession. "Who... or more likely... what is Maggie?" I asked, my voice low and dangerous, a warning wrapped in a question.

Beatrix gulped noticeably. "She's a reticulated python," she replied, her words tumbling out in a rush, as if she couldn't bear to hold them in any longer.

"Tell me you're joking," I said slowly, each word a bullet fired from the chamber of my mounting anger. When she didn't respond, I threw up my hands, my frustration boiling over like a pot left too long on the stove. "Beatrix! That thing should be secured!" It felt like the nicest thing I could say, given that the truth was that I didn't think that Beatrix should have brought a reticulated python here at all in the first place. The idea of a massive, potentially deadly snake roaming free in our already precarious camp was enough to send a shiver of fear down my spine, a cold sweat breaking out across my brow.

"She's perfectly friendly!" Beatrix protested, her voice rising in pitch, a note of desperation creeping into her words. "Maggie wouldn't hurt a fly. Well... maybe a fly. But nothing larger!" She held up her hands in a placating gesture, as if trying to ward off my anger with the sheer force of her conviction.

I pinched the bridge of my nose, struggling to rein in my rising panic, my mind racing with the possibilities of what a creature like Maggie could do if left unchecked. "Right, because that makes me feel so much better about having an escaped constrictor slithering around," I replied, my voice dripping with sarcasm.

Shooting Vincent a glare, as if he were somehow complicit in this new crisis, I turned and began undoing the knots I'd so carefully worked, my fingers trembling slightly with the urgency of the task. As much as I disliked that fuzz-brained goat, leaving him here now seemed like a risk I couldn't afford, a gamble with stakes too high to contemplate.

"I'm taking this guy back to camp before 'friendly' Maggie mistakes him for a furry chew toy," I declared.

As I worked, I shot Beatrix a sidelong look, my eyes narrowing in suspicion, my mind whirling with the possibilities of what other secrets she might be hiding. "How long has she been missing? And please, tell me she's at least somewhere in this general vicinity," I pressed, my voice low and urgent, a plea wrapped in a demand.

Beatrix winced, her face contorting in a grimace of guilt and fear. "Well… we came through the Portal late last night. It was a bit of an unexpected entry. Maggie slithered away in the confusion. I've been searching for hours, but… I don't actually know which way she went," she admitted, her words tumbling out in a rush.

My gut twisted even further, a knot of dread forming in the pit of my stomach like a lead weight. An escaped python, that could be lurking anywhere, while we stood around oblivious. *Wonderful*.

"I'll keep an eye out," I said tightly, my voice strained with the effort of maintaining my composure, my mind racing with the possibilities of what horrors Maggie's presence might bring. "If Maggie's as 'friendly' as you claim, maybe she just found a little nook to curl up in here," I added, trying to inject a note of optimism into my words, a feeble attempt to reassure myself as much as Beatrix.

Beatrix nodded, looking properly chastened, her shoulders slumping in defeat as she seemed to shrink in on herself. "Right. Well... thanks then. I'll just... keep looking," she mumbled, her words trailing off into silence, a half-hearted promise that hung in the air like a wisp of smoke.

With that, she turned and wandered off once more. Shooting Vincent one last irritated glance, he and I began the trek back towards the main camp, our steps hurried.

All the while, I strained my ears for any telltale sounds of scaled movement, my heart pounding in my chest like a drum, my breath coming in short, sharp gasps. *If that snake had gotten itself loose in the camp while we slept...* I shuddered, the thought too terrible to contemplate, a nightmare made flesh.

One crisis at a time, Karen. One crisis at a time, I repeated to myself.

❖

The staccato thudding of Vincent's hooves and his indignant bleating reverberated through the camp like a raucous clarion call, no doubt alerting every soul to the goat's undesired return. Sure enough, Chris emerged from the makeshift equipment shelter, his eyes narrowing as he took in my woolly charge, his expression a mix of exasperation and disbelief.

Despite the precariousness of our circumstances in this harsh world, the constant struggle for survival, I couldn't stifle the upturned quirk of my lips as I drank in his familiar appearance, my heart swelling with a rush of affection and gratitude. It was a moment of respite, a fleeting oasis of comfort.

It didn't matter that two decades had passed since that starry Tasmanian night when I had first laid eyes on the rugged conservationist - Chris still possessed the ability to captivate me utterly, to steal my breath and quicken my pulse with a single glance. Though firmly entrenched in life's journey through middle-age, the passage of time etched in the lines around his eyes and the streaks of silver in what remained of his hair, his physique remained lean and sturdy, a living testament to the rigours of his lifelong active lifestyle. While his thick mane had quickly receded, the closely-cropped salt-and-pepper stubble framing his chiseled jawline only enhanced his undeniably distinguished aura, lending him an air of rugged sophistication that never failed to make my heart skip a beat.

But as always, it was his eyes that enraptured me most profoundly, those fathomless azure pools that seemed to hold the secrets of the universe within their depths. They could convey such intensity, whether meticulously cataloging nature's intricacies with a scientist's keen observation or smouldering with the banked fire of a camping trip. In this moment, they flickered with wry exasperation, igniting with familiar sparks as one questioning eyebrow arched upwards, a silent inquiry that spoke volumes.

"Please don't tell me that menace is back after I just finished cleaning his mess," Chris said, his voice a mix of resignation and disbelief as he jerked his chin towards the brazenly bleating Vincent.

I could only offer an apologetic half-shrug, helpless before the furrowed brow and that all-too-familiar downturned quirk of his lips - an expression I'd been on the receiving end of more times than I could count throughout our decades of shared misadventures across hostile terrains. It was a look that spoke of long-suffering patience, of the endless challenges and obstacles we had faced together, side by side, united in our determination to make a difference in the world.

"Believe me, I wouldn't have brought him if I had a choice," I replied, unable to keep the weary undercurrent from my tone. "But we may have a... situation." The word felt inadequate, a feeble attempt to encapsulate the crisis that loomed before us, the new danger that threatened to upend the delicate balance of our hard-won sanctuary.

The words tumbled out in a rush as I relayed the unsettling encounter with Beatrix and her startling revelation about Maggie's escape, my voice rising and falling with the urgency of the tale, the fear and frustration bleeding into every syllable. I watched the myriad micro-expressions flit across Chris's rugged features as his brilliant analytical mind rapidly processed the implications, the gears turning behind those striking blue eyes as he dissected the new drama with the precision of a surgeon.

"A reticulated python? Loose?" His tanned features tightened, his lips pressing into a grim line. "That's just what we need on top of everything else," he muttered, the sarcasm in his voice a thin veneer over the genuine concern that lurked beneath.

I could only nod in grim solidarity, sharing the pit of familiar frustration and tension roiling in my gut at this unexpected new wrinkle. Vincent, seemingly cognisant that he was no longer at the chaotic centre of our discussion, punctuated the loaded silence with another petulant bleat, his voice a grating reminder of the absurdity of our situation.

Reflexively, I rounded on the ornery creature with a quelling glare that was becoming increasingly familiar, my patience wearing thin in the face of his incessant disruptions. "You don't get to complain, you furry locust," I chided, my mordant words undercut by a surprising swell of grudging affection for the instigator of so much drama, the unlikely catalyst for the strange bond that was forming between us. "At least this way you won't end up as reptile chow," I added, the morbid humour a flimsy shield against the very real danger that lurked beyond the confines of our camp.

Turning back to my husband, I watched the telltale gears engage behind those intense blue gems, his brilliant mind already strategising contingencies like a grandmaster scrutinising a chessboard, the pieces falling into place with effortless grace. For all our years of partnership, the countless trials and triumphs we had shared, I never ceased to be awed by Chris's seemingly inexhaustible poise in even the direst of circumstances, the way he could remain an island of calm in a sea of turbulence.

No matter how dire the prognosis, how bleak the outlook, he could always disengage that brilliant mind from the turmoil of emotion, dispassionately isolating the problem and charting our path forward with a clarity and focus that never failed to inspire me. It was a skill born of necessity, honed over years of facing down the impossible and emerging victorious.

It was that unflappable pragmatism, married with his fierce passion for preservation, the unwavering commitment to the cause that had first drawn us together, that had first captivated my ardent conservationist's heart all those years ago. And though innumerable trials had carved weathered traces across both our world-worn exteriors in the intervening decades, the scars of a life lived on the edge, that searing devotion banked in his eyes remained my eternal lodestar, unfailing and eternal.

"I'll get Nial to help me make a small enclosure near the river," Chris finally said, his voice cutting through my thoughts, his eyes sparking with the beginnings of a plan.

I nodded appreciatively. "I suppose I'm the unlucky goat-sitter until then?" I asked, my tone wry and resigned, the inevitability of my fate settling over me like a well-worn cloak.

Chris grimaced as he shrugged, the gesture a silent acknowledgment of the burden I had unwittingly taken on, the responsibility that now fell squarely on my shoulders.

"Figures," I muttered, casting Vincent a resigned glare.

HALF-TRUTHS

4338.212.2

Having found a new stake to keep Vincent tethered until Chris and Nial could build him a proper enclosure, I led him down to the riverbank, his hooves kicking up small clouds of dust with each stubborn step. The sun beat down mercilessly, and I could feel the sweat beading on my brow as I hammered the stake into the hard, unyielding ground.

I stepped back, admiring my handiwork with a critical eye. The stake was sturdy and strong, driven deep into the earth with a determination that matched my own. It was close enough to the river to allow Vincent access to the water, yet far enough away to keep him from tumbling in and getting swept away by the current.

But even as I surveyed the scene before me, I couldn't shake the feeling that something was missing. The landscape was so bare, so devoid of life and colour. The endless expanse of dust and rock stretched out in every direction.

I knew that we needed to change that, to breathe new life into this barren world. And I knew just where to start.

With a renewed sense of purpose, I made a mental note to speak with Luke about bringing some small trees through the Portal. We needed shelter, not just for Vincent, but for all the creatures that we hoped to introduce to this new ecosystem. Without the protective shade of a leafy canopy, they would be vulnerable to the scorching heat and the relentless dust that seemed to permeate every corner of this land.

I gave Vincent a gentle pat on the head, my fingers sinking into the coarse, wiry fur of his coat. He looked up at me with those intelligent, mischievous eyes, and I couldn't help but feel a flicker of affection for the stubborn old goat.

With Vincent sorted, I turned my attention back to my intended task before Vincent's feast interruption. I had plans to discuss with Grant and Sarah, ideas that had been percolating in my mind.

Making my way back to the camp, my steps were purposeful and determined. As I approached the cluster of motorhomes and tents that made up our little community, I caught sight of Grant and Sarah huddled together at a table outside their own abode. They were deep in conversation, their heads bent over a scattering of papers and plans that littered the surface before them.

I quickened my pace, eager to join them in their discussions. But first, I had a quick detour to make.

Ducking into my own caravan, the cool, dim interior was a welcome respite from the relentless heat outside. I scanned the interior, my eyes searching for the object of my desire. There, nestled among the clutter of nature magazines and bits of equipment, was the item I sought.

I reached out, my fingers closing around the smooth, cool surface of the glass jar. Inside, a writhing mass of tiny, delicate bodies scuttled and skittered, their movements frantic and erratic in the confines of their temporary home.

Holding the jar up to the light, I marvelled at the intricate beauty of the baby huntsman spiders that danced within. They were so small, so fragile, and yet they possessed a resilience and adaptability that awed me.

With the jar of spiderlings clutched tightly in my hand, I emerged from the caravan once more, blinking in the bright sunlight that flooded the camp. I had a new sense of purpose now, a determination to make my case to Grant and Sarah, to persuade them of the importance of starting small and building something sustainable. It had only been a few days but I was already tired of the barrenness and I missed the beautiful Tasmanian wilderness dearly.

As I approached the huddled group, I felt a flicker of apprehension stirring in my gut. Chris had already beaten me to the punch, his shorter frame hunched over the table as he gestured animatedly to the plans and diagrams scattered before them.

Hesitating, my steps faltered as I drew nearer. They were so engrossed in their discussion, their voices rising and falling with an intensity that spoke of the passion they held for their chosen field. I felt like an outsider, intruding upon a private moment of discourse.

I squared my shoulders, my grip tightening on the jar of spiderlings as I closed the distance between us. As I drew nearer, snippets of their conversation began to drift towards me, tantalising glimpses of the grand plans and ambitious dreams that consumed their thoughts.

Grant and Sarah, the esteemed directors of the Bonorong Wildlife Sanctuary, were in their element, their eyes alight with a fervour that spoke of their deep love for the natural world.

But even as I listened, even as I felt the stirrings of excitement and possibility that their words evoked, I couldn't shake the sense of unease that had taken root deep within me.

The enthusiastic siblings were still blissfully unaware of the true nature of their circumstances, still clinging to the belief that this was merely a temporary sojourn, a brief adventure before they could return to the lives they had always known.

I knew better. I knew the truth that lurked beneath the surface of this strange and wondrous world, the reality that we were all trapped here, forever altered by the whims of fate and the machinations of forces beyond our control.

I knew that the truth would have to be revealed eventually, that the bubble of blissful ignorance that Grant and Sarah had wrapped themselves in would have to be burst. But as I watched them now, their faces alight with joy and enthusiasm, I couldn't bring myself to be the one to shatter their illusions.

They deserved this moment of happiness. And so I held my tongue, my lips curving into a smile that felt brittle and false upon my face.

"Karen!" Chris's voice cut through my reverie, his tone warm and welcoming as he beckoned me over to join the group. "We were just discussing the plans for the wildlife sanctuary. Grant and Sarah have some incredible ideas."

I forced a smile to my lips, my hand tightening once more around the jar of spiders. "That's wonderful," I said, my voice filled with a forced brightness that felt hollow even to my own ears. I had already seen the plans, and I did agree, they were ambitious. But there was another matter that I felt couldn't simply be abandoned.

"And what happened to this enclosure for Vincent that you were supposed to be building?" I asked, my voice sharp and pointed as I fixed Chris with a steely gaze.

He had the grace to look sheepish, his eyes skating away from mine as he mumbled some half-hearted excuse about delegating the task to Nial and Adrian. The response caught me by surprise, and I felt a sudden pang of guilt for my harsh tone. I kept forgetting that we had gained another new member to our ranks, a stranger thrust into our midst by circumstances beyond his own doing.

Thankfully, it seemed that Adrian and Nial already knew each other from their work in Hobart, which was helping to keep Adrian somewhat calm. Well, as calm as he could be given the circumstances of his arrival in Clivilius.

Adrian had arrived just yesterday, and like the rest of us, his presence here was the result of Luke. I had heard the whispers, the murmurs of his discontent that rippled through the camp. He had been torn from his life, from his family and his work, and deposited in this world without so much as a by-your-leave.

I could only imagine the pain and confusion he must be feeling, the sense of loss and betrayal that must be gnawing at his soul. According to Chris, who had gleaned a bit more information through his conversations with Nial, Adrian had left behind a wife and two teenage daughters, a life that had been ripped away from him in the blink of an eye.

But as much as my heart ached for Adrian's plight, I couldn't help but feel a flicker of excitement at the prospect of his presence here. He owned and operated his own construction company in Hobart. He was a skilled tradesman and businessman with a keen eye and a deft hand. With his expertise, we stood a chance of not just surviving in this harsh and unforgiving landscape, but of truly thriving, of building something remarkable and enduring.

Catching myself mid-thought, my brow furrowed as I realised that I was once again finding myself justifying Luke's actions, rationalising the unthinkable. He was playing God, plucking people from their lives and depositing them in this strange new world without their consent or knowledge. It was a violation of the highest order, a transgression that should have filled me with outrage and horror.

But even as I tried to summon those feelings, to stoke the flames of righteous indignation that should have been burning within me, I found myself strangely numb, almost apathetic. A part of me, a small, secret part that I hardly dared to acknowledge, even to myself, was almost grateful for Luke's intervention, for the way he was carefully curating our little community, bringing together the skills and talents we would need to build a new life here.

It scared me, this newfound moral flexibility, this willingness to accept the unacceptable in the name of survival. But as I stood there, the jar of spiderlings clutched tight against my chest, I couldn't quite bring myself to care. There were more pressing matters at hand, more immediate concerns that demanded my attention.

"We were just taking Chris through some of the plans that we brought with us," Sarah said, her voice cutting through my reverie. I shook my head, forcing myself to focus on the present.

"I actually brought something that might help persuade you of the need to move quickly on the project," I said, holding up the jar of spiderlings, the tiny creatures within dancing about with renewed vigour at the sudden movement.

Grant and Sarah leaned in closer, their eyes widening with fascination as they took in the sight of the delicate arachnids. I could see the wheels turning behind their eyes, the gears of their scientific minds spinning into overdrive as they contemplated the implications of my discovery.

"I found them in one of the bags of firewood," I explained, my voice growing stronger and more confident as I spoke. "They need a place to call home, a sanctuary where they can thrive and flourish. And we need to move fast to make that happen."

Grant nodded, his brow furrowed with a thoughtfulness that spoke of a keen and penetrating intelligence. "You're right," he said, his voice filled with a quiet determination. "We can't afford to waste any time. Every moment we delay is a moment that these creatures are left vulnerable and exposed."

Sarah chimed in, her own voice filled with a passion that matched her brother's. "We've brought along some plans and designs for the sanctuary," she said, gesturing to the stack of papers and folders that lay scattered across the table. "But we know that we need to start small, to lay the groundwork for something that can grow and evolve over time."

I felt a surge of gratitude and relief wash over me, a sense that perhaps, just perhaps, we were all on the same page. "That's exactly what Chris and I have been discussing," I said, my voice filled with a newfound sense of purpose. "We need to establish a plant nursery and an orchard, to start exploring the properties of this new environment and to provide some much-needed greenery and life to this barren landscape."

Chris nodded, his own face etched with a determination that mirrored my own. "We've been talking about how these projects could serve a dual purpose," he said, his hand coming to rest on my shoulder in a gesture of support and solidarity. "In the short term, we could supply resources for Bixbus, to help keep the camp running smoothly. And in the long term, we could expand to provide resources for the wildlife sanctuary as well."

Grant and Sarah exchanged a glance, their eyes filled with a thoughtfulness that spoke of the wheels turning in their minds. "It's a good plan," Grant said at last, his voice filled with a quiet approval. "From what Chris tells me, the whole area about us has remarkable soil beneath the layers of dust and the hard crust."

"We've seen the coriander plants, Grant," Sarah interrupted her brother, clearly reminding him of the visual witness they had of the soil's remarkable and not yet understood life-giving properties.

Grant nodded, his eyes alight with a fierce and burning curiosity. "I know. And if this soil is everywhere, then I suspect that some of these plans can be fast-tracked," he said, motioning to the folders and diagrams that lay spread out before him.

"What do you mean?" Sarah asked, her brow furrowing in a mixture of confusion and intrigue.

Having already read through the plans myself, I thought I could guess at where Grant was heading, and I chimed in, my own voice filled with a growing excitement. "We can probably bypass the initial soil assessments. I suspect that it really doesn't matter where we begin the site construction. Anywhere along the river is probably going to suit our purposes, at least initially."

Grant nodded, a smile of approval tugging at the corners of his mouth. "That's exactly what I was thinking."

"We need to start really simple and basic anyway, so there's no real harm if we have to relocate as we progress," Chris added, his own voice filled with a quiet confidence.

Sarah nodded, her face etched with a determination that matched her brother's. "We can work together on this," she said, her hand reaching out to clasp mine in a gesture of solidarity and support. "We'll pool our knowledge and resources, and we'll make this happen. For the sake of all the creatures that depend on us."

I felt a lump rising in my throat, a sudden and overwhelming surge of emotion. In that moment, I knew that I had found kindred spirits in Grant and Sarah, fellow lovers of the natural world who understood the weight of the responsibility that we bore.

But even as I basked in the warmth of that realisation, I couldn't shake the sense of unease that had begun to gnaw at the edges of my consciousness. There was something that Grant and Sarah weren't telling us, some piece of the puzzle that was still missing from our understanding of the situation.

Grant threw his sister a curious sideways glance before turning his attention back to me. "We really need to make contact with James," he said, his voice filled with a sudden urgency that made my heart skip a beat.

"Who is James?" Chris asked, beating me to the punch.

"He works at Bonorong with us," Sarah answered, her voice filled with a quiet intensity. "He is our key contact with Brad Coleman."

"Who?" I asked, my curiosity piqued by the unfamiliar name.

"Brad works for EcoSolutions Consulting," Sarah replied.

I felt a sudden jolt of recognition, a flash of understanding that made my heart race. I had seen the EcoSolutions Consulting branding throughout the documents that I had read earlier, the sleek and professional logos that spoke of a well-funded and highly organised operation.

"EcoSolutions," I repeated. "They're the ones who drew these plans up for you, aren't they?" I asked, gesturing to the papers and diagrams that lay scattered across the table.

Sarah nodded. "Yeah. We're supposed to be meeting with them to provide regular updates on our progress of the initial site assessment."

I felt a sudden and sickening lurch in the pit of my stomach, a sense of dread that made my blood run cold. Chris and I exchanged a nervous glance, our eyes filled with a sudden and terrible understanding.

We both knew that neither of us wanted to be the one to tell Grant and Sarah the truth about their situation here, to shatter the illusion of normality and control that they had so carefully constructed around themselves.

"How were you supposed to provide updates?" Chris asked, his voice filled with a sudden and desperate urgency. "Were you intending to cross between Clivilius and Earth through the Portal?"

I felt my eyes widen with shock, my breath catching in my throat at the surprising turn Chris had taken the conversation. I hadn't considered the idea that they could actually have a way to come and go as they pleased, that there might be some loophole or exception that would allow them to maintain their ties to the world we had left behind. *It wasn't really possible, was it?*

Grant opened his mouth to speak, but before he or Sarah could respond, the approach of Paul interrupted our intense conversation. I felt a flicker of annoyance at the intrusion, my mind still reeling with the implications of what Grant and Sarah might have been about to reveal. But as I turned to face Paul, my irritation quickly gave way to curiosity and concern.

"Paul, what brings you here?" I asked, my voice carefully neutral as I studied his face for any hint of what had brought him to our little gathering. There was a seriousness in his expression, a gravity that contrasted sharply with his usual easy-going demeanour. Whatever had brought him here, it was clear that it was no trivial matter.

Paul hesitated for a moment, his eyes flicking between Chris and me as if weighing the impact of his next words. "I need to talk to you about something important," he said at last, his voice low and urgent.

I leaned in closer, my heart beginning to thud heavily in my chest as a myriad of possibilities raced through my mind. In a place like Clivilius, "important" could mean anything from the minor inconvenience of an escapee goat to an impending catastrophe. I braced myself for whatever news Paul was about to deliver, my mind already preparing to formulate contingencies.

"Go on, Paul," I urged him, my voice steady despite the unease that coiled in my gut.

He took a deep breath before continuing, "Tonight, we're planning to raid a large supermarket. We need supplies, and it's our best shot."

I felt my eyebrows shoot up in surprise, my mind struggling to process the implications of what Paul had just said. *A raid? On a supermarket?* The idea seemed almost absurd, like something out of a post-apocalyptic novel. But as I looked around at the barren landscape that stretched out before us, I realised that perhaps it wasn't so far-fetched after all.

Chris, meanwhile, seemed to be taking the news in stride. "A raid, you say?" he asked, his voice filled with a note of intrigue that made me want to shake my head in exasperation. *Trust Chris to find the prospect of a dangerous and potentially illegal mission exciting.*

Grant and Sarah exchanged glances, their expressions mirroring a mix of curiosity and concern. They were still new to the dynamics and challenges of Clivilius, and the mention of a 'raid' clearly piqued their interest, albeit with an undercurrent of apprehension.

I sighed, feeling a wave of exhaustion wash over me. The day had already been long and taxing, and the thought of embarking on a midnight mission filled me with a sense of dread. "I'm feeling a bit of heat exhaustion, so I might retire early tonight," I admitted to Paul, hoping that my honesty wouldn't be seen as a sign of weakness. "But Chris will be there to support you," I added quickly, not wanting to leave Paul in the lurch.

To my surprise, Grant spoke up. "We'll be there too," he said, looking to his sister for confirmation. Sarah nodded, her face set with a determination that made me feel a flicker of admiration. Despite their newness to Clivilius, they were already showing a willingness to pitch in and do their part.

Paul looked relieved. "Fantastic," he said, his voice filled with a mix of gratitude and anticipation.

"What's the plan?" Chris asked, leaning forward with an eagerness that made me want to roll my eyes.

Paul shrugged. "I'm not exactly sure of the fine details yet. But basically, we'll meet at the Portal to receive the goods that Luke and Beatrix bring us."

I frowned, feeling a flicker of unease at the mention of the Portal. The idea of relying on Luke and Beatrix to bring us supplies from Earth felt somehow wrong, like we were crossing a line that shouldn't be crossed. But as I looked around at the bleak and unforgiving landscape that surrounded us, I realised that perhaps we didn't have much choice.

Grant commented on the simplicity of the plan, but I knew that things in Clivilius were seldom as straightforward as they seemed. There were always complications, always unforeseen challenges that threatened to derail even the most carefully laid plans.

"We'll talk about it later this evening at the campfire. We've got a fair bit of preparation to do for it," Paul said, his voice filled with a note of finality that made it clear that the discussion was over, at least for now.

"Preparation… such as?" I asked, wondering what any of us could possibly do to help, given that we couldn't come and go through the Portal like the Guardians could.

"Well, it's likely to be a midnight raid, of sorts, so we'll need to build some additional fires near the Portal so that we have some light," Paul explained, his hands gesturing to emphasise his points.

"I see," I responded, nodding in understanding. I found my mind splitting in two about the idea. On the one hand, Paul was right, we could do with the supplies, and a large supermarket would reap a bountiful reward. Yet, on the other hand, we were contemplating pillaging from Earth. There was no doubt in my mind that with Luke and Beatrix's ability to come and go through the Portal as they pleased, and from basically any location on earth, that they had no intention on paying for any of these goods. Why would they when they can enter the store after hours through their Portal and take whatever they want? No worries for having to battle through layers of security. Simply walk through a wall, and hey presto.

Despite the burst of excitement at the imagery it presented to my mind, the overall idea of knowing that we were essentially stealing, didn't sit too well in my stomach. Here we were again, bordering on dubious ethical grounds, and once again, I found myself unsure that I would fight against the decisions.

But even as I wrestled with my misgivings, I couldn't deny the practical realities of our situation. We were in a new world, a place where the old rules and norms no longer applied. If we were going to survive, we would need to adapt, to do whatever was necessary to ensure our continued existence.

"Makes sense, I guess," I said at last, my voice heavy with the weight of my internal conflict.

"Yeah," Paul said, his hands gesturing to emphasise his points. "Like I said, I've got a lot to consider at the moment, so full details at the campfire later." His tone was one of a leader bearing the weight of responsibility, something that I had come to respect in him.

"Roger that," Grant chimed in, his boyish grin contrasting with the seriousness of the situation. He playfully saluted, which seemed to be his way of lightening the mood.

Sarah, however, didn't seem to appreciate Grant's levity. She cast him a disapproving look, perhaps thinking that the situation warranted a more sombre attitude.

As Paul prepared to leave, I realised that if I wasn't going to debate the notion of plundering a supermarket on Earth, then I may as well take advantage of the situation. Taking a deep breath to give me the courage to not back down now, I pulled him aside for a more private conversation.

Holding up one of the jars I had brought with me, I revealed its contents: baby huntsman spiders. "I captured these little guys in jars yesterday," I began, showing him the jar. "They were in a bag of firewood that was delivered. I've managed to catch a considerable number of them."

Paul looked at the jar, his interest piqued, but he kept a cautious distance from the tiny inhabitants. I could sense his reluctance to get too close, which was understandable given their nature.

In a hushed tone, I confided my deeper concerns to Paul. "I'm worried about their survival in this environment. Plus, I want to start breeding a few species of insects in captivity." My voice carried an urgency that reflected my growing interest in preserving and fostering life in Clivilius, no matter how small.

Paul nodded, his expression one of understanding and support. "I'll mention it to Luke and Beatrix. They might be able to help with getting you some aquariums."

"Terrariums would be better," I corrected him gently, offering a warm smile to ease any embarrassment. It was important to get the details right, especially when it came to habitats for living creatures.

Paul's face lit up with a realisation. "Actually," he said, the idea clearly just hitting him. "The store we are raiding tonight has a pet section. I'll make a mental note to speak with Beatrix and Luke and make sure that they look in that section. Should be something useful in all that."

"Fingers crossed," I replied, hoping that the night's efforts would indeed yield something beneficial for my growing collection of creatures. As a gentle reminder of the importance of this request, I held the jar of baby spiders a little closer to Paul's face, revealing the delicate lives that depended on us.

Paul visibly shuddered at the close encounter, prompting a broader smile from me. His reaction was a mix of amusement and affirmation of the natural instinct to be wary of spiders, even tiny ones.

I laughed softly, and motioned for us to return to the group. As we rejoined the others, Sarah spoke up, her voice filled with a renewed sense of urgency.

"We really do need to contact James," she told Paul, her eyes darting between him and her brother.

My curiosity was piqued, my mind racing with questions about how they intended to make contact and whether they truly had a way to return to Earth. But before I could voice my thoughts, Paul was already in motion.

"Sure. Come with me," he said, ushering Grant and Sarah to follow him.

As a gentle gust of wind whispered across the folders, scattering papers across the table, Sarah quickly began to collect them, her movements hurried and purposeful.

I wanted to follow them, to see where Paul would take them and to learn more about their mysterious connection to the world we had left behind. But before I could make a move, Chris spoke up, his voice casual and untroubled.

"I can mind the folders and plans until you return," he said, reaching out to take the papers from Sarah's hands.

I felt a flicker of annoyance, a sense of frustration at being left out of the loop once again. But as I watched Grant and Sarah follow Paul off into the distance, I knew that there was little I could do but wait and hope for answers.

With a knot twisting in my gut, I watched them disappear from view, my mind racing with possibilities and questions. I was clueless as to how they would make contact, or whether they could go back to Earth, but one thing was certain, they were definitely heading in the direction of the Portal.

"I'll get these plans inside for safety," Chris said, picking up the last folder and tucking it under his arm.

I nodded, barely registering his words as my mind continued to churn with thoughts and theories. "And I'm going for a walk," I said, my voice distant and distracted.

Without waiting for a response, I turned and strode off in the opposite direction, my feet carrying me away from the camp and out into the barren landscape beyond. I needed time to think, to process all that had happened and to try to make sense of the strange and unsettling feelings that had taken root within me.

❖

As I walked off into the distance, the all-encompassing quiet was nearly overpowering, broken only by the soft crunch of my boots against the dry, dusty ground. The silence was eerie, unnatural.

"Not a single bird chirping or insect buzzing in this entire place," I muttered as I walked, my voice sounding oddly muffled in the stillness. If it weren't for the shadow panther attack the other night, I could have been forgiven for thinking that we were the only living things for hundreds of miles in every direction.

The thought hung heavy in my mind, emphasising the desolate isolation of our new environment. Back on Earth, back in Tasmania, the habitats had once constantly vibrated with a diverse harmony of scurrying, fluttering, and calling wildlife. The air had been filled with the songs of birds, the buzzing of insects, the rustling of leaves in the breeze. But here, in this strange and barren landscape, there was only an unsettling cemetery-like stillness, a silence that seemed to stretch on forever.

"At least for now," I murmured to myself after a brief pause, my voice filled with a quiet determination. "Who knows what hardy stowaways or native life might already be dormant all around us, just waiting to be coaxed out?"

I held up my jar of baby spiders, studying the tiny creatures within with a critical eye. They were a testament to the resilience of life, to the way that even the smallest and most fragile of beings could find a way to survive in the most unlikely of places. If these little ones could make the journey from Earth, hitching a ride in the firewood that Luke had been sending through the Portal, then surely there must be other forms of life out there, just waiting to be discovered.

With that thought in mind, my steps took on a purposeful glide, the frontier sun warming one cheek as I continued exploring away from the main camp. To a casual observer, my path might have looked like aimless wandering, a meandering journey with no clear destination in mind. But in truth, my mind was focused, my senses attuned to the subtle nuances of the landscape around me.

I pushed aside the lingering questions about the real intent for Grant and Sarah's presence here, the mysteries that seemed to enshroud them like a cloak of secrecy. Instead, I allowed my optimism to re-emerge with each step, my eyes scanning the horizon for any sign of life, any hint of the potential that lay hidden within this world.

To my experienced conservationist's eye, each featureless rise and shallow valley, every complex patterned crust of sedimentary soil, practically glowed with untapped potential. I could see the way the land yearned to give birth to new greenery, the way the very earth itself seemed to cry out for the nurturing touch of life.

I'm not sure how long I explored, or how many invisible life force patterns I traced through the faint resonance humming through the soles of my boots. But with each passing moment, I felt that symbolic renewal of purpose resound more strongly within me, a clarion call that seemed to emanate from the very heart of this strange and wondrous world.

There simply had to be some natural origin point, a generative place where our focused energies and unconquerable determination could properly take hold and transform the landscape to reflect the living vision growing in my soul. I could feel it, a pulsing, thrumming sense of possibility that seemed to permeate the very air around me.

And then, just as the first whispers of doubt began creeping into my mind, it happened. As I topped yet another low rise, a subtle seismic ripple in the sands resolved into a clear view that took my breath away in one astonished gasp.

Before me lay a shallow basin, nestled between sloping ridges and winding channels carved into the planet's crust. And there, within those naturally circular grooves, sprawled the first unmistakable outcroppings of weathered rock and weak sandy soil.

Past those meandering waves, curved earthen banks arced protectively around a secluded hollow... and in that sheltered cradle, visible even from my current distance, glimmered a series of serene reflecting pools, their waters shimmering like molten silver in the sunlight.

I barely realised my feet were already carrying me forward, drawn irresistibly by those budding promises of an aquatic wellspring sustained in the most unlikely of desert sanctuaries. It was as if some unseen force was guiding me, pulling me towards the very heart of this oasis, towards the source of all life and possibility.

Come here, the whispering waters seemed to sing, their gentle lapping harmonising with the deeper call of the land's eternal dream. It was a melody that permeated every part of my being, resonating with the very core of who I was and what I believed in.

Here... yes, here lay the destined birthplace. Here, amidst the thick moisture and elemental outpourings, the infinite fountains of life's revitalising grace were meant to take form once more under my careful artistic guidance. I could see it all so clearly, the verdant paradise that would spring forth from this humble beginning, the lush and thriving ecosystem that would one day blanket this entire world.

I'm not sure how long I stood there, utterly entranced by the enchanting call of that improbable oasis hidden in the surrounding barrenness. Time seemed to lose all meaning, fading away into the endless expanse of possibility that stretched out before me. It could have been mere seconds or an ageless epoch—all normal sense of time seemed to fade away, leaving only the deep resonance of this sacred space pulsing through my very core.

At some point, Chris's hand landed on my shoulder, giving a gentle squeeze that refocused my single-minded concentration. I blinked, momentarily disoriented, as if waking from a walking dream-state, my mind still lost in the swirling visions of the future that had consumed me.

"Looks like you've found your blissful happy place," he said softly, an intrigued smile on his tanned face as he followed my awestruck gaze towards the distant promise of calm waters and protective banks.

Despite my surprise at his sudden appearance by my side, I could only nod silently, letting the full significance of this revelatory discovery wash over me. Of course, this was the predestined centre, the living green heart our nascent vision of renewal had been yearning for! It was so obvious now, so clear and undeniable in the light of day.

Already, my imagination was painting vivid pictures across the blank canvas before us—raised plant terraces hugging and encircling the existing water basins, watered by continually recycled and nutrient-enriched tiny currents. Gravity-defying trellises draped in curtains of leafy green fabrics, shading and strengthening a series of private divided alcoves.

And nestled within those nurturing embraces, category after category of sample habitats and species displays representing the infinite variety and expressions of reawakened life from our faraway Earth home! This sunken desert grotto would become the flourishing heart of our transcendent restoration endeavour, a living testament to the power of hope and determination in the face of even the most daunting of challenges.

In awed quiet, I looked to Chris, my eyes shining with the fire of newfound purpose. And though no words passed between us, our shared focus harmonised into a singular overarching chord, a resonance that seemed to span the infinite golden-ratio distances of the universe itself.

This was the place where the green world would be reborn anew, where life would once again flourish and thrive in all its myriad forms and expressions. And we would be the ones to make it happen.

TO BE CONTINUED…

Printed and bound by CPI Group (UK) Ltd, Croydon, CR0 4YY
16/05/2024
01008564-0009